THE INNOCENT YEARS

A BETWEEN HEAVEN AND HELL NOVEL

L A MICHAELS

THE INNOCENT YEARS

LML BOOKS Publishing

Cover Design by: Pro Graphics 360
Formatted by: Jackie Brown
Front and back cover images by: loviiiluv
Edited and proofed by: Sadie Faith Anderson

For Mercy Rogers.

Thank you for everything times a million. Love You Always!

Pastiche:

An artistic work in a style that imitates that of another work, artist, or period.

Soap Opera:

An ongoing drama serial on television or radio, featuring the lives of many characters and their emotional relationships.

ACKNOWLEDGEMENTS

There are so many people to thank with this book!

First and foremost, my artist, Luviiilove. Go follow her DeviantArt page. All I have to do is tell them what I want sometimes in the most bizarre details and in three weeks or less there it is almost alive. These characters are practically three dimensional because of you... You go the extra step in making them look as though they were actually related to one another. You're brilliant!

My Filipino "mother" Mercy! You wandered around a grocery store showing off my first book to everyone there. You bought multiple copies of my book for me to sign for people. I cannot ever thank you enough.

Josh... I've not had many people support me for me in my life until lately. Thank you for posting the book announcement on my birthday on your FB page. Thank you for supporting me. Thank you for being my friend. Which I know is not an easy task at times but know that it means the world to me.

Ryan, thank you as well for sharing my cover announcement on your social media as well. Thank you for our conversations and being a good friend as well.

Nikki... I am telling you; Waffle Houses and senators are in our shared future. I'll write the book and you will write the screenplay for the TV movie. In all seriousness thank you for being an awesome friend and business partner over the years!

To my editor, Sadie Faith Anderson, your comments gave me life. Your critiques were done in a way that made sense and didn't destroy my fragile spirit. Thank you so much, and here is to a long future of you editing my crazy thoughts that I have put on to paper!

To Thomas, thank you for being there when no one else was. Your friendship has meant the world to me over the years and your support has as well.

A special thank you to the Antoski family as a whole (Frank obviously included) for giving me an opportunity to get out of a bad situation while I wrote this book. I had to take five steps backwards in order to be motivated to publish it but fate has a way of having things work out.

Thank you to Vicki, Sue Ann, Manny, Alex, my father Ralph, my late mother of course Lisa Marie for making soap operas a staple in our home.

Last but definitely not least... The people who have bought the book! Thank you from the bottom of my heart. I hope that I have captivated you with this novel and you keep coming back for more because I have so much more to share!

From the flames of a fire to the blue skies above, we are all just somewhere Between Heaven and Hell...

LANA – 1963

North Pointe was the largest estate on the largest property in the town of Grosse Pointe. Maids had come and gone from that household for years. Every person who had worked for the Knight family shared a different opinion.

Some thought they were the saviors of Michigan economics. Some thought they stole from another family-named car company. Either way, the family estate itself was utterly beautiful. It was owned by Heathcliff Knight and his late wife Jenny. They were the third generation to call North Pointe home.

Lana Bloom had been the Head Maid of the household for over three years. She was the last staff member hired by the late Jenny Knight. Jenny was a wonderful woman who loved everyone, regardless of who they were. She had been sick for a number of years, and the two had become close at the very end. Lana wished that she had been able to know Jenny earlier. Jenny's husband, Heathcliff, was a good man himself but very much stuck in his ways. Heathcliff cared about his wife and family, but the company was his legacy and very much like a child to him. This was an issue for his actual child, Benton. Benton was nothing like either of his parents. It seemed obvious to everyone, except Benton himself, that he just wasn't the businessman that his father had been.

Jenny let the maid know about Jenny before she passed on. Jenny had requested that Benton and his family move back home. She wanted her family to be reunited.

Unfortunately, Benton had been reluctant to step back from the LA offices with his wife and two sons. Lana was shocked. Family should be with family, no matter what.

Lana herself knew about loss. She had lost a husband right before she went to work for the Knight family. She had been living her life as a comfortable housewife before he had passed on. She was under the impression that she would never have to work, and that he would take care of her. Her husband was shot coming home from a factory one night, by a stranger. He had refused to give up his wallet to the man. He died shortly thereafter at Grosse Pointe General Hospital. She was left to take care of her daughter and loving but aging mother-in-law. She was a strong Latina woman, and she wasn't going to let death get in her way of survival.

The Knight family had indeed been very good to her. Lana worked from eight to four each day. Then, she had two hours to get her daughter Nadia home from school and fed. She then returned to the Knight home to have dinner served for them. Afterwards, she would retire home. She had Sundays off for church. Jenny had heard about Lana's daughter's schooling and insisted that Lana send her to the Saint Agnes school here in town. It was being paid for by the Knight family. Lana couldn't have been more grateful. Yes, working for the Knight's had been a God-sent blessing for Lana Bloom.

"What is for dinner?" Heathcliff asked as he put down the paper down in the home's library. He sat up and went over to the record player.

Lana got up from the marble floor she had been handwashing. "Well, I was thinking of beef stroganoff," she explained.

Heathcliff thought for a moment as he flipped the record on the player. "Yes, that should be doable. Will you be joining us for dinner tonight, young lady?"

The maid put her hands on her waist. "Mr. Knight, you know very well that it is inappropriate for the help to dine with the family. Besides, your son would never allow it."

The retired CEO scoffed. "Do you know where my son is right now?"

Lana gathered her bucket and other cleaning supplies. "I would assume work," she lied. She assumed the bar or the club.

"He is probably at the bar or the club. Either way, it is three in the afternoon, and the man is drinking..."

"Well, I better get dinner started," Lana exclaimed. She enjoyed talking with Heathcliff while she cleaned. She just didn't like talking about Benton with him. She realized very quickly that it was okay for Heathcliff to have an absolutely terrible opinion about his son, but no one else could share it.

With that, Lana walked out of the library and went down the long hall to the kitchen. It was shockingly small for a house of this size. She went to the fridge before she realized that she was not alone. Lana turned and smiled. "Well, hello, Mrs. Knight." It took a minute for Delia to comprehend where she was.

"Oh, hello, Lana. I was just deep in thought," Delia claimed.

Lana was not sure how to feel about Delia Knight. She was the wife of Benton and mother to their children. Even so, she was an outsider within. Heathcliff seemed to have an issue with the fact that Delia was Puerto Rican. Yet strangely, Heathcliff had no issue with Lana herself being Mexican. Lana just assumed that for Heathcliff, it was acceptable for a family to have a Hispanic maid but not a Hispanic in-law. It didn't shock or even upset Lana if she were being honest. "So, what have you been up to today?" Lana asked, politely.

"I've just been here and there..." Delia was holding on to a bottle of wine.

"Well, it is good you have seemed to keep yourself busy..." "Will you be at the parent's night this Friday at the school?" Delia's children went to Saint Agnes alongside Nadia. Lana was unsure of what to think of the two Knight boys...

"She better not," Clifton said as he walked downstairs from the kitchen staircase. Clifton was a typical seventeen-year-old boy. Lana had seen pictures of Heathcliff in his youth, and the mother and son pair looked like twins separated by time. Dark brown hair, big brown eyes, tall, broad-shouldered. Clifton towered over his mother, who was a short woman. "I'm going out."

Delia stood up. "We are going to be having dinner soon. Where could you possibly be going? It's a school night."

The Knight boy took his coat and shrugged. "I said, I am going out."

"You had better not be going to that trashy girl's house," Delia screamed. She was referring to Dallas Bolton. Dallas Bolton was a dark-skinned girl who lived in a not so lovely part of Detroit. It was still unclear how Clifton had met Dallas as they didn't go to the same school.

"I'll do what I want," Clifton said as he marched passed her. As he walked out, his father walked in. Clifton didn't even stop to say hello.

"Where is dinner?" Benton asked, clearly slurring his words.

As Heathcliff already said, it was not even four yet, and Benton was drunk. Though, so was his wife. Lana didn't like to think ill of people, but it was clear these two were not happy together. "I'm making it now," Lana said calmly, "You will be having beef stroganoff. It shouldn't take that long." Benton was home two hours early from work. She suspected he didn't even go in today.

"Dinner should be done by the time I get home. I'm the breadwinner for the family." Benton growled.

Delia put her hand on his shoulder. "Don't worry, dear. I can make you a sandwich while we wait."

Benton quickly moved his shoulder. "I don't want a sandwich. I'm going to the club. I expect dinner to be made by the time I get home." Benton stormed out the back door.

"Well, you better get started," Delia said, shrugging at Lana. She sat back down.

The maid knew better than to expect Delia to side with her, but it still shocked her sometimes. The phone rang. She knew that no one else in the house would answer it. "Hello, this is Lana Bloom speaking... Oh, no, you have the right number. This is the Knight household. I work for them. Is there a message you would like me to take?" She grabbed a pen and paper and then dropped them. "He said what to my daughter? I'll be there right now." She hung up the phone and grabbed her jacket. "I will be back."

Delia looked confused. "What about dinner?" She asked.

"I will make it when I get back. Do you know what your son called my daughter today?" Lana whispered the word into her ear.

"I don't know where Rodrick would have learned such a word," Delia said almost unaffected.

"Well, they want one of you to come and pick Rodrick up. I'm going to pick up Nadia and bring her home." Lana marched out the front door. She tried ridiculously hard to like Delia and Benton, but even if she could get past their drinking, she couldn't get past their, lousy parenting. Clifton was a typical teenager. Rodrick, on the other hand, was the second coming of the devil, and he was thirteen years old...

CLIFF – 2018

Cliff Knight the Second sat in his late father's lawyer's office. Cliff never was fond of his dad. And the lawyer was as big a scum bag as his father had been. Cliff looked at his watch. This was never going to end. His dad had requested that each aspect of his will be read separately to everyone included. It just showed how much time he had on his hands in his last couple of years. Knowing him, though, this was probably planned from the time that Cliff was born. His dad had never been fond of him.

"Sorry. I was on the phone with a client." Monty said. Monty was an older man who looked like Larry King's great-grandfather. As far as Cliff knew, Monty had been his grandfather Benton's lawyer as well. He had never known his grandfather. He died before he was born. "So, let's get to this will reading," Monty muttered. "I have an early flight in the morning and want to get this over with." It was one in the afternoon. "To my biggest disappointment and only son, I am one-hundred percent certain. I leave you nothing."

The Knight CEO stood up from his chair. "I have to get back to work."

"Well, now wait, there is more," Monty explained.

Cliff picked up his briefcase. "I am sure that there is, but I have no desire to listen to the bastard belittle myself or my family." He walked towards the door. "Just so you know, if my father promised you any sort of money post-death, I'm not honoring it." Cliff walked out and slammed the door behind him.

***

Cliff walked into North Pointe and strode into the library. He sat down in an armchair and smiled. His father thought he would have the last laugh, and he didn't. The man died with no power in the company. Cliff only went to his funeral because he was CEO of Knight. His younger sister Phyllis didn't go. His uncle and aunt didn't either. Yes, people from the company went, but half of them either never knew him or only went to make sure he was dead. Cliff was done thinking about Rodrick. He had more important things to think about...

"Thank goodness you are home." Hannah Knight, his daughter, said as she entered the homes library. Hannah had reluctantly moved home a few months earlier after being kicked out of her apartment. "I spoke with Human Resources today, Dad. Why on Earth am I a Vice-President of your company? I don't have that kind of experience."

Cliff stood up, running a hand through his curly hair. "What? Do you think I had any experience when your great-grandmother forced me into the president position? In the amount of time that this company has been around, you may be the only Knight who has actually worked at a dealership on the sales floor. Not to mention your business degree. You will be fine."

Hannah crossed her arms. "So, have you spoken to Aunt Vivica?"

"Not since she went to London for that fashion magazine spread," Cliff admitted. Vivica was his childhood sweetheart. He fucked things up royally back in the '90s when she moved to town. Cliff had proposed to her at the beginning of the summer. She didn't give him an actual answer. Instead, she did what she always did when faced with conflict. Ran for the hills. Cliff hadn't been able to have a proper conversation with the red-haired vixen since then. "I'm sure that she will figure things out soon."

"Well, hopefully. Have you spoken to mom, either? The divorce was finalized, finally, wasn't it?" Hannah asked.

Cliff cleared his throat. "I'd rather not talk with you about your mother and my divorce." Cliff was still shocked that she came to him for the divorce when she had spent years trying to keep what they could now admit was a dead marriage together.

The brunette Vice-President sighed. "Well, you need to speak to someone about it."

She had a point, but Cliff still wasn't comfortable talking to his daughter about it. He was about to respond when the door opened again. "You!" Screamed an all-too-familiar voice. "My best friend has been continent-hopping all summer. This is the second time in a year she has gone into hiding. I don't care what you have to do, but you need to get Vivica back now," Holly O'Dell screamed.

"Did your best friend forget to deposit your paycheck again?" Cliff asked, annoyed.

Holly gave him a dirty look. In addition to being Vivica's best friend and confidant, Holly was also Vivica's maid. "That's not important. My children have been at summer camp, my husband works strange hours in the force, and Lucy is only interested in business. I need human interaction. I've actually resorted to cleaning that damn mansion."

"Holly, why don't you try making friends who aren't your employer? If it were up to me, Vivica would be here right now." Cliff retorted.

"You better pray she doesn't call me at four in the morning again like she has for the past week," Holly screamed.

Hannah put her hands on her hips. "Why on Earth is she calling you at four in the morning? The time difference isn't that far apart."

The maid rubbed her forehead. "She wants to make sure that Lucy isn't around. As I already said. Lucy only ever wants to talk about business…"

MARGOT – 2018

The Fitzpatrick Group was formed in 1966. Initially, they were selling to four car companies. It would be in the decades that came after, thanks to good business deals, that they would grow into what it was today. This was in large part to Brandon Fitzpatrick, but his daughter Margot arguably was what put the family at the top of its game. Margot Fitzpatrick-Sherman-Lance-Fields-Roe-Johns had been Metro Detroit Businesswoman of the Year three years in a row and a record ten times in the twenty-five years. It wasn't because of her great personality and kindness towards others. It was because she was a ruthless bitch who chased every dollar she saw. Margot could make money off a dead goldfish if she found the right angle.

"Mrs. Fitzpatrick, there is someone here to see you."

Margot hit the switch on her intercom. "Tell them they can wait until I'm ready," Margot said as she brushed the hair on one of her prized collectible ponies. She had been collecting them ever since they came out in the eighties.

"They said they aren't going to wait."

The CEO got up from her chair as the door opened. "Lucy Kingsley, you have a lot of nerve, demanding to see me after you went to work for my good-for-nothing, thankfully now ex-sister-in-law."

"Who the hell is Lucy Kingsley?" Perry Fields, the second son to Margot, asked, standing in the doorway. "Hello, Mother."

Margot crossed her arms. "Hello, Mother? I haven't seen or heard from you in two years, and this is how you greet me? What do you want? Money? I'm assuming it is money."

"Funny thing, not everyone is obsessed with money like you are. That said, I will be working in the building again. I'm moving back to Grosse Pointe." Perry explained."

"Where on Earth do you plan on living?" Margot asked as she sat back down.

Perry rolled his eyes. "At the mansion."

"Oh, no... I just finally got your Uncle to move out. I want to be left alone." The CEO stated.

The son sat down across from his mother. "You are forgetting that the mansion belongs to Grandpa Brandon and Grandma Nadia, right? I saw them a few weeks ago when I visited them in Florida. They already said I could move back in. Not to mention- what the hell do you need that entire house to yourself for?"

She could think of any number of reasons. Margot admittedly was actually a little lonely since her younger brother Nial moved out. He stupidly went to the resident Godfather of Grosse Pointe and cashed in a favor to have his ex-mistress's boyfriend or whatever killed. The police didn't suspect Nial in the slightest, but Margot was tired of his bullshit lately and needed breathing space.

Margot's family was far from the smartest group of people. There were years of bad choices made, dating back to when the company first started to find its ground. The biggest mistake was ever getting involved in the Knight family's drama back in the sixties. Her own family were idiots, but the Knights were just fucked up. It took a brief affair with Rodrick Knight back in the mid-eighties to figure that one out. Out of her two sons, Perry had the better business sense, though, and she was willing to give him another round.

"All right, you can stay. You know the rules though, no whores, no Knight's, and no Weston's." Margot put her hands on her desk.

"Mother, don't all those things basically just describe Vivica and possibly her sister?" Perry wondered.

The boy was clearly maturing because it didn't take him long to put that one together. If asked, Margot's brother Nial would still be trying to put two and two together. "Good," Margot breathed out a sigh of relief. "So, we are on the same page. Well, I have an appointment coming in, and I'm sure you are busy yourself." She turned around and faced the window. Margot was not one for goodbyes, even when they were just meant as a pleasantry.

Perry stood up from his chair and nodded. "I will see you tonight, then."

"I suppose, but I'm not having family dinner with you," Margot stated.

"When did you ever?" Perry said aloud.

LUCY – 2018

The eldest Kingsley daughter, Lucy, sat in the lobby of Margot's office. It had been a while since she had been inside this building. Back when Vivica divorced her husband, Nial, Margot had used the chance to get Vivica out of her company.

Vivica had never been fond of Margot, so this was something that she had been fine with. Lucy, not so much. Sure, Lucy was getting paid on a weekly basis. However, since the separation of the two companies, Lucy had basically been unemployed. It looked terrible on her resume. It didn't help that Vivica agreed to revamp their business under a different means. They were a party planning firm. Vivica had mentioned something about cosmetics, but then ran for the hills when her on-and-off-again lover Cliff Knight proposed to her. Lucy was now stuck with the daunting task of figuring out what to do next by herself, with very little help from Vivica.

Lucy looked at her phone. There was a text from her younger brother, Xander. It said, *I'll be home late from training*. Xander had been in the police academy back in New York and graduated when their father, Alexander Kingsley, was arrested for money laundering and tax fraud. At the time, the Kingsley children were looking to rent a house together, along with their teenage sister Langley. Lucy had money, but in the wake of her father's imprisonment, she had to reinvent herself from heiress to self-made businesswoman. Unfortunately, because of this, there was a change of lifestyle in terms of finances.

Lucy was about to put her phone away again when she got another text from Langley. Langley was supposed to be getting a summer job to afford the lifestyle she demanded. It was late August... Lucy sighed. Her younger sister, Langley, had yet again not gotten a job... She put her phone in her purse and looked at the wall clock. The blonde had no clue what was taking Margot so long. Lucy only had a few questions to ask her, which was dangerous, considering Margot's hatred for Vivica. Still, with the redhead MIA, she had no choice but to seek outside help from the town's other resident red-haired vixen.

The door opened to Margot's office opened. All of a sudden, she was back in the present. The office suite was overly bright with everything done in whites. Reality never felt so cold. Margot's personal assistant was clearly lost in something on her tablet. For a moment, Lucy foolishly thought that it might have been Margot. Instead, standing in the doorway was a young man. She assumed he was a new VP or something. She had to admit he was rather cute- short curly red hair, tall, but with a slight summer tan. Lucy tried not to stare but couldn't help it. She got up from her seat, blushing profusely. "Excuse me, but do you know if Margot is in there?"

"Unfortunately," Perry said. He, too, looked at Lucy for an extra-long second. "Do you have a meeting with her?"

"Sort of... I mean, it's really just a few questions. I used to work here, but Margot threw us to the curb. It's Margot's fault I'm in Grosse Pointe in the first place..." Lucy realized she was rambling.

Perry laughed. "Strange. Margot normally drives people away from Grosse Pointe." He crossed his arms. "What company do you work for?"

"*Weston-Kingsley*. It's a relaunch of a cosmetic company from the early 2000's. I'm Lucy Kingsley. My business partner is Vivica Weston. I'm sure you have heard of her."

"Vivica is your business partner, and you are going to Margot for help?" He looked at her again. "You must be relatively new to town."

Lucy smiled. She could sense a bit of ego in his tone. The blonde had to admit it was kind of sexy. "I've actually lived here for over five years now. Are you new to town? I've never seen you before."

"Definitely not new. I grew up here. I just moved back today, though." Perry looked at his phone. "My movers are actually on their way to my house. I need to be there to meet them." He got out his wallet and took out a card. "I'd love to continue this conversation sometime. Possibly over coffee." He handed her the card and started to walk towards the elevator.

Perry Fields, the card read. Lucy put it in her purse. She once again looked at the clock; she didn't have all day. Lucy knocked on the door and walked in. "Margot, hi, sorry to bother you. I just need a few minutes of your time to go over a few legal details. I sent you them a few months back. I never heard back, though."

"Does anyone wait for me to let them in anymore?" Margot glowered as she put the pony-brush down, from where she was stroking her luxurious locks. "Well, sit down." She said as she put the pony-brush into her drawer.

Lucy had always respected Margot more than Vivica ever did. Their dynamic was still different, though. Lucy was a business acquaintance, practically a stranger. Vivica was her ex-sister-in-law three times over. Margot had admired Lucy upon their first-time meeting, but the admiration went away as soon as Lucy chose to work for Vivica. Lucy was just doing what she had to in order to get this damn business off the ground, especially since Vivica had decided to go MIA for the entire summer.

Lucy inhaled a deep sigh. "So, I just need you to sign off on a few property names so that I can announce them in the relaunch happening in September."

Margot stood up and looked out the window. "Well, I could give you those properties, but I don't see why I should. *V Cosmetics* was a hit company back in the day- until Vivica fucked it up by divorcing Nial." Lucy said, "Nial divorced Vivica, I thought."

"Who has time to keep track of those sorts of details? Anyways... The only way I am going to sign off is if Vivica relinquishes her 15% share from the company," Margot explained.

Lucy's jaw dropped. "Why on earth does Vivica have 15% of the company?"

The CEO sighed. She turned back around to face Lucy.

"Every damn time she divorced Nial, she got five percent. Those two idiots kept the same prenup through each marriage. Nial only had about ten shares left, but I made him give those to me. My parents own fifty-one. I need those shares to get controlling interests in the company, which I really should have. I can make this company billions every year, but that isn't enough for Brandon and Nadia, apparently..."

Lucy had met Brandon and Nadia on a handful of occasions. They were the complete opposite of their children. Humble, kind, and genuine. She suspected they were not exactly proud of the way their children turned out.

"I will speak with Vivica about it," Lucy sighed. This meant having to stay up all night to reach her at the right time, hoping Holly wasn't keeping the line busy...

SISTER MARY NEWMAN – 1963

Saint Agnes Church was one of the oldest in the state. Meanwhile, the adjoining school was not much younger. Sister Mary Newman had come to the congregation a few years back. She was not sure of what to think of the town of Grosse Pointe. She didn't seem to like it, but she knew that God had a plan for her, and His plan somehow would involve Grosse Pointe, Michigan. Apparently, teaching eighth grade was one of those things, as well.

Today was definitely a test from God. After all, Rodrick Knight chose to call his classmate Nadia Bloom a whore. Sister Mary Newman had asked him in the hallway if he knew what that term meant; and he couldn't give her a straight answer. Sister Mary knew that any other nun or teacher would have smacked him for saying that- not only in the house of God but to a young and clearly innocent girl. However, Mary didn't believe in hitting, even if Rodrick deserved it. He had only been in her class for a few months, but he was already the worst-behaved student. He was a Knight, though, as the other faculty had mentioned, so there was no controlling him. They hadn't been able to control his father, and they hadn't been able to control his older brother before them.

Mary looked at Rodrick, who was staring right back at her. The boy sitting at the other end of the row was Brandon Fitzpatrick. He punched Rodrick in the eye after hearing him call Nadia the name. Mary had never met Brandon's parents before. They worked two jobs. They managed and ran a bar

Monday through Saturday, and Sundays were the only day they had to put together the steel business they were working on. Mary had often read notes explaining such things in detail from the boy's parents or when Brandon's mother Ida called on the phone.

It was 5:30 pm, and all the other children had been picked up. The sun was still shining for another few minutes at least as the sunset started outside on the crisp fall day. Mary had no idea who was going to pick up either child. She had phoned the Fitzpatrick's bar and left a message with a waitress. She called the Knight household and got the maid, who apparently was Nadia's mother. Lana Bloom had already come and went. She had to be back in the Knight household to finish dinner. Mary had considered asking her to take Rodrick with her but realized that it probably wasn't the smartest of ideas, even if it would have gotten the boy out of her hair.

Finally, someone knocked on the door, and she asked them to come in. "Finally,," Rodrick yelled and got up. "What the heck took you so long?" He asked the woman.

His mother, Delia, looked at the teacher. She was wearing sunglasses indoors and had the slight smell of wine on her breath. "What exactly happened here?"

Mary stood up. "It's nice to see you, Mrs. Knight. It seems that Rodrick has been using words he shouldn't again."

Delia looked at her son. Mary didn't need her to take the glasses off to tell that her eyes probably looked furious.

"What did you say this time?"

Rodrick looked at Mary. "Well, am I going to tell her, or are you?" he asked.

"He called his classmate a prostitute, but that isn't the word he used..." Mary explained.

"That's not the word I used!" Rodrick screamed, like a little brat.

Delia rubbed her forehead, then put her hands on her hips. "Rodrick Knight. You know better than to use such language at school, or anywhere that could embarrass your father." She smacked him hard on the shoulder. "I'll make sure his father finds out." She grabbed his wrist and took him out of the classroom.

The nun had more to say, but she realized that Delia purposely yanked him out to avoid her listening to what she had to say. Mary didn't know how to feel about Delia. That seemed to be a common theme with the Knight family. "I hope you both have a pleasant evening..."

The mother waved goodbye. Another young woman, a strawberry blonde, walked in. She was tiny but pretty. "I'm here to pick up my younger brother. I'm sorry our parents couldn't come, but Mother had to tend to the bar, and Father was preparing for a business deal."

"Oh, it's fine. Brandon technically did nothing wrong. I would just prefer he didn't use his fists to solve a problem." Mary explained to the woman.

Susan turned to her younger brother. "Brandon, you know better than to turn to violence in public. When Dad finds out..." She turned back to the nun. "I'm Susan, by the way."

Sister Mary Newman smiled. "I believe we have seen each other at Mass before."

"I'm sure we have. I almost never miss church. It's the one day the bar isn't open," she explained.

"I've heard many good things about the bar your parents own," Mary explained, trying to make small talk. She could sense that Susan was rather nervous for some reason.

The two siblings looked at one another. "Our parents don't technically own the bar," Brandon murmured. "They just run it for the old woman who really owns it."

Susan patted her brother on the shoulder. "Yes, our father is trying to get into the steel industry. It's been a journey."

"I wish him well on his journey. Maybe one day he will be as big as the Knight family in town."

Brandon couldn't help but laugh at that. "Dad wishes. He idolizes the Knights..."

LANGLEY – 2018

Langley Kingsley had originally been from Manhattan. She had moved to Grosse Pointe back in early January of this year. Her summers used to involve trips to Europe and extended stays at her family's Long Island home. This summer, however, she spent lounging between the Weston pool, the Knight pool, and the Fitzpatrick pool... Today, however, her best friend Harry Knight decided they would slum it with the locals.

Langley scowled. "Why on Earth would you want to go to a public pool? It's so filthy..."

Harry Knight said, "You said I needed to attempt making more friends this summer. We only have a little bit longer before the school year starts. So far, I have made no new friends."

The blonde girl put her sunglass on. "Well, why couldn't we have done it at a mall or something?"

Harry shrugged. "I mean, we could, I guess. It's not like we are at some public pool, though. We're at the yacht club."

"Any pool that is open to strangers is public in my eyes. I mean, Lord, Mrs. Templeton is in the shallow end right now, and I don't think she has showered in a week." Langley noted.

Grosse Pointe might have been a wealthier suburb of Detroit, but it wasn't the same as being in Manhattan itself. She longed for the days of being able to do nothing all day without a care in the world. Now she was broke.

Langley sighed. "We need to start working on my love life while we are at it."

"Why? You and Brad have been getting along really well," Harry thought out loud.

"Harry, your cousin is hot as F, but he won't make anything official." She turned and noticed a boy who was taking his shirt off. He had a natural tan about him and short curly hair. A contender, but he wasn't looking at her. He was looking at Harry, who wasn't even shirtless. "Don't look now, but that guy over there is checking you out." She got out her phone and started texting.

Harry turned a little and then turned back. "That's Preston Costa."

The blonde continued to text. "Great, go chat with him."

"Langley, his dad is a huge mob boss. I doubt he is gay."

"He can't be gay because his father is a mob boss? That's not prejudiced at all, Harry." She was looking at her social media, and all her old friends were on vacation. She hadn't spoken to any of them since her exile to the Mid-West. She wasn't jealous. Just pissed off. "You should go talk to him. Who hasn't slept with an organized crime boss's son?"

The young Knight looked at the blonde girl. "Who said I was looking to sleep with him?"

Langley remembered a few months back; Harry had vowed that he was now saving himself for the right person after his first sexual encounter with another boy ended in a court case. His second sexual encounter was with her, in order to get him to calm down. She personally didn't understand the concept of abstinence but was willing to support her friend. His cousin? Not so much.

Langley was about to continue speaking when Preston walked over. She looked at Harry. "Do you need anything?" She asked. She knew that Harry wasn't going to say anything.

"Oh, I just wanted to say hi." He looked at Harry specifically. "We go to school together, right?"

"Umm well, sort of..." Harry was tongue-tied.

The Kingsley girl sighed. "If you go to Saint Agnes, then yes, he goes to school with you. I will be attending there as well in the fall. I'm Protestant, though." Not that she had been to church in several years. She was only transferring to Saint Agnes because she couldn't handle the public school any longer.

Preston nodded his head. "That's cool. You're Harry Knight, right?" He looked at Harry.

Harry blushed. "Yes," was all he managed to say. Langley knew that Harry had always been an overly nervous person. It didn't help that throughout most of the summer, men had come up to him, often asking for sexual favors. Harry had been blackmailed throughout the last school year with a sex tape of his first sexual experience with another guy. The guy in question, Todd Roberts, had been sent away because of it. Harry was able to get off. People argued it was because of who his family was. Even so, Harry didn't deserve any of it, to begin with.

"So, what is it like to be the son of a criminal?" Langley asked, trying to move the conversation further. "My father was involved with the New York Mob scene from a financial standpoint. Probably won't be seeing him anytime soon..."

The tan boy looked at her, confused. "Who said my family was involved in any crimes? My mother owns an art gallery, and my father is in the shipping business."

These were both excellent coverups for crime, Langley thought. She had friends back in Manhattan whose parents were involved in the big-league mob, and they always gave similar answers. "So, then, when are we hanging out? I'm casually seeing Brad Fitzpatrick. Harry is single. Three's a crowd, but four is a party. You should come over to Brad's house tonight for an after-dinner swim. Doesn't that sound fun."

"I will consider it." With that, Preston turned around.

Langley put her sunglasses back on. "He has a nice ass."

"We don't know if he is gay." Harry slightly whispered back.

"Oh, he is definitely gay. He wasn't checking out my girls. He wanted to check your boys out, though."

"How on Earth are we friends?" Harry asked.

The blonde shrugged. "I ask myself that constantly. Love you!"

HANNAH – 2018

Hannah had her own office... She insisted on not getting special treatment. Sure, other VP's had offices, and hers was not even that large, but something about it made her feel uncomfortable.

Back when Hannah was in college, she had tried so hard to get on the ground floor of a lucrative business. The main issue was that none were lucrative. She graduated, and then, Hannah couldn't find a job anywhere. That wasn't going to stop her from moving out of North Pointe and on her own. That is- until her supposed friends kicked her out onto the street, and she was left homeless and jobless. Instead of turning to her favorite Aunt, Vivica, she went back to her father for a small loan. He wouldn't just hand over the money. Instead, he offered her the very job she had now. Hannah wouldn't accept it. Instead, she went for a position as car salesperson at a Knight-owned dealership. The brunette girl's sales had gone above and beyond what anyone had expected. That's when her father offered her the position again.

Hannah still didn't want to take the job. But then, the guy she liked, Xander Kingsley quit to take a job with the GPPD. It didn't help that Xander, for no real reason whatsoever, went to her twin sister Hope. But once, Hannah and Xander had slept together, the night of Harry's birthday, after a drunken night of 'getting to know one another better'. Hannah suspected that Xander had not told Hope about this. She honestly questioned if she was better off not being with him if he would just randomly go to her sister. That's when he walked in...

"Hey, how is my favorite ex-co-worker?" He joked.

Xander had the most amazing baby blue eyes and blond hair. He had a baby face, but it worked in his favor, somehow. Hannah didn't know what attracted her to him in the first place. Besides, she knew that Hope couldn't have possibly been attracted to the same things.

"Fine. How are things with Hope?" She gave him a dirty look. Hannah had tried her hardest to avoid Xander for most of the summer. Hope had moved out of North Pointe in late Spring and was living in the same hotel as her. While Hannah missed her Aunt dearly, she was glad that Vivica had gone MIA because it made it so easy to avoid her home, where Xander was currently living with his siblings.

The Kingsley boy frowned. "Fine, I suppose. I've missed hanging out with you, though."

The Knight girl could tell something was going on. But she couldn't figure out what it was. She just didn't trust Xander anymore. "Well, you have Hope. So, you shouldn't be that sad. We look identical. Only, I'm not a psychopath."

"I knew you were mad." He crossed his arms. He had puppy dog eyes when he looked sad. Hannah couldn't help but moan silently. "It's nothing personal, Hannah. I like you both, but I just feel like we make better friends. Hope is a little different."

Was Hope a little different? She had heard variations of that her entire life. The past ten years or so had been from boys. Hope was a better kisser. Hope had a better ass, Hope's breasts somehow were perkier... Hannah knew what Xander meant, and honestly, it kind of made her want to throw up.

"I'm not interested in being played with. We slept together, Xander."

Xander rubbed his forehead. "I honestly had forgotten." She could tell he was biting his tongue at this response. "You and I just seemed like we were such good friends. You never seemed to give off a flirty vibe, and honestly, we were both so drunk that night."

"So, how is the GPPD?" She asked. She honestly could have cared less, but she was done listening to him try to justify things.

"It's beyond awesome. I mean, the only time I ever get to see action is when Mrs. Templeton calls the police on your Aunt's house. She'll think Holly is breaking in or that Langley is a hooker." He cackled, throwing his head back. Hannah didn't give him the satisfaction of laughing back. Xander continued. "It never really works in her favor, though. Holly's husband is the one I'm shadowing right now."

Hannah nodded. She sat down at her desk and started to log onto her computer. "Well, that is nice. Mrs. Templeton is the town nut, so nothing really shocking there." Hannah honestly didn't have anything else to say to him. The few times they interacted over the summer; it became increasingly obvious that he wasn't the same guy she thought he was. Hannah quickly realized that she didn't want to define herself by her relationships in the same way her Mother and Aunt had their entire lives. Hope and Hannah would never be close, but she wouldn't go to battle with her for a man. She *won* Xander, as terrible as it sounded, and Hannah wasn't going to fight her on it. Speak of the devil woman...

"Xander, there you are!" Hope said, bursting into the room. "I said I was only going to be five minutes with Daddy, and you go and find yourself in here..." Hope said with a creepy smile on her face.

Hannah honestly never remembered her calling their father "*Daddy*" past age ten. She clearly was putting on an act.

Whether it be for their father or Xander, that was another question.

Hope turned to her sister. "So, then, how are you enjoying your new job? It must be so much nicer than asking if people would like a box for their chicken at that grocery store."

"I haven't worked at that grocery store in a year... I'm still getting used to the change, though, which is why I need to be left alone right now. I need to prep for a meeting." Hannah did have a meeting, but as of right now, she was just sitting in on it.

Her twin Hope walked right over to Xander and hung herself from his neck. "It's just so nice to see my sister finally get a big girl job. We were all so worried about her."

The sad part was that she was probably right. Hannah's mother never could understand why she wouldn't want to exploit everything that life had given her. Her father understood not wanting to work for *Knight* but thought she was foolish not to use any contacts they had through the company to find work. Harry didn't voice his opinion, and Hope voiced her own all day and night, even though she was happy to see her leave.

"If you two wouldn't mind?" Hannah looked at them.

DELIA – 1963

Agreeing to move to Michigan had been a struggle for Delia. She had grown up in Seattle but had been going to school in Northern California when she first met Benton. They quickly fell for one another and even quicker had a child. She had definitely loved him at the time, but she wasn't so sure if she was ever *in love* with him. At this point, with two teenage children, it seemed like a silly question to even ask herself.

Delia and Benton had a very stable marriage compared to others in their social circle, as far as she was concerned. When they had lived in California, she had looked after the keeping of the house, and Benton worked. He drank, but it didn't bother her. Delia herself enjoyed one or two glasses of wine a day- but never more than three. Once or twice every so often, she would have a fourth. It wasn't anything terrible, though. She knew how to remain a functioning member of society. It was her husband who would cause scenes. Again, though, it didn't bother her.

Delia sat at the kitchen table, looking at Rodrick. She never could understand why he was the way he was. She punished him often. Delia tried not to get his father involved, considering that would just lead to physical punishment. She was at a loss, though. "We won't tell your father about this, but I'm not going to keep protecting you."

"You beat me with a spoon for five minutes. How do you consider that protecting me?" Rodrick held a rag filled with ice on his back.

"If your father had served you the punishment, he wouldn't have had to use the spoon, and we would probably be in the emergency room half the night." Delia pointed out.

Benton walked into the kitchen and looked around. "Where the hell is dinner?"

"One of the staff is going to pick something up. Lana had to deal with family issues tonight." Delia explained, this boy was her son and he was turning into a monster. Delia hated admitting it to herself but it was the damn truth.

That's when Delia's husband walked over to the fridge. "I've been waiting for dinner all day." He took out a beer. "Dinner better be here soon. Honestly, the nerve of that maid sometimes. It's been a long day."

Delia walked over to her husband and casually took the beer out of his hand. He didn't seem to notice. "Why don't you tell us about it?"

"Just more nonsense. I don't know what Father was doing the past few years, but there are a lot of things in that company that need restructuring. Even worse- that will take years to do. We just aren't making enough money." He leaned against the fridge. He noticed his son holding the rag of ice. "What happened to him?"

"I tripped." Rodrick was trained at this point on what to say.

Benton ignored him. "Oh, so then that Irish guy came back today. He really wants us to use his metal company for the cars. I'm not taking the gamble, though. I know for a fact that none of the other companies have even taken meetings with him. The fact I continue to humor him is shocking to me."

"Well," Delia said, "He is probably just trying to make a name for himself." she pointed out.

"I have no issue with people wanting to chase an honest dollar. I just have an issue with foreigners coming here and trying to take the hard-earned money that we earned first."

Delia honestly had no clue what he was trying to get at. She often wondered if he had an issue with the fact that her parents were not from here. She knew that Heathcliff did.

"Where is Lana?" Heathcliff scowled as he stormed into the kitchen. "I don't smell food."

Delia felt like a broken record... "She went home early. Her daughter had a stressful day at school and needed to be tended to."

Heathcliff sat down at the kitchen table, next to Rodrick. "Well, I hope she is all right. You are in her class, aren't you, boy?"

Rodrick looked at his mother, then back at his grandfather. "Yes. She is a nice girl. She spends all her time with that Fitzpatrick boy, though..."

"Fitzpatrick?" Benton said, turning to his son. "That's the poor son of a bitch who wants to get into the steel business. Well, it makes sense the maid's daughter would be friends with those Irish slobs."

"Benton, I want you to strike a deal with that Fitzpatrick guy," Heathcliff said, looking at his watch.

Benton stormed over to his father in a rage. "What on Earth are you on? Why should I give money to those foreigners?"

"They will take a lesser bid. It's exactly what we need right now to save money going into the fourth quarter. Fitzpatrick will have his five minutes of wealth and then go broke by this time next year." Heathcliff wouldn't take his eyes off his son.

The Latina wife wanted to scream sometimes. Delia couldn't believe the things that would come out of Heathcliff and Benton. She looked at her younger son, in the hope that he would say something kind. Maybe it would give her hope for the Knight men.

"It's probably for the best this way. Those Fitzpatricks shouldn't be in this town anyway. It's too good for them." Rodrick crossed his arms.

Nadia rubbed her forehead. "Rodrick, go upstairs and study until the butler brings the food." She had hoped he learned his lesson from this afternoon. However, it was clear that wasn't the case.

SUSAN – 1963

Susan, the older Fitzpatrick child, had taken her younger
brother into the bar their family managed on the outskirts of
town. The two siblings had remained silent on the way home.
Susan was still unsure of how their parents would react to
Brandon going after the Knight boy. They both knew that their
father Seamus had been trying to get into business with
Benton Knight for months. Their parents were not sure of why
the Knight family- or any of the big four- would not jump at
taking advantage of their steel. Susan and Brandon knew that
it just wasn't a lucrative business deal, unfortunately.

Susan had often heard stories of their father's journey
through childhood in Ireland, to marrying their mother Ida,
moving to America, and traveling to Michigan. Her father had
thought he could find work working in the auto industry.
Unfortunately, he didn't have the skills needed. Instead, he
worked two jobs, one as a bartender at the bar they currently
ran. When the owner's husband passed on, she wasn't able to
run the bar herself at her age. She offered Seamus and Ida a
partial partnership in the business. They humbly agreed,
knowing that it would keep the bills paid while Seamus
worked on his side project with a few friends and investors at
nighttime. The Fitzpatrick daughter had high hopes for her
father. She wasn't sure that his dream would ever be
accomplished, though.

"Girl, get me a drink!" Mrs. Templeton screamed from a
barstool. Susan had just walked in with her brother, and

already, she was back to work. She walked over and poured the old bat a shot of whiskey.

"Here you go." She looked at Mrs. Templeton with a fake smile.

Mrs. Templeton yanked the drink off the counter and swigged it. "I'm not tipping you for doing your job. Now stop looking at me. I'll call for you when I'm ready for another drink."

The brunette girl couldn't help but roll her eyes. She turned around, and Ida was standing behind her. Her mother looked overworked. Which she was. Susan frowned. "Sorry, it took so long. The car is acting up."

"Well, hopefully, your father will be able to afford a new one soon. He had his meeting with Benton Knight today. I think it went well, based on what your father says." Ida had always been overly optimistic.

"Mother, we might need to talk about that deal. Brandon might be the one who needs to tell you, though..." Susan explained.

Ida looked over at Brandon, who was sitting alone at a booth, studying. "What did his teacher want? Brandon better not have been acting up in class. Though he never seemed to have that issue before. I hope nothing is wrong."

While Susan knew what Brandon had done was noble in principle, it didn't change the fact that it might have hurt the Knight deal. "Well, again, I think that Brandon should be the one to tell you..."

"Girl, I want another shot!" Mrs. Templeton screamed from across the bar.

Ida rolled her eyes this time. "I heard that woman only comes here because she was banned from the yacht club," The mother whispered.

Susan could believe it. "Where is Dad, by the way?"

"He went to pick up an order for the family business."

Family business? It was hardly a family business. They didn't have a business. They had unpaid debts to people and a ridiculous amount of metal in their basement. Susan sighed. She really did hope that something would work out for her parents. She knew that Seamus would never give up on this pipe dream, and Ida would continue to support him like a loving wife- even if they were living on the streets one day because of it.

HOLLY – 2018

Holly, Vivica Fitzpatrick's maid, dragged down a suitcase from the redhead's second floor, into the living room. Holly was going to pick up Vivica from Paris. It took her all summer, but she finally was able to track her calls down. Vivica made the mistake of using a landline, for once. Holly had forced her husband to help track the calls after the first month. Holly wasn't playing games. She needed her best friend and employer back. She was bored, and Lucy was already starting to drive her crazy again.

As Holly walked across the room, she noticed Brad sitting on the couch. "Why aren't you spending time with your girlfriend?"

Brad looked at her. "Well, I mean, I don't think I'd really call her my girlfriend. At least not yet. We haven't really made things official."

"You live under the same roof. How much more official do you need to make things?" Holly rolled her eyes as she stopped dragging the luggage. She had packed the one thing that would be sure to get Vivica back home- with all the proper threats involved.

"I mean that is sort of a circumstantial situation. It's not like we sleep anywhere near one another," Brad pointed out.

Holly knew he had a point. Vivica had moved Langley to the other wing once she and Brad started getting close. It wasn't that Holly was advocating a sexual relationship out of Brad and Langley. It just confused her to no end as to what

Vivica thought was going to happen. Brad had been the President of the Abstinence Club at his boarding school. He wasn't interested in sex before marriage. "Do you want to go to Paris, to drag home your mother?"

The blond boy shrugged. "I should probably stay here. She will come back when she is ready, though, Holly." If only that were true. Holly had played this game before. Vivica was more than likely still in Paris. It would take about five minutes of fake arguing before she made a run with Holly to the nearest airport. "Suit yourself. I'd say that Lucy is in charge until I get back, but then again, I doubt anything that crazy will happen." That boy was more behaved than her seven-year-old...

***

"Holly, I don't have time to go searching for Vivica throughout Europe right now," Cliff stated as he tried closing his front door behind her.

Holly put her foot in the door, halting his exit. "So, what you are saying is that you are giving up on her?"

"What I'm saying is that I don't have the time right now. There is a slight auto crisis starting to brew. You know very well that I want Weston back and living here," he admitted.

Holly could tell he was still being genuine.

The maid shrugged. "Fine, but don't be shocked when she takes it as a sign."

"Then don't go after her. She always returns, Holly. This isn't the first time she has gone MIA after being presented with something life changing. You weren't around when I went away for our first summer together, or when Tiffany and I got married, or when Tiffany came back from being kidnapped. Those are just three examples. I promise you, Vivica will return." Cliff assured her.

Holly realized that he was right. He probably knew her more than anyone. In her mind, Holly herself knew Vivica the best, though. The red-haired vixen had a history of oversharing things that had nothing to do with what was relevant. She remembered her first week with Vivica- almost six years ago now...

HOLLY – 2013

Vivica screamed, "Where the heck is the box with Laura's clothes in it? She keeps texting me to send her a bunch of sweaters while she is in Australia. How cold could it possibly be in Australia?" As she screamed, the woman descended the staircase.

Margot looked at her once again Sister-in-Law with disgust. "I have no idea where my nieces' clothes are. Half the shit you brought from your house still needs to be sorted. The delivery drivers said they had at least two more trips to make. I told them not to bother..." She looked at Holly, who was a little confused.

This was only a temporary job, she kept telling herself. Holly's husband would be off disability soon enough, and she could go back to finishing up her degree. She wouldn't be a maid for the rest of her life. Holly had limited interaction with the Fitzpatrick family but had, of course, heard of their exploits. She watched as the two red-haired in-laws bickered with one another. That is when Nadia walked in. The family matriarch and the town saint. "Will the two of you shut the hell up?" Clearly, saints didn't all speak the same. "I can hear you from the kitchen. I'm trying to bake cookies with Brad."

"Who the hell is Brad?" Margot mumbled.

Vivica struck her a dirty look. "Your nephew..."

Margot looked out into space for a moment. "My nephew's name is Rod, and then there is your daughter, Laura."

"How on Earth can you forget Brad? Rod is Nial's first son. You literally sat next to Brad at the wedding. It was Nial's idea for you to be his God-mother." Vivica spat out. Nadia got in-between the two. "Enough out of both of you. Brandon and I will be here for another week before we go on our travels. We are going to act like a civilized family, even if it kills us." She marched her way back into the kitchen.

Vivica looked at Holly. "Who is she?"

Margot turned around and remembered that the maid was there. "Oh, she is just one of the new maids… I hired her this morning." She looked at her watch. "I'm going to be late for a conference call because of you." She grabbed her coat off the rack and marched out of the house.

The maid looked at her new employer. *Was she her employer?* Margot had hired her, but Nadia and Brandon technically owned the house. She wasn't really sure about any of this. She had never been a maid before or knew anyone who had been one.

"Hi," Holly managed to say.

"Can you believe her?" Vivica said as she made her way into the living room. Holly was unsure if she was supposed to follow, but then, Vivica continued to talk. "Did she make you sign the non-disclosure agreement on her ponies?"

Holly quickly ran into the next room. "Ponies? You have stables here?" She thought the lake was in their backyard. *Where on Earth could stables go?*

Vivica laughed. "There are no stables. No, Margot collects those plastic pony toys. She has thousands of them. They are all lined up in two rooms. She has *all* of them. She was in her twenties when those came out…"

"Oh, well, that is interesting." Holly wasn't sure if she should give a genuine opinion on how weird that was. "I should probably get to cleaning." Holly had no idea where the cleaning things were or what she was supposed to clean. The house was cleaner than the hospital if she was honest.

"Oh, take a break. If Margie hired you, then you are probably mentally exhausted," Vivica stated. She got into her phone for a second. She looked down at her feed. "Well, it looks like my bitch of a sister is hosting a party. I never got an invitation."

"Your sister is the one who came back from the dead, right?" Holly made the mistake of asking.

Vivica shot her a dirty look. "Unfortunately, she was never dead. Just kidnapped. I mourned over her for nothing. Next time she dies, I'm spitting on her grave."

Holly couldn't tell if she actually liked this Vivica woman or not. Vivica's mouth clearly had no filter. Yet, she seemed to be more honest than most people she had met. It was slightly shocking that Vivica hated her sister as much as she did, though.

"So, how old is your son?" Holly asked.

"Ten. Though, I feel like I just gave birth to him a few years ago. I know that can't be right, though. My daughter is off traveling somewhere instead of doing school. Which, I guess I can't complain. I myself never use my college degree. I have the most wonderful nieces and nephews, though. You would love Hannah, especially. I adore her. She is so much like me but so much her own person, which is a good thing. Hope is very much her mother's daughter, but I love her just the same. Harry is Brad's age, and they were raised as brothers up until the bitch came back..." Vivica laughed and looked out into space for a few seconds. "You will like working here. I think we will get along really well."

The new maid somehow had to agree. She didn't know why, though. It was almost an instant connection.

LANA -1963

"I can't believe you work for that little shit's family," Midge Bloom screamed.

Lana loved her Mother-in-Law, but she had a mouth on her worse than Benton or his child, Rodrick.

"I should go beat him with my cane." Midge got up from her chair, but Lana stopped her.

Lana said, "We need to remember that I do work for the child's family, and we need the income. Rodger's life insurance is not going to last forever."

Rodger was Lana's late husband and Midge's son. Midge had moved in to help with Nadia when he passed away.

Nadia sighed. "I'll survive. I just don't understand why Brandon punched him." She sat down on the couch in their living room.

Lana kissed her daughter on the forehead. "It doesn't excuse his behavior just because you can handle it. Still, though, thank you for not going overboard like your Grandmother. Heathcliff is a good man. It's his son and his family that are the issues."

The grandmother, Midge, moaned. "We should boycott *Knight!* We can buy one of those foreign cars."

"With what money?" Lana sighed. "Besides, if it weren't for *Knight's* insurance, Rodger wouldn't have had life insurance." Lana rubbed her forehead. "Why are we having this conversation right now? I'm not selling the car." She was going to continue, but there was a knock on the door. She went to open it. "Oh, hello, David."

"Hi," David said, stepping into the doorway. "I just wanted to check on the rent payment. I've kept my father away for as long as I could, but he wants it. I'm really sorry, Mrs. Bloom." Lana could tell he looked sincere, maintaining his eye contact.

She went into the kitchen and came out with a tin can. "Here is all but one-hundred dollars. I should be able to get that to you at the end of next week."

David smiled. "I think that this should be able to cover you for another week or so if you need it."

"Thank you."

Midge looked at David. "Are you still seeing that girlfriend of yours?"

The landlord's son blushed. "Oh, well, we actually decided to stop seeing one another a while ago."

"Oh, did you hear that, Lana? David is single. Isn't that too bad?" Midge bluntly stated.

Lana shot her Mother-in-Law a dirty look. Lana knew that she meant well, but she doubted David would ever want to get involved with a widow who had a teenage daughter.

"Yes, it is sad. She seemed nice the few times I met her." Lana looked at her watch. "Time for dinner."

"Why don't you invite David over?" Midge suggested.

"Yeah, mom, why don't you?" Nadia asked.

The landlord's son blushed. "I don't think I could impose on your family dinner."

Midge laughed. "Oh please, we always have more than we need. I've lived with Lana long enough that I've started to adapt to her Spanish ways. I always make enough food for leftovers for a week."

"I wish you would stop making so much food." Lana rolled her eyes. She looked back at David. "Really, I don't want you to feel obligated."

"Well, to be honest, I probably have just had a sandwich for dinner. If there is a chance of a hot cooked meal, I might be interested." David admitted.

"Well, then it is settled. Nadia, go set another place at the table." Midge told her Granddaughter.

SUSAN – 1963

Susan's shift was finally coming to an end for the night. She looked over to her brother, who was mopping the floors. He was grounded for the next century. Susan couldn't help but feel bad for him. He would probably never be able to go out with his friends again. Of course, if it had been any other child that Brandon had punched, then he would be a hero in his parents' eyes. It had to be the son of a Knight, though. All she really wanted to do was get home, watch the news, and then do a little bit of journaling.

The door opened, and a new-but-familiar face to Susan walked in. It was Brandon's teacher, whom she had met with earlier that day. Sister Mary was walking over to him.

"Hi, Susan, right?"

Susan was stuck in her tracks for a minute. She hadn't noticed earlier, but the teacher had the most beautiful eyes she had ever seen. She realized she hadn't said anything in a minute or so. "Um, yes... My name is Susan. You are Brandon's teacher, correct?"

The nun nodded. "Yes. Sister Mary Newman, but please just call me Mary. I feel like everyone calls me by my full title. It gets weird sometimes. I hope it stops, soon."

"Are nuns allowed to come into bars?" Susan immediately felt terrible about asking her that.

"Yes." Mary giggled. "I'm allowed to come in. There are many things I'm allowed to do, actually. To be honest, when I originally got the calling, I was nervous because I thought I would do nothing but go to church all day. I was definitely wrong."

The Fitzpatrick daughter nodded. "Well, that is good to know. Would you like a drink?"

"Well, maybe just an iced tea," Mary explained.

Brandon walked over to them, speaking in a hushed tone. "Sister Mary, what are you doing here?"

Mary looked at her student. "I thought I should do more exploring of the town. I've been stuck at Saint Agnes since I got here, I feel."

The two Fitzpatrick siblings looked at one another. "This isn't really Grosse Pointe. It's more of the outskirts of Grosse Pointe and Detroit," Brandon explained.

Susan wished her brother would stop undermining where they lived. It was a nice enough area. They didn't need a mansion like the Knights family to be happy. Their father sure as hell thought they did, though. He almost seemed to cry a little over the notion that Brandon might have destroyed his life's work. She honestly was getting a little bit tired of hearing about his get-rich-quick schemes. The bar needed work. It could be so much more successful than it was, but heaven forbid her father realize they had a business venture.

No, he had to do better than his father had...

She put the iced tea down in front of the nun. "I hope you enjoy it. It is on the house. Just don't tell my father." The man could be very hypocritical. He would neglect the bar almost daily, and yet the minute profits were down; it was an issue.

"Brandon, why aren't you mopping?" Seamus asked as he walked out of the kitchen. Brandon went back to his punishment, mopping the floors until they were sopping wet. Her father looked down at the nun. "Hello, sister, what brings you in here?"

Mary put her hand out, but the man didn't shake it. Susan never saw her father shake a woman's hand. It was rather sexist, in her opinion. She assumed the Knights' men would just be, just based on their upbringing alone.

Sister Mary said, softly, "I'm actually Brandon's teacher."

It took her father all of a second to put things together. He sighed, narrowing his eyes at her. "I need you to understand that Brandon doesn't normally go around hurting other students. He is being punished, so don't worry."

"Oh, don't worry. I trust that Brandon has learned his lesson. I'm happy that he stood up for Nadia." Mary explained.

"Well, the boy should have known better. People like Rodrick Knight and his father are important to this town. They don't have the time to be getting into fights." Mary looked at Susan and took another sip of her iced tea. "I hate to tell you this, Mr. Fitzpatrick, but Rodrick is in fights constantly. He normally starts them himself."

Seamus struck the nun a dirty look. "I don't believe it. The wealthy have better things to do than fight. Fighting is for the poor…"

Susan knew he meant that fighting was for people like his family. Seamus's father had forced him to box. Seamus hated it. Yet, he didn't seem to grasp himself that his family didn't seem to like anything about the way he treated them. They were sick of walking on eggshells because the company needed new business cards, or the company needed new supplies. The company didn't exist. The auto companies weren't interested in getting involved any more than any of the lumber companies. Her fathers dream was never going to come to fruition.

HARRY – 2018

Before the end of last school year, Sister Mary Newman had given Harry the diaries of Susan Fitzpatrick. Susan was a closeted, secret lesbian that Mary had befriended in her youth. Susan had died from cancer much too soon. Reading her diaries, Harry could see that very easily. The woman didn't have an extraordinary life, but she dealt with so many things. The issues she dealt with in her everyday life included the beginning of the Knight and Fitzpatrick feud. Harry had heard both sides of the story from so many people over the years, but here was documentation of the things going on as they actually happened—discussion of his grandfather as a teenager as well as the teenage Brandon and Nadia. The town's beloved couple were at a one-point humans. It was surreal, to say the least.

It was odd to read about places he had visited so many times, as well as locations that no longer existed. The bar that the Fitzpatrick's ran had burnt down in the late '70s, long after they had struck it rich. A diner his father and aunt frequented as teens was built in its place. It was odd to read about the Fitzpatrick family living in anything other than a mansion.

"Give me that book. We need to party every last second away," Langley said as she slammed the book shut in her hands.

"Langley, what party? It's literally just the three of us." Brad pointed out, walking out with pop for all three of them.

The blonde sighed. "Well, Preston Costa might be joining us." She turned to Harry and winked.

Brad looked at his cousin. "Why on Earth would Preston Costa be coming to my house?"

"I invited him," Langley stated.

Yes, Langley did invite him. Harry wished she hadn't. He still had no idea if the guy was gay or not. He really wasn't interested in a relationship with anyone, though. After everything that had happened with Todd Roberts the year before, he just wasn't ready. He knew the reputation that Preston had. The guy probably wasn't into guys, and even if he was, he was still Preston Costa. Sure, he was cute. Well, no, really, he was hot.

Harry couldn't deny that. He was extremely hot. The teenage Knight boy would be lying if he said he hadn't noticed him in the past. The issue was that Preston had never noticed him back. Not until now. Not until after Harry happened to come out of the closet, not by choice.

It was funny. Harry knew that there were a couple of kids that identified as bi in his class. Two were in a relationship. There was Todd, who had been openly bisexual himself. Then maybe one or two gay guys who were both in relationships with guys from public schools. Harry had never been close to any of them. The two girls in the relationship had reached out to him after he was outed. He appreciated their sympathy, but it was clear from the moment they spoke that they weren't going to be besties anytime soon.

Harry had always told himself, the number one reason (aside from his insecurities) for why he never came out was because he didn't want to be labeled by his sexuality alone. He was so much more than that. At least he thought he was. The good thing when he was forced out was that most people didn't really seem to label him that way. Though he took the rest of the semester off, so he really didn't know how things would go. Especially at his Catholic school. He would know soon enough, though.

That being said, Harry soon realized that there were a lot more gay people around than he knew. Or at least- people who didn't mind sex where they could get it. Harry though, was not interested at all. He received texts and messages on social media day in and out from guys he kind of knew of- but not really at all. They would claim they had admired him from afar for years in class and wanted to meet up. Langley had taken it upon herself to monitor all his messages. His father's lawyer did as well, and they both advised him against anything. Langley more colorfully, though.

That was why Harry just wasn't interested in whatever Preston Costa was after... If anything at all. Preston probably identified as *straight,* but he didn't mind *experimenting...* Which was code for closeted gay or bisexual and never coming out. It didn't help that most every guy interested was also twice the size of him and would more than likely beat him up if he ever said anything. Which again, was a turn-off, if he had been interested.

"I don't think he is going to show up, Brad," Harry sighed. "We don't have anything to worry about. Unless he wants to go after Langley." He realized suddenly that wasn't the right choice of words.

Langley sighed. "Well, we are doing something fun. Let's play a prank phone call on Mrs. Templeton."

Brad put his hand on her shoulder. "Let's leave the woman alone for a day or so. She is crazy and rich enough to eventually figure out who is pretending to be the Save the Immigrants Foundation people."

"I never get to have any fun," Langley rolled her eyes.

Harry, the Knight boy, could tell that things between his best friend and cousin were not going so well. Langley wanted more than just someone to talk with. Brad was far too pure for her. It was hard to relate to Langley sometimes. Brad was practically his brother, and Harry had to side with him more than her. He could tell that Brad had sort of started treating him the same after Langley chose to have sex with Harry a few months back.

"I think I'm just going to go home. You guys should have some alone time," Harry stated. He grabbed his backpack and the book out of Langley's hand.

That's when someone walked in through the patio door. It was Preston. He was wearing a black t-shirt and a pair of green swim trunks. It was different than what he had been wearing earlier. He waved to Harry, but it could have been Langley, depending on how you looked at it... Or even Brad.

"Hey, Harry." Preston sad.

Harry's heart stopped for a second.

"Brad, I want a drink," Langley said.

"Here." Brad put one in her hand. Langley quickly threw it behind her. "Okay, let's go get you another drink," Brad said, annoyed. The blonde couple walked back into the house together.

The curly-haired boy stretched his arms behind his back and looked at Preston. Preston was smiling, and he had to assume it was at him. That- or he was an admirer of birds or trees or maybe even the sunset... It had to be one of those things. "I didn't think you would come," Harry said.

Preston smirked at him. "To be honest, I wasn't so sure I would either. That blonde friend of yours seems a little aggressive..."

He wasn't wrong about that, Harry thought. "Well, I mean, feel free to use the pool, I guess. I was actually just about to go home."

His phone went off in his pocket. It was a text from Langley saying that if he went home, she would use her social media following to make his life worse than Todd ever had. He couldn't even see her from the patio door window.

How could she hear this conversation?

"Well, that's too bad. I thought we could hang... You know, all four of us. For some reason, I thought there would be more people here." Preston admitted.

Langley hadn't been able to get anyone to come. She didn't have any friends at Saint Agnes, and she had hated everyone at Grosse Pointe West. The only other people she knew in town were her brother and sister. None of whom were interested in hanging out. Well, Hannah probably would have, but it would have been awkward.

Harry sighed, "Yeah. Langley seems to have trouble making friends around here. She is from New York."

Preston nodded. "My dad is from there, too. He seems to have the same issue. He seems to not mind your Brads' father Nial all that much, though."

There was definitely a lot to unpack in that sentence, but Harry chose to ignore it.

Harry murmured, "If you have other things to do right now, go ahead and leave." He wasn't sure if that sounded rude or not. Harry wished that Langley hadn't gone inside.

"You have really nice hair," Preston said, sort of casually.

"Oh, um, thanks. It's sort of unmanageable. I hate cutting it." It took him a moment to realize that might have been a compliment.

Harry's phone went off again. Langley said, *Go fuck yourself with that comment about New York, but compliment Preston back.*

"You have nice... Skin." If Preston wasn't gay and he mentioned him having nice eyes, lips, muscles, or hair, it would have been either awkward or ended with him in the ER.

The mob son laughed. "Thanks. That's nice of you. I don't really do anything special to make it nice."

"So, you are on the football team, right?" Harry asked.

Preston nodded. "Yeah. Were you thinking of trying out?"

Not in a million years. "No... I'm more into books." He had to admit that he was into the way that guys looked in football uniforms. Basketball uniforms were more his thing, though. Which he was pretty sure Preston also played.

Langley burst outside, where she had clearly been eavesdropping, "I just called Mrs. Templeton and told her that I donated money in her name at the Detroit African American Society." She looked at Harry like he fucked up his chance.

LUCY – 2018

Lucy was on the phone. "Well, Holly, just get back as soon as possible. Your husband called a little bit ago, and he is not exactly thrilled that you bolted off to Europe to find Vivica. I don't think he likes Vivica very much... Yes, I am aware that you are an independent woman who makes her own choices... Okay, I'll talk with you soon."

Lucy hung her phone up from talking with Holly. She was sitting in Vivica's living room, trying to do some work. It wasn't going very well. Lucy could hear Langley from the kitchen flirting with Brad, and that made her uncomfortable for a number of reasons. She didn't really want to think about her teenage sister's sex life. Lucy also didn't need to be worried that Langley would hurt Vivica Fitzpatricks child. Which could hurt her own job. Xander also snuck in through the front door with Hope a little while ago. Then, some boy with the last name Costa showed up. Even odder, the Costa boy claimed Langley invited him. If anything, else couldn't get worse, Lucy was interrupted by Holly's husband, who showed up, wanting to know why the red-haired nutcase was taking his wife away from her family yet again.

Lucy was about to draft an email when the doorbell yet-again chimed. No one else in the house seemed to want to get it, so she got up and walked into the foyer. She opened the door to find a short Asian woman. "Can help you?" Lucy seemed confused.

"Your neighbor is a racist!" The Asian woman screamed.

Lucy had to assume she meant Mrs. Templeton. "Ma'am, the entire town knows this. Why is this a shock to you?"

"That coocoo lady hired me to cater to her book club for the week. I show up, and she starts screaming, *Get Yoko Ono out of my kitchen!* Lady, I'm not Yoko! Then I tell her I'm from the Philippines and she changes her tone. Apparently, her best friend in the world is Filipino, and she put her hand on my arm in a creepy way. I smacked her and told her I was going to inform all her neighbors she is a racist pervert."

"Well, I think the cat is out of the bag on Mrs. Templeton's views towards minorities. Thank you for the information, though." Lucy said.

The woman turned around. "I know a pie lady who drives me crazy. She is Filipino herself. I will send her to Mrs. Templeton, and they can have a creepy relationship along with her Filipino friend. I don't need this!" She said as she marched down the driveway. As she did, though, someone else walked up. A hunky redhead with great eyes and a sensual smile that said *fuck me roughly*. It was Perry Fitzpatrick.

"Hi" Lucy said a little confused. "What brings you here?"

"Oh, well," Perry sighed. "I wanted to meet with Vivica. She was an old friend of sorts." Perry explained. He then looked back at the Asian woman who was now next door, talking to the neighbors. "Why was Howard's Catering talking with you?"

"The lady who was just here? I guess she didn't know Mrs. Templeton was a racist and wanted to inform me." Lucy explained.

Perry laughed. "It's nice to know some things never change around here."

Lucy gestured for him to come in. They walked into the living room. "So, how exactly do you know Vivica, again?"

Brad walked in from the kitchen. He did a double take.

"Oh, hey Perry, long time no see."

Perry quickly stood back up and walked over to Brad. "How is my little cousin doing? Not so little, I guess anymore. Have I really been away for so long?" Lucy was confused. "Wait, are you a Knight?"

"A Knight? Uh, definitely not. I'm a Fitzpatrick, just like Brad," he explained.

"I have to go get something from my room." Brad ran upstairs.

Lucy put two and two together. "I heard that Margot had a son. I just didn't realize he was you."

The red-haired man chuckled. "Well, she isn't exactly proud of me."

"Why not?" Lucy asked hesitantly.

He shrugged. "I'm too much like my grandfather, as she puts it. Not enough like her. I've been away from home because of that. I've worked for different parts of the company while away. I finally decided enough was enough and moved back, though."

Lucy nodded. "So, you like Vivica?"

"I mean, she has been my Aunt on and off for most of my life. She is a good person. A little spacy and dramatic- but still better than my mother." Perry admitted.

The eldest Kingsley, Lucy, nodded. "Yeah... Unfortunately, Vivica is still out of town, though. I've been semi-house sitting, semi-watching Brad, and semi-bumming off of her." Lucy still wanted to look for a place to rent, but it became painfully awkward when Vivica went running off, leaving her to get their cosmetic company in order.

Perry laughed. "Well, Vivica's house has always been a place of people coming and going."

Suddenly there was another knock on the door. Lucy sighed and went to get it. Why was this house so popular tonight, she wondered?

"Oh, for crying out loud, what do you want?"

Mrs. Templeton looked up at her, with her hunched-over back. "Where is that black lady who works for the whore?"

"They are both out of town. Why?" Lucy asked annoyed

"I'm throwing an ice cream party, and I wanted the black lady to know that she is not invited." Mrs. Templeton explained.

Lucy blinked. "Well, am I invited?"

Mrs. Templeton scoffed. "Certainly not. This house, in general, is not invited, but the black lady is definitely a big no-no. Also, if an Asian woman shows up here, tell her she should come back. I have a pie to go with the ice cream. Ice cream and pie. They just go together like brown people and prison."

Lucy slammed the door shut. This was a really messed up street...

LANGLEY – 2018

Langley, the youngest Kingsley daughter, knocked on her semi-boyfriend Brad's bedroom door. "I'm coming in!" Langley screamed as she busted the door open. She scowled at him and sneered. "What on Earth is wrong? I swear you have become more and more distant with time. Do you not want to be with me?"

Brad sat on his bed and didn't look up. "Langley, we are in like completely different places in life."

Langley rolled her eyes and sat down next to Brad on his bed. "We are literally the same age. How on Earth are we any different?"

"I mean, you have done a lot more in terms of sexual stuff..." Brad looked at the girl.

The blonde girl was a bit taken back by this. "I don't know why this bothers you so much. You didn't have an issue with it back when we first started to get more serious."

Brad shrugged. "Well, I don't know. I mean, it's obvious you want more from me than I'm willing to give."

"I can live without sleeping with you," Langley stated.

"Okay, well, even if that is true, I can't believe you would invite Preston Costa to my house. I can't stand that kid," Brad admitted.

How on Earth was she supposed to know this? Langley actually made an effort to get to know Brad, but even so, this was a random fact. "Well, I'm sorry. I didn't think that it would be an issue. He seems to be pretty normal."

"His father is a well-known mob boss," Brad explained.

The girl shrugged. "So, my father is a criminal too. Your parents have both been MIA all summer as well. Why do you even care?"

Brad sighed. "It's a very complicated situation. I don't know if you have put two and two together yet... But a lot of people in this town tend to be related in some way or another."

Langley looked at him, confused. "It's not that different in Manhattan. People who travel in the same circles tend to be related."

"Yes, well, when I was born, my last name was Costa for the first five months of my life," Brad admitted out loud.

"How is that even possible? I don't remember reading anything about your mom being married to Anthony Costa." Langley knew most everything about Vivica. She had been following her life in the gossip columns for years.

The blond boy stood up. "Jackie Costa didn't want baby's father to be a mob boss. So, she planned to fake his death. However, my father owed my dad a lot of money and had helped deliver me. Why? I don't know. When Jackie ran off, he was paranoid. My mother had given birth the day before and was still recovering. So, my father faked my death and gave Anthony me. So, for the first five months of my life, my name was Preston Bradly Costa. Then Jackie returned home with the real Preston in her arms, wanting to take back Anthony. It was an ordeal; my father could have and probably should have gone to jail, but my aunt blackmailed my mother into letting him go free."

Langley sat on her bed for a long minute and tried to make total sense of the monologue given to her. "You make NYC families look normal. Fuck... You had a screwed-up life. I'm so sorry." She really was. She knew that Brad had been uncomfortable with the idea of being anything like his father, but things were starting to make more sense. "Is that when your parents divorced the first time?"

"Yes. Uncle Cliff is the reason why. I don't blame him, though. For the most part, he kept away until my mom was single. Then he would start to get close to her, but then Aunt Tiffany would always get in the way. Except for this time. This time, Aunt Tiffany had apparently given up on trying to keep them apart. I hope things work out for them because I can't keep the charade up of being happy."

The youngest Kingsley seemed to understand where he was coming from. Clearly, there was a lot more to his past than meets the eye. "Well, I'm sorry for inviting Preston over. We can kick him out if you would like."

Brad walked over to his window and looked outside. Below them, outside, Harry had a smile on his face as he talked to Preston, and it didn't seem forced. "That's the happiest I've seen Harry in a while. I think we can let things go. That doesn't mean his parents won't totally freak out, though. The Knight family has been trying to run the Costa's out of town for decades." Whereas the Fitzpatrick's ironically had been playing buddy-buddy with them.

MARGOT - 2018

As Margot sat in her kitchen, she checked her phone for Vivica's updates. It had been a while since she had received anything from her ex-Sister-in-Law. It must have been nice for her to be radio silent. Margot wasn't foolish though... The moment she got comfortable, the whore would be back and making her life miserable. Margot scowled, turning to her tablet to read the paper. Her son walked downstairs and grabbed some food the cook had prepared for them. He sat down quietly across from her.

"Good morning." He said.

"You're late," She pointed out. Margot hadn't been waiting up for her grown son, but she had been binge-watching something in the library when he got in. "What girl were you with last night?" She didn't even look up.

Perry rolled his eyes. "What does it matter to you?"

"It didn't. I just wanted to confirm that you were indeed with a girl." Margot smiled. She knew he was. Her son was not one to work more hours than he had to, and most of his friends had left town years ago. The ones left had settled down.

The red-haired son groaned. "I'm not a gay, mother."

Margot finally looked up. "Well, who said you were? I'd be okay with it if you were. Did you hear that Cliff and Tiffany's boy was?" "I got the alert on my phone when that unfortunate video appeared. I clicked off almost immediately."

Perry wanted to change the subject. "If you must know, I was just talking with Lucy Kingsley last night. You know of her, correct?"

Lucy had so much potential and wasted it on Vivica. Margot regretted not just giving her a place with the Fitzpatrick group several years ago. Looking back, so many complications could have been avoided. Vivica's damn party planning business would never have gotten off the ground had Lucy not become involved.

"The girl is a lost cause. I wouldn't get involved," Margot lied. If anything, she was doing this for both Lucy and Perry. They were both equals in her opinion. She changed the subject. "So, Perry, I looked at your first assignment. You are going to be attempting to buy out Templeton ice cream?"

Her son shrugged. "That woman is like five hundred years old, and aside from a few nieces and nephews, she has no family. What is the point in that crazy old bat continuing on with her ice cream empire?"

"It's a Michigan legacy and an Empire, as you pointed out. You realize how difficult that woman is?" Margot pointed out.

Perry shrugged. "Everyone has a price."

She would never admit it, but if anyone could get through to the old pile of bones, then it would probably be her son. Margot herself could easily go after Templeton ice cream, but she already dealt with Vivica on a regular basis. She didn't need two crazy bitches to go up against.

DELIA – 1963

Clifton walked down the foyer stairs as Delia walked out from the drawing room with a glass of wine. It was ten AM on a Monday.

Delia asked, "What are you doing home? Don't you have school?"

"It's a holiday... It's not even noon. Why are you drinking?" Clifton asked.

Delia gave her son a dirty look. "It was sent to us as a gift. I was just tasting it to see if I liked it." They both looked at the glass filled, which was practically to the top. Delia quickly changed the subject. "If it's a holiday, then where is your brother?"

The older Knight son shrugged. "How the hell would I know? I don't spend time with the brat." The doorbell rang. He looked at his mother. "You should probably get that." He walked out of the room.

Delia put the glass down on a table in the center of the room. She walked over to the door and opened it. Standing in the doorway was a nun that looked familiar. "Do I know you?" She asked.

Sister Mary Newman smiled. "Hi, we met the other day. I was wondering if we could talk about your son."

"What did Clifton do now?" Delia asked.

"Not Clifton. Rodrick. I'm his teacher if you remember."

It took her a second, but Delia started to remember who she was. "Oh, right. Um, yes, please come in." She took Sister

Mary into the drawing room and gestured for her to sit down. Delia hated the drawing room. It was so dark, and the sun never seemed to shine into this part of the house. Delia had no clue if her father-in-law was in the library, though.

She breathed out a heavy sigh, staring at the woman. "So, what did Clifton do again?"

"Rodrick... Well, you see, his behavior has gotten a little unruly as of late, and I'm not sure what to do." Mary admitted.

The brunette woman groaned as she sat down, with her morning drink in hand. "Have you ever considered doing your job? His father has no issue with beating him, but I'd rather not have to be in the house when it happens. That's why we send the boys to Catholic school..."

Mary coughed. "I really prefer not to use physical forms of punishment."

"Neither do I, but what exactly are we supposed to do with a childlike Rodrick? His father's family is full of one psychopath after another. His grandfather might act like the nicest man on the planet, but he hates me. Why does he hate me? I'm not blonde with blue eyes and the lightest skin ever. Yet, he flirts with the maid all day... Just like his Rodrick does with her child Nadia, I suppose."

Delia knew what went on around the house. She just never said anything out loud. This was probably the first time ever that she had actually admitted it to anyone else. Sure, most of the town knew what her family was capable of. It didn't mean that they themselves acknowledged it.

Heathcliff walked into the room. He noticed the nun and strode on over. Delia wasn't sure what he was up to.

Heathcliff said, "Hello, sister. What brings you to our home this afternoon?"

Mary cleared her throat. "I was just talking with your daughter-in-law about Rodrick."

Heathcliff nodded. "Well, I trust that young Rodrick is doing well in school?"

"His grades are all right. A solid B student." Mary admitted.

The patriarch looked at Delia. "Well, that right there is an issue on its own. Wouldn't you agree, Delia? Rodrick is a Knight. Knight's get A's."

"I have no way of controlling Rodrick's studies," Delia said. "Especially when you put that television set in his bedroom. He watches it until the broadcast ends..."

Heathcliff sat down. "Well, I wasn't going to put a TV in the drawing room or library. I didn't want him going into my office either anymore. Do you enjoy TV, sister?"

"Well, I rarely watch it," Sister Mary admitted nervously.

"Delia, fix your child's grades..." He walked out of the room.

Delia went right for a drink. "You sure wouldn't like a little drink? You look like you could use one."

HANNAH – 2018

Working in the family drawing room had become a distraction. There was a TV in there, as well as in the library and her bedroom. So, Hannah had decided to move out to the patio. It was probably a foolish choice, considering that it was a nice day. It was also a bit windy, and she had a lot of paperwork. One piece of paper started to fly. She Hannah up to go after it but Harry caught it instead. He set it on the table as he sat down.

"Thank you. So, how was your night?" Hannah asked.,

"It was cool. You should have come over." Harry stated.

"I was working late. The person who had my position before me didn't leave things very well. I think he retired, too. I don't know… Besides, I wouldn't have wanted to deal with Hope being there." Hannah explained.

Harry started looking out into the yard. "I mean I think she was there, but she wasn't outside with Langley, Brad, Preston and I."

"Who's Preston?" Hannah took off her glasses, squinting at him. She didn't know that Harry had a new friend.

It was good for Harry to venture outside of his cousin and that Kingsley girl. Hannah didn't hold Langley accountable for her brother's actions. She genuinely liked Lucy. That said, Langley was a bit wild… Even for her standards.

The curly-haired Knight blushed. "Oh, well Preston Costa… You know, Anthony and Jackie's son."

Hannah blinked. "The one who was expelled from that French boarding school?"

Harry gasped. "He was expelled?"

"Well, that is what I heard. Why was Preston Costa there, regardless? If Aunt Vivica found out, she would kill Lucy for letting a Costa in that house. It would be almost as bad as letting Mrs. Templeton in the house."

Hannah knew how much both her parents and Aunt hated the Costa family. They were clearly in organized crime. The entire city knew it but did nothing about it. The same could be said about Mrs. Templeton's bigotry, though...

"Langley invited him over..." Harry admitted.

This made sense, Hannah thought. She said out loud, "Well, I'd recommend telling Langley that if she doesn't want Vivica to murder her, then she better not invites him again." She thought about that for a second, and it sounded a tiny bit hypocritical, given the circumstances. "Why did she even invite Preston over? I thought she was with Brad?"

Harry got on his phone. "Um, well, he wasn't there for Langley. He was there for me. I think he might be into me."

"Anthony Costa has a gay son. I guess it is possible." Hannah immediately realized what she said and regretted it. A few months ago, the same would probably have been saying about their own father in regard to Harry. "I mean..." "I know what you mean. Regardless, I don't even know if he is gay or bi or whatever. I mean, he might have been flirting with me, but I don't know." Harry explained. He blushed. He continued to look at his phone.

The older sibling thought for a moment. She wanted to be happy for Harry but knew that most people wouldn't be. They probably would have been happier for him if he brought home an older man like she had at his age. A Costa *was* a different story. "Well, I'd be willing to meet him if you ever bring him around."

Harry turned red. "I don't think it is a very smart idea to bring him around the house. I mean, Dad has been supportive of me, and with Mom being at the European doctor exchange until December, I think he will continue to be. But, still. A Costa? Plus, again. I don't even know if he likes me."

"Who are you texting?" Hannah asked.

"Preston. He wants to hang out, but I don't know..."

"Harry, the only way you are going to find out if he likes you and you like him is if you spend time with him..." She rolled her eyes. She looked at her own phone. There was a text from Xander. He wanted to *talk*. "Why don't you just leave me alone?" She mumbled.

The younger brother looked at his sister. "Well, I can leave if you want."

Hannah looked up. "No, not you. Xander. He keeps texting me, saying he wants to talk. We ran into each other the other day at the office, but then Hope turned up as well. I'm over him, though. I'm not interested in sharing him with Hope, which I think is what he wants." She was really shocked by Xander. She thought he was a good guy. Part of her still wanted to believe he was.

BRANDON – 1963

Brandon, the red-haired boy, crossed the street from Detroit to Grosse Pointe. He was just trying to stay away from his house. His father was still livid with him for getting into a fight with Rodrick. It wasn't his fault that Rodrick was the scum of the earth. It shocked Brandon that his mother was angry, though. He honestly thought that she would have understood. Susan understood, but they had both grown up watching their father go after a dream that he needed to let die already. They both felt bad thinking that, but it was the truth.

As Brandon continued to walk, he noticed the olive-skinned beauty he defended the other day sitting on a bench.

He quickly walked over. "Hey, Nadia!" He said with all the confidence in the world. She was reading a book. "What are you reading?"

"Just some silly romance novel." She slammed the book shut. Nadia looked at Brandon. "You didn't have to defend me against Rodrick. You do know that, right?"

Brandon sat down. "I didn't need to defend you. I just couldn't deal with him in general anymore. Rodrick is the most obnoxious guy I've ever met. Ever since he transferred to Saint Agnes, I've wanted to sock him."

"You aren't alone in that," Nadia admitted out loud.

She was probably right. Brandon and his friends were all sick of him. The issue was that most of their Dads worked for his Dad and were afraid of the consequences. Brandon had the advantage that his father didn't work for him; he just wanted to *be* him.

Supposedly, Benton was worse than Rodrick. That was the rumor, at least. The older brother, Clifton, seemed somewhat reasonable, though.

As he was thinking this, a familiar brunet boy walked by. "Don't look up," Brandon whispered to Nadia.

"Oh, look, the help's daughter and the Irish boy. Who said you two were allowed here?" Rodrick asked.

The red-haired boy looked around. "Who said we were allowed on a public street? Um, society, I suppose…"

Rodrick rolled his eyes. "Poor people can be hilarious sometimes. People might get the wrong idea from seeing a Hispanic walking around a nice area."

"My mother and I are meeting for lunch in a little bit," Nadia said. "I was just doing some reading. What on Earth are you walking around for?"

Rodrick rolled his eyes. "I'm just getting out of my house for a little bit. You only know North Pointe because that's the place where your Mommy cleans toilets…"

"Why don't you leave us alone, Knight, before we do the same to you?" Brandon said as he sized him up. He could tell that Rodrick was backing off, but it didn't seem to be out of fear. More like a lack of interest.

"You're going to make me clean toilets?" Rodrick said, bored by the response. "Well, why should I get in-between the trash?" With that, he strode off, scowling.

Brandon looked at Nadia, assuming that she would be sad. Instead, she just folded her arms with a scowl.

Brandon murmured, "He really doesn't bother you, does he?"

Nadia looked at him. "Not even slightly. He is annoying, just not worth getting hung up over."

"I'm not hung up on him," Brandon stated.

"I never said you were. It's just in my case; it's easier for me to keep my distance. My mother works for his grandfather and the rest of that deranged family," Nadia explained.

Brandon could actually feel for her in that way. "Yeah, my father wants to work with the Knights really bad."

"Well, why doesn't he apply at one of their factories? They are always hiring." Nadia pointed out.

Was Brandon really going to explain this to her? "My father doesn't want to work for Knight. He wants to work alongside of Knight. He wants to distribute steel for their cars. Mind you, he doesn't have a business yet, and he wants the Knight family to fund the entire thing, with no guarantee that it would even work."

The girl looked confused. "How would that even work out, then? You need to provide something in order to get something back."

Brandon looked annoyed. "Trust me, my sister and I explain this to him all the time. My mother acknowledges it as well- but never to his face. In his mind, the Knight family will be jumping at the thought of working with him once he can come up with the right presentation. He has been trying to do this for years."

MARGOT – 2018

Margot spoke into the phone. "No, the hospital hasn't filled your position yet, Nial... They think you are on vacation. You are on vacation, aren't you? Nial, so help me if I find out you are with Vivica... So, help me little brother."

The redhead looked at her computer to see what time it was. Her idiot little brother wouldn't stop talking. She wanted to remind him that most of the town was not exactly fond of him, so no one was really looking for him.

"Yes, Nial, I do think it is worth reminding that after the third marriage to the same woman, it is no longer considered being romantic..." Not that she found any of the three other marriages to be, either.

Margot remembered the first time that Nial brought Vivica home. It confused the entire family because they had already known her, obviously. At that point in time, her parents considered her their "niece". She never considered Vivica to be her cousin, though. It didn't change the facts, though...

Vivica's mother, Gail, had been married to her half-Uncle, DJ Brash until he died in an accident on a construction site, at one of the Knight dealerships.

DJ had always been the lone reminder of both her parent's old lives before they had money. It was hard to imagine that when she was born, they had only been living in the mansion for five years or so. DJ stopped coming around as much when Gail came into his life. Nadia and Gail couldn't stand one another. Nadia wanted DJ to live with them at the mansion. Gail wanted to pretend to live a middle-class life because of her daughter... Vivica. Gail was so worried about her daughter's mindset from having lived in Beverly Hills since birth. Personally, Margot herself could have cared less. It did seem like Gail was obsessed with not being wealthy in a bizarre way. It was so weird that years later, Vivica learned her father had been sending her money that Gail hid. She would have probably murdered Nadia if she ever did that to her. Well... She would have had Costa's people do it.

She tried to remember how they ever got first involved with the Costa family. It had to have been around her first marriage. Anthony was still working for his father at that point. She never really liked Anthony's father. She respected Anthony, though. He was an old-fashioned kind of gangster. It was too bad he married a woman as bad as Vivica, but for all the wrong reasons...

Margot looked at the time again. She realized with a jolt that she was going to be late for a meeting. That's when the door opened. She assumed it would be her assistant, but instead, it was her nephew...

"Bradley, what on earth are you doing here?" She asked, confused.

"Oh, uh hi, Aunt Margot. I was just wondering if we could talk." Brad said as he closed the door.

"What about?" Margot asked, realizing she wouldn't make the meeting.

Brad stood there for a moment. "Well, it's just that Preston Costa is back from boarding school... He might be interested in someone I care about, and I'm worried. I know you and dad are friendly with the Costas, though."

Preston Costa... That boy would always go down as one of Nial's more stupid ideas. She loved Anthony Costa like a brother herself. She would have just been honest with Anthony and told him the truth about his kid. Though, the prospect of not having to take care of a baby did make sense to her. She made nannies do all the hard work with her sons Joshua and Perry.

"Well, it depends on what you mean. Do I think that a teenage boy alone is dangerous?" She thought about that for a moment but then shrugged it off. "Not particularly... That said, a Costa... Well, their reputation exists for a reason. They, however, are some of the best people I have known. Much better than the Knights, that is for sure. The only decent Knight is Tiffany and possibly Rodrick." She looked at her nephew, who still looked concerned. "Is Preston after that blonde girl you have been spending time with? Her father is Alexander Kingsley... If she were caught dating him, she could possibly destroy any shred of hope he ever has of getting out of prison. You may wish to remind her of that."

"It's not Langley that he might like," Brad explained.

"Well, who on Earth could he possibly be courting?" She crossed her arms.

Brad coughed. "I'm not really sure it is my place to say. I mean, I don't know if Preston really likes them or not..."

Margot put two and two together. "Well, this person may wish to realize that Preston comes with a lot of baggage because of his family." She knew from Tiffany that Harry was far from stable due to his social anxieties.

"I'll have to let the person know..." Brad explained.

LANGLEY – 2018

The blonde girl, Langley, picked up her class schedule. "Are any of these teachers decent?" She handed the paper to Harry.

Harry looked at the list for a moment. "They are all pretty nice. You know you have actually to go to class, here, right?"

Langley scoffed. "If you are referring to the amount of time, I went to class at Grosse Pointe West; it was because I knew that I deserved better. I still got an A in all my classes. I took a speech class. How did that even happen? Where is Brad?"

"He had to run an errand, but he said that we should watch his football practice, and then can all meet up after," Harry explained as he looked at his own schedule. "We have three classes together!"

"Shoot," Langley said, as they strode down the hallway. " I knew I forgot something. I wanted to make sure we had all the same classes. Hopefully, any that I don't have with you, I have them with Brad."

Harry frowned. "If you have them with Brad, that means I won't. Which means I will be by myself."

She hadn't thought of that. She knew that Harry needed both to get through this year. "Well, maybe you will get Preston in some of your classes."

"I don't think that he likes me, Langley. At least not in the way you seem to want him to." Harry waved to a teacher.

This boy needed a serious confidence boost, but Langley had literally been trying to do that since the day she first met Harry. "Well, don't worry. If he isn't the guy for you, then someone else will be."

With that, the two walked outside over to the bleachers. Langley wasn't ready to go back to school. It felt like summer just started, yet it still felt like she did nothing. Sure, if she had gone to South Hampton, all she would have done was watch *The Young and the Restless* and reality shows all day while she tanned and shopped, which is basically what she did here. She did jokingly put in a few job applications. Lucy demanded her to that... None of them (luckily) called her back. It helped that she wrote *Langley Kingsley, daughter of convicted money man Alexander Kingsley. Did my Daddy steal from you?*

The two sat down, and that's when Langley noticed Brad walking out on to the field. The girls in the front row all sat there, cheering on their boyfriends. Brad had tried on multiple occasions to get her to interact with them. Langley had nothing in common with any of them. She once again thought back to the friends that she left behind in Manhattan. They went shopping and they went to parties together, clubbing with fake ID's. She was sure that these girls would probably do similar things, but she was also sure they were the type to sneak around their parents to do so. Langley was used to parents who hid in the background, mothers who were MIA while the father paid off teachers and cops to keep their children out of trouble. That was her family, in a nutshell. She would listen to Xander go on and on about his "morals". She was this close to reminding him of his own school days. Not to mention- he was stringing along one twin while he clearly liked the other. The most awkward part of all was the fact that these two twins were Brad's cousins and Harry's sisters.

The two of them watched in silence for about five minutes, trying to keep themselves amused by something neither of them knew much about. Langley sort of knew football. Football and basketball were big on Sundays back in Manhattan. It was a great way to have one last party before returning to work and school on Monday. Langley wasn't entirely sure if her old school had a football team, though. They had Lacrosse, Polo, Water Polo, Tennis, and Golf team, though. Football and basketball were more poor-people games, though, that rich person paid a lot of money to watch. Polo and Tennis were sports you played for college applications, not because you had a genuine interest. If you did, then you probably were skipping college and training for a professional career, and you ate, slept, and breathed those things.

Grosse Pointe and Manhattan were nothing alike. As much as Langley tried to find the similarities; they just weren't there. Sure, there were some extremely wealthy families, such as the Knights and Fitzpatricks. But the whole place was just so suburban. Anything that happened to the Knight or Fitzpatrick families were talked about for years. Even the low-income families would get in on the gossip. That didn't happen in New York. The poor rarely interacted with the wealthy on that level.

Langley continued to stay inside her head until she noticed Preston walk out on the field... Harry turned to her at the same time she turned to him. They had been watching Brad's practices for a while at this point. Preston had not been at any, and yet, he was dressed to go out on the field. Brad had been made Captain this year. Surely, he would have told her about this. The field went silent; Brad went over to the couch and seemed to get into an argument. Brad then walked in their direction as the rest of the team broke for a break themselves.

Langley stood up. "Brad, why is Preston here?" She asked right away. As much as she thought that Harry and Preston would make a cute couple, she still was worried about how it might affect Brad.

"Apparently, he made the team. You know, without even trying out... "Brad growled through his helmet.

"I didn't know that Preston was into football?" Harry frowned.

Langley was unsure about why Harry was frowning. "Well, I mean, you only hung out once. He isn't going to tell you his life story, sweetie..."

Harry shrugged. "I mean, it isn't just that. It's just how many gay football players do you know?"

Langley knew of a few from some of the clubs she used to frequent in New York... "Harry, I think you are trying to find reasons as to why you and Preston wouldn't work."

"Well, that might be for the best." Brad pointed out.

This was going to be a complicated situation. Langley sighed out loud. "Brad, why don't you give Preston a chance? He could be an asset to your team. You won't know until you practice with him."

The blond boy scoffed. "It's just... I don't know everyone else had to work so hard to make it to Varsity. The team got an awfully large donation this year outside of the other Alumni donations. I wonder if it was from his parents..."

She understood where he was coming from, but then again, her own father donated a building to get Lucy elected Treasurer once... As she thought of a decent response, Preston walked over.

"Brad, I just wanted to thank you and the other guys for letting me on the team. I was on a soccer team back in Italy. It was nothing big, but it was pretty good." Preston explained.

He shot Harry a lusty look.

Brad crossed his arms. "What do you playing soccer have to do with my football team?"

"They call football *soccer* in most other countries, Brad. It's the same thing..." Langley even knew this. She could tell he was becoming rather tense. "Why don't we go get a drink from a vending machine together..." She took Brad's hand and left Preston and Harry alone.

HARRY – 2018

"Do you mind if I sit down?" Preston asked.

The curly-haired boy gulped. Harry knew that there was padding, but Preston looked so hot in his football uniform. He couldn't help but look at him. "Oh, yeah, sure."

"Brad doesn't seem to like me, does he?" Preston wondered.

"I mean, it is an awkward situation..." Harry admitted. Which it was.

"We were babies, and there was something among our parents..." Preston pointed out.

Harry got what Preston was saying, but he knew Brad all too well... He wanted to be the opposite of both his parents.

"I mean, if it means anything, I think you are a good guy."

The Italian boy smiled. "That does help me, actually."

The youngest Knight boy blushed. "So, you like football? I guess that will make you popular among the girls." Harry realized very quickly that he sounded like a Mother, saying that.

Preston laughed. "I suppose... I'm not holding my breath, though. I got out of a relationship in my old boarding school. It's one of the reasons I moved back."

"Oh, do you miss her?" Harry asked.

"Who said it was a her?" Preston asked.

Harry's eyes opened wide. So, he was into guys? He wasn't sure how he was supposed to react to this. He was happy, but why? Harry wasn't even sure if he himself was ready for a proper relationship. Todd Roberts left him a mess after last year. It wasn't even that Harry thought that Preston was like Todd. It was just that Preston was Preston. Well-toned, amazing brown eyes, a nice tan, and perfect jawline. When did things such as jawlines even start to matter to Harry? A year ago, he was the shy kid in the back who would listen in on the girls in his classes who gushed over Shawn Mendes and Harry Styles, and wish he could give his own opinions.

Harry was a different person. He had no choice. When he looked back at the outcome of the sex tape, he couldn't help but shutter. In a blink of an eye, he went from being a wealthy nobody to someone on the level of a Kardashian.

Something he never had any interest in being.

"Yeah. I'm gay..." Preston said.

"Are you out?" Harry asked. He wondered if that was an appropriate follow-up question.

Preston shrugged. "More or less. I mean, my family knows. People back at the boarding school knew—a few close friends. I'm trying to keep it on the down-low here, though. Mainly because I don't really want to deal with the backlash... I'm not opposed to anyone knowing, but you know, with Catholic school and all."

The Knight knew exactly what he meant. "Well, you know, hanging around me isn't going to help. I'd say anyone with access to the internet knows I'm gay."

"Which I have no issue with. Again, I'm not hiding myself. I just don't really feel like transferring schools again," Preston explained.

"If they took me back this semester, then I doubt they will have an issue with you." Harry pointed out though he realized that his father had to make as many demands to get them where they were today. "We should hang out…" Harry said out loud.

Preston smiled. "I'd like that. Can we maybe not do it with Brad and Langley, though? I mean no offense, but Brad isn't going to take very kindly to us hanging out, and your blonde friend is a little pushy…"

There wasn't any denying either of those claims. Brad was not happy about being around a Costa, and Langley was indeed very pushy. A quality that he personally admired in her, but it didn't change facts.

"Yeah. I mean, we could hang just you and me. Just… You know, just hang out."

The tan boy looked confused. "As opposed to what- not hanging?"

Harry's romantic life had basically been non-existent. He had no idea if people referred to dates as dates anymore. He didn't want to come out and say the word *date*, though, because Preston could just want to be friends. Gay guys could be friends with one another. "I'm just rambling."

"You're pretty cute when you ramble." Preston smiled as Harry clearly started to blush.

Langley walked back over. "Harry, good news, we are going to lunch… Brad wants to focus on football practice without distraction." She looked annoyed and yanked his hand.

Harry waved goodbye to Preston as he realized he didn't set a time to hang with Preston, nor did he have his phone number.

LANGLEY – 2018

"I'm going to level with you. Your cousin is driving me up a damn wall," Langley stated as she looked at a menu.

Harry sighed. "I really hope you two don't break up." It would make things a tiny bit awkward for several reasons.

The blonde girl brushed her hair out of her eye. She wasn't thinking of breaking up with Brad. She also didn't think that Brad planned to break up with her. At least she was hoping he wasn't. They were just from two different worlds, and they were still trying to work out how those worlds could collide properly.

"We will be fine. Brad just really doesn't like Preston. Which I totally understand, now that I know the reasoning, but still. It's not like the world is going to end if he is forced to interact with him. Your Mother and Aunt interact with each other all the time."

"That may be a poor example. My mother hates Aunt Vivica with a passion. The same goes for Aunt Vivica's feelings towards my mother," Harry admitted.

"Well, still... Brad's parents are beyond fucked up. Nial clearly isn't the brightest man outside of his medical practice. That doesn't mean Brad is going to turn out like either of them. I don't have a secret sister hiding somewhere, and he is not trying to rebel against his storybook-romance parents like Nial and Vivica. Even if those things were to happen, who really cares?"

The young Knight looked at her, confused. "I think you are trying to justify something, but I don't want to come out and say it if I'm wrong…"

She knew he knew what she was getting at. She wanted to sleep with Brad. She, at the very least, wanted to see Brad naked. Langley had purposely walked past his door in a towel on multiple occasions. Her room wasn't even close to his by design from Lucy and Vivica. "I want him so bad." She put her head on the table.

SUSAN – 1963

The weather was starting to get colder. Susan loved autumn. It was her favorite time of year by far. She could spend hours walking the streets of Detroit and Grosse Pointe as she watched the trees start to turn colors. She was walking down Bell Street, which happened to be the street that the Knight family lived on. The strawberry blonde looked at the ancestral home and rolled her eyes.

This was what her father dreamed of. This is what her father insisted they needed in their lives. She didn't need that, though. All she needed was stability. One day, she would leave home... Susan just was unsure of what she would do. Women were not career people, and she never saw herself marrying a man. Yet, she wanted to marry. It confused her sometimes. She got out of her head and continued to walk when the front door of North Pointe opened. It wasn't a Knight exiting the house, though. It was Brandon's teacher... Susan smiled and waved.

"Susan Fitzpatrick?" Mary said as she walked over. "What are you doing here?"

"Oh, I just love taking walks. It gets me away from the bar and my father..." She admitted out loud.

Mary nodded. "He seems like he means well. I understand the concept of wanting better for one's family. I just think that there are better avenues to go about it if I'm being honest. The Knight family is not perfect."

Hearing it from someone else, no less a nun, didn't change the fact that it was like listening to a broken record.

"Yes, Brandon and I are more than aware. We would be happy just focusing on the bar or something else. We don't need a thirty-room mansion.... What were you doing at North Pointe? If you don't mind me asking."

"Well, I was just meeting with Mrs. Knight. She is an interesting woman. I also met Heathcliff Knight. I've actually met him in passing a few times. There are definitely a lot of layers to that man." Mary explained.

"Are nuns supposed to gossip?" Susan asked.

"I suppose it does sound like gossiping." Mary blushed. "You know, I'm the youngest nun at Saint Agnes. I didn't mind it at first, but people have this idea of what a nun is supposed to look like. Old, mean, and apparently bald. I hate hiding my hair." Mary admitted.

The Fitzpatrick girl blushed. Mary did have wonderful hair. At least from what she could see under her habit. "Well, maybe we should hang out sometime." She admitted.

She never asked people to hang out. Especially, not girls as pretty as Mary... Did she just think that Mary was pretty? She never thought of girls as pretty, at least not in the way she thought of Mary.

Mary was about to answer when North Pointe's front door opened again. It was Delia Knight. She ran over to the two girls or, more accurately, she wobbled. Susan couldn't be sure, but she dealt with enough drunks on a daily basis to recognize the body language.

Delia said, "Sister. I was just thinking... Maybe you would like to come over for dinner tonight."

The nun turned to Delia while still looking at Susan. "Oh, that would be lovely. You know, my friend, Susan, would love to come as well."

Susan looked at the nun and the rich Knight wife. "Oh, I couldn't possibly impose..."

"No. Please come," Delia slurred. "The more, the better. My husband just called from the office. He has to go back to the LA offices for the next day or so to handle something. Heathcliff rarely likes to eat with me when Benton is not there. Plus, there is no telling if Clifton or Rodrick will be there." Delia admitted.

The strawberry blonde played with her hair. "Mrs. Knight, you realize that my younger brother is Brandon Fitzpatrick, correct?"

Delia's eyes widened for a moment, but she blinked. "Well, look at this as a peace offering. I wouldn't bring him, though... We don't need to cause any more tension. Let's just look at this as three girlfriends having a night out."

The word *girlfriend* made Susan's hair stand up on the back of her neck, but she smiled. It would be nice to get away from the bar for the night. Plus, she had no doubt that her father would let her go. She wasn't sure if she would tell her father, though...

CLIFF – 2018

The family patriarch, Cliff, walked out the front door of North Pointe and looked across the street at his Weston's house. There had been no word from Holly if she had found her or not. He was starting to worry that Vivica didn't want to be found. They spent years dodging their feelings, and now they had the chance to be together. He guessed it made sense that it wouldn't be easy. It never was, with her. He remembered the last time they had the chance to be together...

CLIFF – 2010

Vivica packed up her boxes and was packing up her clothes. She touched a framed photo of herself with him, the girls, Harry, and Brad. She frowned.

Weston finally turned around and looked at him. "Don't worry. I will be out of here very soon."

Cliff marched over to Vivica and sat her down on their bed. He sat down next to her. "Vivica, why are you leaving?"

"Your wife just came back from the dead... Or being kidnapped or whatever... I can't keep you from her," Vivica explained as she started to cry.

It had been so long since seeing Tiffany, and yet he couldn't deny his attraction to her was still there. Even so, he loved Vivica. He wanted to be with Vivica.

"What if I said I don't want you to leave?"

"Clifton Knight, you have three children downstairs that are spending time with their mother right now, for the first time in years. What are you going to do, ask her to leave?" Vivica got back up and walked over to the window.

It didn't change his feelings for Vivica, though. "I could divorce her. She could still live on the property, either in the other wing or the Guest House out back."

The redhead turned around. "You expect me to live with the woman who stole you from me once already? She is about to do the exact same thing. Tiffany already thinks you are just going to go right back to her."

"Well, where are you going to go?" Cliff asked. He stood up and stood right behind Vivica. "What- are you going to move back in with Luke?" He wondered. The last thing he wanted her to do would be to go back with his cousin.

"I've booked plane tickets for Brad and myself. We are going to go visit Laura at her boarding school," Vivica explained.

It only took a moment for Cliff to put two and two together. "The boarding school near where Nial has been living?"

Vivica turned around. "I have no interest or desire to be with Nial again. You know that as well as I do. Two marriages to him were enough. The only good thing he ever did for me was give me my children... At least, two of them."

"They will always be your children, Vivica. You helped raise them." Cliff assured her.

"I will always be their Aunt, and I will always be here if they need me. They have Tiffany, though. Why would they want me? Don't worry; I will leave instructions for Tiffany on Harry's anxiety medication and doctors. I'll also explain to her that Hannah needs personal time with her or you; otherwise she won't ask for it. I can already tell that Hope is going to settle in the easiest with Tiffany, which she should. They all should. Tiffany is their mother. I'm their Aunt. It doesn't make me love them any less, though." Vivica wiped the tears with her sleeve.

"What about the love I need from you?" Cliff asked out loud. The door opened. It was Tiffany. "Oh, hello, dear." It was so natural for him to fall back in line with being married to Tiffany. Yet, he still wanted Vivica.

Tiffany looked at Cliff and smiled. She was acting as if Vivica wasn't even in the room. "The children are hungry. I thought we could take Hope, Harry, and Hannah to the club for lunch. We used to love doing that just you and I before I went away."

The red-haired sister turned to Tiffany. "Hannah and Harry hate the club. What about Brad?" "Well, Brad and you both have packing to do." Tiffany pointed out.

Cliff quickly took Tiffany into the hallway before Vivica could respond. He knew that this wasn't going to end well. He looked at his wife. She was still beautiful. She would always be the woman he fell in love with, yet she wasn't the love of his life. At least he didn't think that she was anymore.

"I realize that you have been through a very traumatic event, but Tiffany, that was just rude."

The doctor looked at the CEO in confusion. "Well, Cliff, they do need to move out. Harry and Hannah are already confused. Hope is the only one who seems to grasp that I'm their mother! I'm so sorry to disrupt your life with *my* sister..."

He fell in love with Vivica first. They knew each other from twelve years old. It took him forever to grasp his feelings. Then when he finally did, his father got involved. Rodrick did everything he could to keep them apart. Then Tiffany came to town, and he couldn't help but fall in love with her. He did fall in love with her. She was a more mature version of Vivica, and yet she wasn't Vivica. When he finally decided that he made the wrong choice, Vivica married Nial, and Tiffany announced she was pregnant. He assumed it was the world telling him that Tiffany was meant to be his wife. Yet now he looked at this woman he thought he was in love with and questioned if he really did. He did though at least he thought he was.

"I'll have a moving company get the rest of my things. Brad and I are leaving." Vivica said as she walked out of their bedroom. "You might not want to believe it, Tiffany, but I'm glad you are alive, and I'm glad that the children have their mother back." She started to walk down the hall but looked back for a moment. "Goodbye, Cliff." She then turned back and started walking again...

CLIFF – 2018

The Knight CEO looked at his phone. He was reluctant, but he decided to try and call Vivica. The phone rang, but it went to voicemail after two rings. He sighed. Maybe it was time he concluded that Vivica and he were just never meant to be together forever. Then his phone rang again, but it wasn't Vivica. It was Holly, though. He quickly answered.

"Any updates?" He asked

"I'm on her trail. She was in Italy but now apparently is in Paris. It's going to be a matter of getting into a club tonight. I'll get her, though." Holly explained.

Cliff wanted to say he was surprised that Vivica was that hard to find. But he knew his Weston. She always ran off when things didn't go her way. She ran off to New York the summer that he was forced to spend in Europe. She ran to Nial when he married Tiffany. That was her nature.

"Well, please hurry."

HANNAH – 2018

Hannah knew this would happen. As she walked down the hall at KMC, people smiled at her but acted as if she didn't belong there. Hannah knew that she didn't belong there, but she wasn't going to join in on the silent version of hazing. The Knight daughter finally made it to her office and jumped as she walked in. Hope was sitting at her desk. Hannah realized once again that she had a twin, a fact that everyone on the planet made sure to remind her of.

"Good you are finally here. I'm just letting you know I've decided to take an internship in London. Xander is yours. I don't want him anymore."

Hannah looked at her idiot twin sister for a long minute. "What makes you think I want him now that you are leaving? In case you didn't notice, once he chose you, I stopped perusing him."

Hope got up from behind Hannah's desk. "Oh, trust me. I know you did and that's when I realized we had nothing in common. I like my boys to be a little less goody-goody. I guess that is the best word. I'm all for saving the world and helping animals but not to the degree that Xander is."

"So, you are admitting that you only liked him because I clearly liked him?"

"Well, I will never publicly acknowledge it, but more or less yes." Hope nodded in a bitchy way.

This was typical Hope. The worst part was that she would leave her office, break up with Xander (if she hadn't already)- and still been made to be the hero of this. Meanwhile, Hannah would be the screw-up. Even over their younger brother and his sex tape. Which she knew wasn't his fault but still...

"I slept with Xander on Harry's birthday."

Hope turned and looked at her twin. She smiled. "Hannah, you are about to get the boy. Why on Earth do you feel the need to make things up?" She asked.

"Who said I was making things up?" Hannah imitated Hope's overly cheerful way of speaking. "Technically, he hadn't made things serious with you. At least that is what he alluded to." Hannah said.

"I have to get going..." Hope explained. She grabbed her purse and slammed the door on the way out.

The supposed screw-up sat at her desk. Hannah smiled. After years of coming in second to the great, brilliant, supposedly kind-hearted Hope, she finally was coming in first. It didn't feel as great as she wanted it to. Hope still won. Hannah had gotten over Xander for the most part and yet, now, he was available again. She wasn't sure she even wanted him anymore. Especially with how close Harry was with Langley. Obviously, it shouldn't matter, but the last thing she needed was to discover that Xander really was a terrible guy and to have a bad falling out with him. She wasn't going to deal with all of this...

She needed her Aunt's advice. Vivica always knew exactly what to tell her. Even when Vivica herself clearly didn't believe what she was saying...

HANNAH – 2011

Hannah had been sitting in the drawing room for what seemed like an eternity. It had only been around three hours. Harry and Brad were keeping themselves occupied while Hope was out seeking pity from her friends.

Hannah still couldn't believe that their mother was supposedly back from the dead. She was there when the car exploded. She heard Tiffany scream. It just made no sense. They weren't allowed to see her right away because no one could believe she actually was alive.

The door finally opened. But instead of it being her Mother or Father, it was her Aunt. She came and sat down next to her. "How are you holding up?"

"Fine. I mean... I don't know." She looked at her Aunt. Hannah could tell that Vivica was not in good shape after seeing her sister alive herself. "How are you doing?"

Vivica smiled at her niece. "It doesn't matter how I'm doing right now. I need to make sure that you and everyone else is doing all right."

"That's not right, Aunt Vivica. You deserve to have your opinion heard. Just because Mom came back doesn't mean anything. We don't even know all the facts as of yet. She could have been hiding from all of us." Hannah pointed out.

The redhead laughed. "Oh, trust me, dear, your mother would not have stayed away from your father if she knew I was around... Or you, and your brother and sister." She added in quickly. "I don't mean to be petty. I just want you to have a good relationship with her."

Hannah wanted to. It was just that Harry had no clue who she was, and Hope was literally hanging on her the moment that she returned. It was hard to feel one way or another. She was three years old when her mother went away. Hope had always believed in the idea of a nuclear family. Hannah never really needed that. She had her Father, Aunt, brother, cousin, and even Hope. That was all she needed. Their grandfather on occasion would show up and that was when things got a little out of hand.

Vivica kissed her on the forehead. "Regardless of what has happened, it doesn't change all the fun we have all had over the past several years."

It wasn't as if her Aunt had been married to her father the entire time that Tiffany was away. She had married Brad's father again as well. She was also in the middle of a divorce from her other uncle, Luke, when her mother first died. Vivica and her father never seemed to have a chance together. It was Hannah who finally had convinced her Aunt that her father was ready to move on and that they could all be a happy family.

"Are you hungry? We can all go get lunch at the diner. Or maybe the boys can go play at the park and we can go for a walk?" Vivica suggested.

Hannah was about to answer when her father walked in. "Honey, your mother would like to see you and Harry," he explained. Hannah could tell that he wasn't sure how to feel in this moment.

"Aunt Vivica and I were already going for a walk with the boys," Hannah explained.

Cliff rubbed his forehead. "Well, maybe you could all do that in a little bit? Your mother hasn't seen you in so long."

"Your father is right, dear. We can go once you have spent time with her." Vivica smiled.

Hannah looked out the window. "I don't know what to even say to her..."

"Just talk about school. Tell her all about your friends and drama club. Tell her about play rehearsal. I know she will get a kick out of that story you told me from the other day." Vivica told her.

The brunette Knight shrugged. "I guess..." Hannah got up and walked towards the door.

"Is she staying the night?" Vivica asked Cliff.

"Yes. I mean, I don't know..." Cliff sighed.

Hannah walked into the foyer, down the hall to the kitchen. She sighed and opened the door. Her mother, Tiffany, was sitting at the kitchen table.

Hannah smiled. "Hi, mom." She said reluctantly. It felt weird to say *Mom* after all these years.

Tiffany looked up from a photo album. "Hope, I'm so glad you are back."

"I'm Hannah, actually." She explained. She went to sit down across from her mother.

"Well, I'm still getting used to this, sorry. I named you. Did your father ever tell you that? He picked the name Hope and I picked Hannah. I'm sure that he has told you. I doubt your Aunt ever told that." Tiffany said, half trying way too hard and half sounding bitter.

Hannah took a deep breath. "I've never actually heard that story. So, um, what would you like to discuss?"

"Discuss? Hannah, I haven't been here in forever. I want to know everything. I assume you are cheerleader, doing debate and ballet, like your sister?"

"I do absolutely none of that." Hannah said very annoyed.

Tiffany frowned. "Oh, well that is fine, I suppose. Your sister is just impressive, is all. What do you do?"

Vivica walked in. "Oh, she does a lot. She is in the drama club, she is a student rep, and she does a lot of volunteer work around town. You would be extremely impressed with her." She kissed Hannah on the forehead again.

"I see. Well, that is all impressive as well, I guess." Tiffany stated.

HANNAH – 2018

Impressive ... Hannah always wanted to smack her mother when she remembered that. She knew it was wrong to feel that away about anyone really but really. How were Hope's hobbies any more impressive? Why did Hope always to get more attention? She looked at her reflection in the window and could tell she needed to calm herself down.

Hannah quickly got on her computer to try and distract herself. An ad for a grocery store popped up in the corner of her screen. Jordon Food Store... She worked there for a year and a half before being *fired*. Well, not fired but forced out by a crazy, sexist, and racist manager who couldn't handle the fact that she was Latina. It took her the longest time to realize that she was being targeted. It didn't matter that she was wealthy or a Knight. She was Latina. So, that made her unwanted in the eyes of this manager. Hannah had no choice but to get out of the situation.

She clicked off the screen and got up from her desk. She was starting to get dizzy when she walked to her office door. Hannah opened the door but passed out on the floor before she could step out...

LUCY – 2018

The eldest Kingsley walked into Vivica's kitchen. It had been quiet without Vivica and Holly around. Yet, it was louder because of Langley being Langley. Lucy was unsure how much of Vivica verse Langley she would be able to take once the redhead did return home.

Lucy knew she needed to find a house of her own. She also knew they needed to find an office space for their business. All these things would be so much, more comfortable with Vivica around. Sure, she could be actively looking for a house by herself, but the fact was that with Vivica away, it made it less of an issue. It was when they were all together that things became awkward.

Xander sat at the kitchen table, eating a bowl soup. "What's up?"

"Nothing much. I was just getting ready for a quick phone meeting. I thought I'd have a cup of tea. What about you?" She asked.

"Eh, just relaxing. I get to work the night shift, but I'm not tired at all. Apparently, Hope is leaving for England..." Xander said out loud. He sounded a bit annoyed.

The blonde girl looked at her brother. "Are you going to fight for her?"

The blond brother shrugged. "I would if she seemed interested, but she told me in a sort of bitchy way. I don't know how to describe it. Either way, it leaves more time to focus on work."

"Well, what about Hannah? I know you two had a short will-they won't-they..." Lucy. Pointed out.

"I might have blown things with her. I don't know. I like her, but I'm a few years younger than both of them. I don't want to get married right now. I want to get my career going before I even think about that. Dad's lack of common sense already put me a year or so behind. Plus, there is part of me that still wants to be on the NYPD someday." Xander admitted.

Lucy knew Xander had wanted to be a cop since he was young. It started off as a simple cop and robbers' game he used to play with his friends, but it turned into something more. Xander always wanted to be one of the good guys. Sure, their father's lack of morals probably put gave Xander a much deeper perspective about what good vs. evil truly meant. That said, Xander was his father's son. Xander acted like a true Kingsley man, and that did worry Lucy. He needed to learn that women were not meant to fight over a singular man just because they were willing.

Xander sighed. "I better get going," he said as he put his bowl in the sink.

The blonde sister got a text message. It was from Holly. She was about to burst in on Vivica. Lucy remembered the first meeting she had with Vivica five years earlier...

LUCY – 2011

How could she be so stupid? Lucy asked herself as she got on the elevator at The Fitzpatrick Group. She took a plane all the way from Manhattan, all based on a five-minute conversation she had with Margot Fitzpatrick... Lucy should have known that Margot was all smoke and mirrors. Lucy never had a job waiting for her. Not to mention, Lucy was in the hotel business. She wasn't even sure whatever the heck the Fitzpatrick's even did.

Lucy wanted to scream, but that's when someone else got in the elevator. A redhead. Lucy swore she looked familiar, but Lucy couldn't figure out from where. The redhead looked at her, and Lucy got the message. "What floor?"

Vivica looked at the button, which was already pressed. "Oh, I guess you are already going to the lobby. Sorry, I've just got so much on my mind right now. I just had my marriage annulled. I just got engaged, this will be my third time marrying this guy... Lord knows my mother would have been proud."

Lucy didn't know how to respond. "Well, congratulations on the wedding, I suppose."

"My fiancé decided to give me a company for our engagement present. I mean, I wanted to start this business, but I wanted to do it slowly on my own. Not jump right into it. So, I have like three months to plan the most boring hospital gala on the planet and then also my wedding."

"Well, that really shouldn't be so hard. I always had to deal with double bookings and what have you at the hotel chain I worked at," Lucy admitted.

The redhead smiled. "Really?"

The blonde shrugged. "Well, yeah. I did it all the time. It's not that hard."

"Right, but I need to budget... I'm just used to Nial or Cliff, or Luke or whoever giving me a credit card and telling me to go to town." Vivica admitted.

Right off the bat, Lucy could tell this woman had no clue what she was doing in terms of running a business by herself.

Lucy asked softly, "What career path were you in before this current company?"

"I've been an international cover and runway model. I briefly owned a cosmetic company back in the early 2000s, though." Vivica pointed out.

Lucy thought, *Models, cosmetics, and party planning didn't exactly go together...* That's when elevator made it to the lobby. She received a text message from her father. He had been trying to get into contact with her for the past month since she randomly quit her job. Lucy knew that his fears meant that he was in, more considerable trouble than she thought. She gulped... "You need help." She said flatly to Vivica.

Vivica shrugged. "I suppose. I mean, I will probably just get some workers or something. I should be able to get most of the work done myself."

"No. Sweetheart, look, you have absolutely no idea how business works. That's fine. I do. I have a Master's in Business. We will get you the tools that you really need in order to succeed. I'm proposing a partnership." Lucy explained.

"I really don't think I want a partner. You do seem to know what you are doing, though. How about an Assistant role?"

She wasn't going to be an assistant. Lucy had some standards left. That's when her father's lawyer sent her a text. He was claiming it was a wellness check. Lucy took a deep breath. "If I'm going to be your assistant, I'm going to need an upfront signing bonus and..." She wrote down a number on the back of a business card in her pocket. "This amount a year."

The redhead took the card and quickly looked back up at the blonde. "My husband can afford it." Vivica smiled.

Lucy had to admit she was shocked. A personal assistant, even a good one, didn't make that much money in Manhattan. Yes, she was about to be paid that much money in Michigan. Her lifestyle would quickly readjust itself.

Lucy's lower lip trembled in disbelief, but she hid it by ducking her head down, struggling to keep her composure. She was so excited; she could scarcely hide it. "We need to get papers drawn up right away. I'm actually based out of New York right now. I'll have to prepare myself to move."

Lucy had enough saved to move. She knew that once her husband and his lawyers actually looked at the deal, there would be some renegotiations, which would be fine. After all, she doubted she would be able to afford to live in Grosse Pointe, but there were several semi-close cities she would be able to live comfortably in.

It then hit her. Lucy would be leaving Xander and Langley. She had helped raise the two of them, and now she was running for the hills, away from both of them. Was this going to be easy? She knew that she couldn't possibly take them with her. Alex Kingsley would never allow for all three of his children to leave the state. Especially with how things were playing out. No, Lucy knew that she would have to make this journey alone without the absentee redhead. Lucy trusted her younger brother to take care of Langley. There was also an excellent chance that her father would never even get arrested...

Vivica explained, "I just texted my husband. He is having his lawyers write something up right now. We can actually go wait in my office right now and start talking strategy."

LUCY – 2018

Back to the present moment, the blonde received a text message. She assumed it was from Holly and was hoping that it was good news. Maybe she had snagged their redhaired friend. Instead, however, it was a message from a number she hadn't heard from in months. It was her father's lawyer. He was insisting upon having a sit down with them in Manhattan.

Lucy hadn't been back to Manhattan in three years, it seemed. She stopped going around when it became more obvious that her father was going to end up in prison. It wasn't as if she never intended to return. It was just she had no intention of doing so on her father's terms. She quickly texted back, *No*.

LANA – 1963

The maid, Lana, couldn't figure out what her employer's wife was up to. Why on Earth was her employer inviting Nadia's teacher and Brandon's older sister? That made no sense in her mind. Lana went along with it, though. That was what a maid was expected to do. She was preparing a chicken as if it were a Thanksgiving celebration... For three people. Heathcliff was dining out that evening. Lana was told that Benton was in California for business, but she suspected he was there for other reasons.

Lana supposed that if that were the case, maybe Delia deserved a nice night off for herself. After all, Lana noticed that Delia had not drunk anything the entire afternoon, which was a step-up from her normal bottle that she'd be done with by dinner. Lana had to negotiate a weekly order of boxes of wine to be quickly replaced so that it never looked as if Delia was drinking that much. Lama did suspect that this demand was not a smart thing. It made Delia think she was drinking a lot less than she actually was.

"Is dinner almost prepared?" Delia asked. "I want things to be perfect for my guests tonight!" She wore a green dress with her hair done up. It had been a while since she had seen Delia make an actual effort. Even when they had important business clients over, it became obvious when she wasn't trying very hard. Lana was never sure if that was because of Benton or Heathcliff.

"Yes, Mrs. Knight," Lana said. "I should have everything done within the hour. Your get-together should go over well. I have set up some appetizers in the library."

Delia smiled, which was rare for her. "Good... Good. This will be a nice evening."

Clifton walked downstairs. He was wearing a white T-shirt with a pair of jeans that had a rip in them. Delia caught wind of this.

Delia asked, glaring, "Why on Earth do you have a hole in your pants?

"I don't know, Mom. I'm going out. Don't wait up." Clifton explained.

Delia marched over to the back door and stopped him from exiting. "You are not going anywhere in that outfit. You are a Knight, not trailer trash."

Lana suspected that Delia was referring to the girl that Clifton was supposedly seeing. *Dallas Bolton.* She happened to be black. Which apparently was not okay with the Latina mother.

Clifton sighed and folded his arms. "Get out of my way, Mother. I'm just going to hang out with some friends. Why would I dress up just to see them?" He pointed out.

Delia hissed, "Well, are you going to their homes? I don't want any of these people getting the idea that my son cannot afford a pair of pants that don't have a hole in them."

Clifton rolled his eyes. "We are just going to hang around the park for a while and then maybe get a bite to eat."

The maid expected suspect that Delia wasn't prepared to fight. "Just try to be back before ten." The Latina Knight explained.

Moments like these, Lana was unable to really consider her full feelings. No, Clifton shouldn't speak to his mother like this. However, Delia needed to demand respect, in her opinion. Lana's child, Nadia, would never dream of speaking to her in this way. Even so, as the maid, it wasn't her place to get involved. She wasn't Delia's friend. She never would be. That wasn't how the maid-employer relationship worked.

"Yeah, I'll try…" Clifton told her, sounding a little defeated for some reason. Lana presumed he himself wanted a mother who would stand up for herself. Delia just wasn't that type of mother.

DELIA – 1963

Delia couldn't believe her son just embarrassed her in front of the maid, of all people. Delia was trying to come up with a quick excuse for Lana when the doorbell rang.

"Would you like me to get the door, Mrs. Knight?" Lana asked.

"No. I will get it myself..." Delia explained with a little more confidence. She wasn't going to let any Knight man get in the way of tonight. That said, she had no clue where Rodrick was...

The Latina Knight walked down the hall from the kitchen to the foyer. She turned on the chandelier lights before opening the door. The nun and her friend both arrived at the exact same time, standing in the doorway, looking at her. Delia wondered if they had come together.

She would find out later. "Hello, welcome to my house. Please, come in," Delia said with confidence.

The nun didn't seem that enchanted by Delia's house. She hadn't earlier either. Delia was honestly glad. Whenever the family had new people over the house, they always overly gushed about how glamorous the house was. The Fitzpatrick girl, however, had that look she had seen time and time again. At least in her case, I seemed a little more genuine. The nun clearly didn't care about gaudy looks or luxury- she was only here to meet Delia, and to become friends.

"You have such a beautiful house," Susan admitted out loud.

"Yes, it really is a wonderful home," Mary added in.

Delia smiled politely. She still missed their home in California. "Oh, thank you both so much. I try to keep a nice home." Delia had tried to put a mirror up in the foyer once. Heathcliff screamed at her for changing anything about the house... It wasn't her house. "Please, follow me into the library. I have refreshments." Delia explained.

The two women followed behind her as they walked down another hallway. The two of them passed several doors before finally making it to the library. Mary's eyes widened. "You have so many books in here."

She never had really paid attention, Delia admitted to herself. The Knight woman honestly wondered how many of these books actually had ever been read. She suspected they were just for decoration. The only books that really got any use were the Encyclopedia and dictionary.

"Please sit," Delia told her guests. She noticed a bottle of wine. It was only now that she realized she really hadn't had a drink all day. "So, Susan, tell me about your family?"

Susan clearly looked a little taken back by the question. "Oh, well, we run a bar on the outskirts of town. That's really it."

Delia said, "I heard that your father had a meeting with my husband. My husband and his father are considering working with him." That was probably more information than she should have given out, but it was too late to change things now.

The strawberry blondes' eyes widened even more. "Really? That's honestly a relief if it actually comes to fruition. My father has been trying to get someone to invest in his business ideas for a while."

Delia really wished that she hadn't said that. Now, if and when the business deal did happen, this girl was going to think that Delia approved of her husband's shady business moves.

The woman kept it cryptic. "I truly hope that it works for him."

The door opened, and Delia's own eyes widened. "Rodrick, what on Earth are you doing here?"

"I live here." He said, looking pissed off. "What are you doing here?" He rolled his eyes.

"I'm having a dinner party with a few... Friends." She knew it sounded presumptuous to call these two women friends, but she didn't know what else to call them.

Rodrick looked and saw Sister Mary Newman. "Why are my teacher and a Fitzpatrick in my house?" He demanded.

Delia had forgotten their shared connection. It was at that moment that something snapped in Delia. "Now, go upstairs and study. Make a good impression for your teacher..." She said this with authority instead of kindness.

The younger Knight son wanted to respond, but he knew he had just been defeated. "Have the maid bring something up for me."

"You can eat in the kitchen when she tells you dinner is made." Delia crossed her arms. That was the last straw. She wouldn't have her sons treating her like dirt. Delia didn't care if her sons were Knight men anymore. They were still her sons.

HOLLY – 2018

Holly was outside of a hotel room somewhere in Europe. It had been a restless journey, but Holly had finally found the redhead. "Open up!" She screamed as she knocked on the door. "I know you are in there, and I'm taking you home."

Her husband was livid with how long Holly had been gone. She had pointed out that he once spent months away from home undercover. She realized their situations had its differences, but this was her best friend.

Holly growled, "I swear to God, Vivica. I will bust down this door." She continued banging on the door."

The door finally opened. "Why on Earth is the maid banging on your door?" Nial asked.

Holly's eyes widened. She realized that Nial was at least a hundred and fifty pounds heavier, with a bulging belly and a massive face. But at that moment, she pushed him aside and walked into the room.

"What in the actual fuck is going on here?" Holly demanded as she found a blonde woman sitting on the bed. "Who on Earth are you?"

"My girlfriend. Meghan." Nial said as he crossed his arms. "Vivica's room is down the hall..."

Holly looked around for a moment, realizing the desk clerk probably got confused. Vivica's last name was still legally *Fitzpatrick*.

"Well, in that case... Meghan- run from this loser as fast as you can."

With Holly, she walked out of the hotel room and slammed the door shut. She then started walking down the hall, realizing she had no clue which room Vivica was actually in. It didn't matter though, because another door opened, and a redhead popped out.

"March right back in there. We need to talk!" Holly ordered.

Vivica rolled her eyes and did as she was told. She went and sat on a couch and gestured for Holly to sit next to her.

"I'm surprised it took you so long to find me," Vivica said with a coiled smile.

"I got lost in Monte Carlo..." Holly admitted.

"Who on Earth paid you to come here?" Vivica wondered

"You are forgetting I have copies of all your credit cards, right? Do you even check your bank balance?" Holly could easily tell that Vivica had little idea what she was talking about. She sighed in frustration. "Why on Earth is Nial here?"

Vivica shrugged. "He wanted to introduce me to his new playtoy. I didn't ask him to come. I have no idea how he even found me."

Holly took a sigh of relief. "Well, we need to get you back home."

"I don't think I should go. I think Cliff and even Brad are better off without me." Vivica admitted. "Lucy, for sure, is better off without me."

The maid looked Vivica in the eye. "Look, normally I would have a list of reasons for why you need to run back to town. I don't this time. Cliff desperately misses you, but he's no longer married to your bitch of a sister. Harry has literally spent the entire summer with Lucy's sister and Brad. The three of them seem to get along. Hannah even seems to be adjusting to her job."

The former Fitzpatrick girl sighed. "So, then, no one needs me back in town?"

"Mrs. Templeton and Margot have no one to call a slut or whore anymore, if that makes you feel any better..." Holly smiled.

Vivica's phone made a shrill, *pinging* sound. She got up and looked at the screen. "It's from Cliff... I've been purposely not responding. Can you please read it for me?" She handed the phone to Holly.

Holly read the text, and her mouth gaped wide open. She jumped right up, pulling Vivica off her feet. "Scratch that, you are needed right now. Hannah collapsed at KMC while on the job. She has just been admitted to Grosse Pointe General Hospital."

The redhead didn't even need to think twice. She went into her closet and grabbed her luggage. "We might need to pick up a few more bags. I bought more clothes..."

Holly threw the bag aside. "Get the idiot doctor down the hall to gather your things. We need to get going!"

HARRY – 2018

The curly-haired Knight boy sat down in his corner of the library. He was reading from the diary of Susan Fitzpatrick. Sister Mary Newman had given him her old journals to read, and while he was able to read them over within a few days, essentially. He had already reread them multiple times. It was hard to believe that this woman had lived in town and had been involved with the Fitzpatrick and Knight families. Sure, this was before his late grandfather Rodrick was head of the family, and before Margot was even a thought. Still, it was outstanding that the life she lived in such a short time was full of intrigue. Susan wasn't your average Fitzpatrick; after all, she was a Fitzpatrick before they came into money.

When Harry was younger, he remembered his Grandfather and even Great-Grandmother refer to the Fitzpatrick clan as *new money* in a dirty way. Yes, here, he could see that at one point, his Great-Grandmother Delia had such great respect for Susan. Harry suspected her later disdain came from the treatment that they gave Susan. He had yet to really share any of this with Brad. It changed his perspective of the family as it presently stood.

Harry closed the diary and looked up. There was a pair of big brown eyes looking at him from across the room. Harry got up and walked over. This was unlike him; Harry never made the first move.

"Hey..." Harry said.

Preston smiled back. "Hey."

The Knight boy looked at the empty seat and wanted to ask if he could sit down... "So, um, would it be ok if I..."

Preston rolled his eyes. "Would you like to sit down, Harry?" He laughed.

Harry took that as the best offer that he would probably get. He sat down, blushing quietly. "So, what brings you to the library? School doesn't even start up again until next week."

Preston responded, "I'm just prepping for some of my AP classes. My math and science classes will actually count towards college credit." Preston said as if he were proud of himself. He lowered his eyelashes, waiting for Harry to be impressed. But Harry was taking the same AP classes...He didn't intend on telling Preston this, though.

"That's pretty cool," Harry said, with a smile "I just never see any actual students in here during the summer unless they are getting tutored. I love to read here."

The Costa son smiled. "Yeah, I love libraries. My house is a little chaotic during the daytime with my family's businesses. Plus, my sister is still home from boarding school for the next few weeks."

Harry didn't know how to let the conversation flow naturally. He kept waiting for Langley to text him or to pop out of somewhere to take control. Then his phone vibrated. It wasn't Langley. It was his father.

Harry glanced down to read it. All he saw was in all bold letters- *Hannah had been admitted to the hospital.*

"Oh, fuck..." Harry said, louder than he intended. "I've got to go... Shoot, I walked here. I can run... Or no, I'll order a car, but it has to be Knight. I can't be driven in a non-Knight car..." Harry's stomach started to rip apart inside. Tears bit at his eyes. He swirled around, unable to know what to do?

Preston jumped up. "Harry, what do you need, and where do you need to go? Take a second to calm down."

Harry couldn't breathe. "My sister is in the hospital. I walked from the house, though, instead of taking my car..."

Preston grabbed his hand. "Come on; I'll drive you. Don't worry. I have a Knight car," he explained.

***

The two boys rushed into the visiting area of the hospital, where they found Cliff sitting with Brad, Langley, and Lucy. Harry knew that his other sister was on her way to England. He had no clue if she had even left yet, but considering her lack of a relationship with Hannah, he doubted she would be there.

Harry's mind wasn't on Preston anymore, so he completely forgot that the boy had come in with him. Brad and his father both looked confused and annoyed at the same time. They glared silently at Preston's entrance.

Harry ignored it. "How is she doing?" Harry asked his father.

"She is with a doctor right now. It seems that it was stress-related." Cliff told him. He once again looked at Preston. Harry could tell that his father knew exactly who the boy was. "Who is your friend?" He asked.

"Oh, um, this is Preston... Costa. We have been hanging out a little bit as of late." Harry admitted.

Preston put out his hand to shake Cliff's. When he did, Cliff clearly wasn't thrilled about it.

Cliff's lips trembled up with a fake smile. "Well, it is nice you came along, I suppose?"

"Where is my niece?" An all-too-familiar voice screamed.

"Vivica, you are going the wrong way!" Another familiar voice said. The maid quickly yanked Vivica down the hall and over to what apparently was her entire family.

Vivica looked at Cliff, and Cliff looked at Vivica...

"Weston?" Cliff said with a loving smile.

Harry walked up to his aunt and hugged her. Brad nodded to her in a *nice to see you again* kind of way. "Hello, everyone." Vivica said.

VIVICA – 2018

It had been months since the redhaired vixen had seen Cliff Knight. The last time she had seen him, she was still trying to get out of his marriage proposal. She then spent months banging her head on walls around Europe, wondering why the hell she would turn down the one damn thing she had wanted her entire life. It wasn't until this moment that she finally had an answer for him. "I accept." She blurted out.

"You accept what?" The bitchy blonde teenager who had been spending all her time with Brad said.

"I mean... How are you, Cliff? Where is Hannah?" She wondered.

Cliff groaned and responded. "She is just meeting with her doctors right now. I only texted you his morning, how on earth did you get here so quickly?"

Vivica shrugged. "Oh, you can get on a plane and be anywhere within a number of hours," Vivica said that as if it made a lick of sense. "We clearly have a lot to talk about," Vivica said, as she looked at the peanut gallery. The redhead could already tell that Lucy was about to get out paperwork for her to look over. The blonde assistant turned business partner had words for her. There was five years of aggression built up and Vivica was ready for it when it finally cam

"Can we maybe speak in private for a second?" Cliff nodded.

The two walked down the hall together. He was still the most beautiful man she had ever seen, she thought to herself.

Cliff cleared his throat. "So, what did you need to talk about?"

"I'm sorry... I didn't mean to abandon and ignore you the entire summer." She admitted.

Cliff shrugged. "It isn't like I haven't done the same to you in the past."

She knew he was referring to their first summer as a couple. Or that summer after they graduated high school...

"I thought about you the entire time, though. I do want to marry you," she explained.

Cliff's face lit up. "So, then, you are finally accepting my proposal?"

"Well, I suppose," Vivica murmured softly. "I'm going to lose out on a large chunk of money from my last divorce from Nial. Which I think will disappoint you more than me. I do, though. I've wanted to be your bride since I was twelve years old." The redhead admitted.

"They are finally engaged!" Holly screamed out from the next room.

Vivica looked around the corner. Holly was clearly listening in. This didn't shock her. She was always being noisy. "All right... You can all come out..."

"We have the wedding of the century to plan!" Holly shouted.

Vivica quickly noticed Lucy start to whimper. Vivica said, "Don't worry, dear, we will get our cosmetic company up and running before the engagement. The wedding will take a few months to plan, obviously." Everyone looked at her, shocked. "What? I've been waiting for this day since I was twelve, as I literally just said... The first time we tried this, it ended in disaster; the second time was a sham, so the third time is the charm. We are making sure nothing gets in the way. Which reminds me, I should call my bitch of a sister," she proudly said. That's when Vivica noticed Preston Costa standing next to Harry. She whispered to Cliff. "Honey, why is that mob boss's son here?" Cliff shrugged.

A doctor finally walked over, rubbing his forehead. "Hannah is ready for visitors. Only one at a time, though. She is still recovering. It was a stress-related incident. She will be able to explain things more in detail."

Cliff looked at Vivica. "Would you like to come with me?"

"I honestly was coming regardless if you wanted me to or not, so yes," Vivica explained.

HANNAH – 2018

The female Knight looked at the ceiling of her hospital room. She couldn't believe this happened again. The last time she had passed out from stress was right before she had quit that horrible job. Yet, she was still being triggered... The door opened, and she turned. Hannah immediately sat up, wincing in pain.

"Aunt Vivica!" she practically screamed.

Vivica quickly gave her a tight hug. "Oh, I've missed you. How is my favorite niece and soon to be stepdaughter, again?"

"I'll be fine. It's just stress." Hannah admitted.

"Hannah, if you are this stressed, I want you to take some time off from work," Cliff told her, stepping into the room behind Vivica.

Hannah sighed. "I can't just take a leave of absence from work, Dad. If I do that, then people are just going to claim nepotism. Which they already do. I'm plenty capable of my job. This job didn't cause my stress. My stress is from my last one."

Vivica nodded, trying to understand. "I imagine that selling cars all day can be rather stressful." She sat at the foot of her bed.

"It wasn't from selling cars... This was from when I was working for that grocery store. The therapist I was seeing at the time diagnosed me with hypersomnia. I was emotionally tired all the time and would just pass out randomly. I became so reliant on energy drinks. She kept urging me to quit my job, but I needed the money." Hannah immediately looked at her father. She knew he wasn't going to like that answer. It was before the two of them started to rebuild their relationship. Hannah had thought that Cliff wanted her to be truly identical to Hope down to her personality. Just her mother had wanted.

"Hannah Knight, why on Earth did you stay at a job that was mentally destroying you? If you had come to me, I would have helped you out," Cliff explained.

Hannah sighed. "As much as I know, I could have come to you. I couldn't have come to you and mom. At least, not as she was at the time," Hannah said. It was true. Tiffany had been so judgmental of her during that time, and that was one of the main reasons she moved out. Hope, who had failed three classes in one semester, was a perfect saint- and yet Hannah was still the screw-up. It hadn't been fair.

Her Aunt looked at her father. "We shouldn't be stressing her out further. We all have our reasons as to why we don't speak up. Now just tell me what or who was stressing you out at that grocery store. There is a Costa in the hallway. We can take care of this situation right away."

Cliff looked at Vivica, startled. "Vivica, we aren't the Fitzpatrick's. We aren't going to handle our situations by hiring a hitman."

Hannah's eyes widened. "There is a Costa in the hallway? It wouldn't happen to be Preston Costa?" She had a small smile on her face. She was hoping that meant Harry was spending more time with him.

"I think that is Preston," Vivica lamented. "I swear- children in this town grow up so fast... Why do you ask?"

"Oh, no reason... That said, is he here with Harry?" Hannah further pondered.

Vivica smacked her forehead. "My nephew better not be falling for a Costa..." The head of the family looked at his fiancé. "What? A Costa... There is no way that a Costa would ever be with a Knight."

Knight."

"Oh, like you two have room to talk. No one wanted you to be together, either," Hannah reminded them both.

Vivica stood up from the bed. "That's a bit of a different situation. Neither of us have ever intentionally killed anyone. Anthony and Jackie Costa, on the other hand... Well, I'd be less concerned if Harry said he and Mrs. Templeton were getting it on."

"You realize that if either of you get involved, Harry is going to have the world's worst panic attack, right?" Hannah pointed out.

Cliff sighed. "She is right. We will just have to trust that Harry knows how to make good choices."

"I'm going to have Holly follow them around town..." Vivica explained. "I just don't want him getting hurt."

LANGLEY – 2018

The youngest Kingsley child said nothing on the way home from the hospital. She already knew that Brad was furious that Preston showed up with his cousin. Langley, being Langley, though, couldn't stay silent for very long. She knocked on his door and didn't wait for him to say anything. She barged in without a response.

"Langley, I could have been getting changed," Brad screamed. He was actually about to start doing just that.

"Don't tease me... How are you doing?" Langley asked.

Brad sat down on his bed. "I'm fine, I guess. I'm just worried about Harry being with that idiot..."

Langley sat down next to her boyfriend. "We need to let Harry find that out for himself. Until Preston gives us any reason to worry, we still need to think the best about him. If Harry and he are going to date, we should be respectful."

"Well, how do we even know that will end up happening? We don't even know if Preston is gay." Brad looked at Langley. Langley tried to hold back a knowing expression, but it wasn't working. "Langley, what do you know?"

She wished Brad could separate his parent's stupidity from his own life. He was absolutely nothing like them. On top of that, Preston really didn't seem to be like his parents. Sure, Langley didn't actually know Anthony or Jackie, but she had gone to school with other kids who weren't like their parents before.

Langley drew in a deep sigh, and said, "Preston told me Harry came out as gay. I don't think they are dating, though. Who knows, school starts back up in a few days and they'll have more time to spend with one another... Personally, I have no issue with it." She looked Brad right in the eye.

"I hate it when you are right," Brad said. "Still, it doesn't change the fact that Harry gets freaked out in Pontiac, of all places. What happens if Preston invites him over, and Anthony Costa shoots someone up?" Brad pointed out.

Langley wasn't really sure how to answer that. She shrugged her shoulders. "He will have a fun story to tell the other nuts in the loony bin one day..." She said sarcastically. Brad wasn't going to let up on this.

There was a single knock on the door. "Who is it?" Brad called. "Come in.

It was Vivica. "Oh, Lanyard, you are here..."

Langley gave the redhead a bitchy look. "It's Langley."

"Lawndale, yes... Anyway, I just wanted to spend some time with my son. I haven't seen him in months."

That was her choice. Why was Langley expected to leave because of that reason? Langley sighed. "I will talk with you later." She kissed Brad on the lips before giving Vivica a dirty look and leaving.

VIVICA – 2018

She watched as Laminate left the room. Vivica didn't know why, but that girl just set off a bunch of red flags in her head when it came to Brad. "So, how are you doing, sweetheart?"

Brad shrugged. "Fine. I suppose. I'm happy you're back in town, though."

"I don't plan on leaving again anytime soon," Vivica promised. "I just needed a little while to make sure being with your uncle was best for me," Vivica explained.

"Is he really still my uncle still at this point?" Brad wondered.

"Well, he is still Harry and the girl's father. So, I guess. I'm sure he would be fine with you just calling him Cliff going forward, though." She would have suggested just *Dad* when Nial was around. Vivica knew better than to say that though around Brad, who got stressed out about both her and Nial. "What is your final opinion on my engagement?"

The blond son turned and looked out the window. "I want you to be happy. I know that Cliff is what makes you happy."

Vivica knew he wasn't saying his whole feeling on the subject, and that was concerning her a bit. "Brad, if you don't want me to get married to Cliff, you need to speak up now."

Brad turned to his mother. "I just know you only just divorced Dad a little while ago. I don't want you to marry Cliff, and then realize quickly you love Dad or Luke Knight again."

The mother put her hand on her sons' shoulder. "I will never marry Nial again. Your aunt would probably come after me with an ax, and Holly would join her. Luke is a fond part of my past, but we are just not soulmates.

With that, someone else knocked on the door. This time it was the maid who peeked into the room with wide eyes. Vivica scowled. "Holly, I'm trying to have a private moment with my son."

"I actually have football practice in the morning. I need to get ready for bed." Brad explained, moving away from her.

Vivica sighed. "I love you." She walked into the hallway with Holly. "Well, way to ruin a moment." Vivica crossed her arms.

"Oh, relax... Now that you are home, you can be a full-time mother to him, which reminds me. I really need to pick my kids up from summer camp..." Holly nodded her head, just remembering that. "I think they were around six years old when I dropped them off. I'm hoping they are thirty by now."

"So, what else do I need to be focused on, other than Hannah and my nephew's mobster boyfriend?" Vivica asked.

Holly looked at her point-blank. "Mobster boyfriend? Harry's dating Preston Costa?"

If only she knew. Of all the gay teenage boys for Harry to fall for, he had to find a mobster's son. "I just wish that there was another way to show that I support Harry without it involving a Costa... If he wanted to watch *Xanadu* all day long, I'd have no problem. Oh, or *Valley of the Dolls!*"

The maid rolled her eyes. "You know how bitchy redhaired hags can be..."

The two continued to walk until they made their way downstairs. Then, they sat on the couch next to one another.

The maid said, gently, "Vivica, I think the best thing for you is just to allow Harry to be himself. If he wants to watch old camp classics, then let him find them for himself. If he wants to rock it out to Madonna or Cher again, it is up for him to find those on his own. He could be a hardcore Republican for all we know, but it is up to him to find that information out himself."

Vivica had no issue if Harry was a Republican. She assumed the Republicans and LGBT community would have different views, though. She finally realized what Holly was trying to say. "If Harry wants to be a log cabin Republican then I will support him."

"It's like talking to a redhaired wall with you sometimes..." Holly smacked her forehead.

CLIFF – 2018

The Knight CEO knocked on his son's door.

"Come in," Harry said. Cliff did without hesitation. He looked at his son and sighed. "I'm not dating him," Harry said.

"Yes, but you are spending time with him. Which, in many ways, concerns me just as much? You go from hiding in your room all day and night to hanging around that New York girl- and now a Mob bosses' son. You do realize that is what he is. The Costa's might have a few legit businesses, but it doesn't change the fact that they are still an organized crime family."

Cliff remembered back in the late '70s when Grosse Pointe started kicking out all the other crime families. The Costas somehow managed to stick around. It sent a message to the other families, as well as the town itself. When Anthony came back to town after years of exile, it only got worse. It only escalated further when he married that nut, Jackie.

Cliff still remembered the wedding of the two. Nial Fitzpatrick was the best man... It was a mockery to Grosse Pointe, Saint Agnes, and dare he say it- even the Fitzpatrick family. They had risen from their past only to be dragged down again, thanks to Nial and Margot's relationship with the Costa family. Then there was the baby swap...

"Look, you need to be careful around him. I really don't want you around the boy or his family. I know I can't force you to stay away from him, though. My father tried his hardest to keep me away from Vivica. To the point where he sent me to

Europe every summer. He even orchestrated getting Vivica a modeling contract with the Madwell Agency."

"Your father orchestrated all that just to keep you and Aunt Vivica away from one another? Harry asked, confused.

"He had his reasons..."

Lately, Cliff wondered if the only reason he didn't want Harry spending time with Vivica was that her late stepfather was secretly his uncle. There wasn't was a blood connection between the two themselves, but was Rodrick so obsessed with keeping DJ out of the family that he tried keeping *her* out? He still hadn't told Vivica. He still hadn't even heard the entire will of Rodrick's. Which he was sure had nothing but insults towards him, Vivica, and possibly the rest of the family.

Harry didn't look that concerned. "Well, I'm not dating him. I mean, yeah, he is cool and all, but I mean... How do you know if you like someone?" Harry blurted out.

Cliff had no idea how to answer this for a number of reasons. He took a deep breath. "Well, you just sort of know. I mean, there is a difference between finding someone attractive and wanting to be with them forever. Sometimes you don't want to be with them, but you are just interested in exploring the prospect." Cliff didn't know if that made any sense.

"Did you see yourself with Mom for the rest of your life?" Harry wondered.

"I did for the longest time. When I married your mother, I thought it would be forever."

When he thought she had died, he remembered hearing the news that Tiffany and Vivica had been in a car accident. He was more concerned about Vivica than Tiffany. It hadn't then when he realized that as much as he cared for Tiffany, she wasn't his one true love. She was the woman he was meant to have his children with, but that was about it.

It took Cliff a long moment, but he started to realize just how much he and his family hurt Vivica throughout the years. He allowed for so much verbal abuse from his father. His Grandmother Delia had been so kind towards her, but, in her later life, Delia had expressed that she was only kind to Vivica because she had made him happy. Delia told Cliff and Tiffany once that she was delighted that Cliff *grew up* and married a doctor instead of a model. She had been losing it a bit when she made these comments, but still, it hurt him a lot to hear this. He knew how much Vivica cared for Delia.

"Dad, if I did date Preston, would you be angry? I mean, I legit don't think we will date. I'm just wondering. Will you support me?" Harry looked at his father in the eyes.

The father sighed. "I'd support you if you even if you dated that couch we talked about before. Just be careful."

***

After getting off the phone with Hannah at the hospital, Cliff had a lot of work to do. He not only had a company to run, but he also had a wedding to plan. Cliff was sure Vivica would do most of the planning, but it would be up to him to finance and secure a lot of it.

The door opened, and he already knew who it was before he turned around.

"What is my Knight up to?? Vivica asked as she sat on his lap.

"Just work. What is my Weston doing over so late at night?" Cliff wondered.

Vivica looked at him and started laughing. "It's not even nine... Have we really gotten so old that this is considered *late at night*?"

"Weston, you look the same as you did when you were sixteen." He admitted.

The redhead smiled at him and kissed his neck. She then pulled away, and Cliff wished she hadn't. "I spoke with Brad about us getting married. Did you speak with Harry?"

He tried, but he was more concerned about the Costa boy. "Yes. I know that Harry will be very happy to have you as his stepmother."

She shrugged. "I don't need to be his stepmother. I can still just be his aunt just like before. I never tried to replace his mother, and I never will try to. Even if my bitch of a sister thinks otherwise."

Cliff couldn't help but laugh. Then he started to feel guilty. Tiffany tried her hardest when it came to raising Harry, but his personal problems made it difficult for them to connect properly. At least that is what he would tell his doctors when they would question what was going on. There was a long period in which Harry refused to leave the house except to go to school. It all started when Cliff and Vivica separated. Cliff thought it had more to do with Brad leaving than Vivica, though. Brad had been the one who got Harry to venture out of the house and do things. Once a boarding school separated the two boys, it freaked Harry out and was too much for him.

Really, it was Nial's fault for sending Brad away. Cliff never understood why he would want to send his son away.

It did make him feel less guilty about his illegitimate son, who was forced on Nial shortly after his first divorce from Vivica. Nial was never really a family man in general. He treated his daughter Laura like a princess when she had been younger, but she still broke away from the family, and no one knew exactly where she was.

Tiffany tried, but she, for whatever reason, expected her three children would all just ease up through life, similar to herself before the kidnapping. Cliff learned very quickly when they got back together that Tiffany was never hurt; he had moved on with Vivica. Instead, she was just upset that things didn't go right back to the way things had been the moment before the car accident. She wanted her life to go back exactly as it had been before, which was more than understandable and really shouldn't have been an issue. The main issue was that she went from raising two very young girls and a baby to raising two teenage daughters with completely different personalities and a son with a million social and mental issues that were not an easy fix. Vivica had to give up modeling to take care of Harry. Cliff had tried to allow her to hire a nanny, but she wouldn't allow it. She wanted to be there for Harry as well as Brad and the girls.

They were very unconventional, but they acted as an extremely nuclear family. Cliff went to work each morning; they would come home and play with the boys, help the girls with their homework, and spend time with Vivica. Vivica, with the help of a cook, prepared all the meals, including homemade lunches for the children. She spent time helping Hannah with all her after-school activities. Vivica also made sure that Harry didn't just sit alone in his room. Vivica and Cliff both made sure they acted like a regular family. Nial was still in and out of Brad's life, and by that point, Laura only was around during holidays.

It was only at this moment that Cliff realized, Vivica was needed in this household again. He looked into her eyes. "I love you, Weston."

"I've always loved you, Cliff. We really need to worry about both the boys, though. I don't trust that Lysistrata girl though with Brad."

"You mean Langley?" Cliff asked, confused.

The redhead shrugged. "Isn't that what I said? Either way, we need to get Langley away from both the boys."

He knew she wasn't going to like his response, but he was going to say it anyway. "Vivica, you realize that no one in our lives wanted us to be together. Yet, we were both what the other one needed."

The redhaired vixen tried to come up with a proper response. "Well, it's a bit different..."

HANNAH –2018

Hannah sat up in her hospital room, thinking about everything that had led her to this point. She thought about it all often, which she knew wasn't a good thing. The Knight daughter realized it was better to let herself move on. That is what people always told her to do: *"Move on."* They would hear about the torment that she and her co-workers went through, and the response was that *"Oh, well, he was just an older man who didn't know any better. Feel bad for him. Be ashamed with yourself for not being okay with how you were treated."* It apparently was still acceptable to be a bigot so long as you were old.

Hannah had dealt with Mrs. Templeton since her birth. She remembered a lone emergency where Vivica had been out of town, and Cliff needed a babysitter but couldn't find anyone else. Mrs. Templeton ate a literal bucket of ice cream while they watched a documentary on Hitler and some weird knock-off of *Gone with the Wind,* where the South had won the war...

She wanted to go home or at least somewhere where all the lights were off. At least somewhere where she couldn't hear someone screaming in pain down the hall. That's when the door opened.

"Don't worry, Hannah. This is just a general check-in that the city is enforcing," Xander said as he walked in and closed the door. He was wearing his police uniform. Hannah had to admit he looked sexy. "Hey, Hannah. I hope I didn't wake you. Langley and Lucy both sent me a series of texts, but

I couldn't answer them while I was at work. I ran over as soon as I heard. Are you alright?"

This was the Xander who Hannah had fallen for a few months back. But she couldn't do this right now... So, no, she wasn't ok.

Hannah turned away and scowled. "I'll be better once you are gone. Hope's in England."

"Yeah... I know. Look, I only agreed to date her over you because she asked first. That's really it. The longer I spent with her, the more I realized she really was well... The way you described her. "

"An obnoxious bitch?" Hannah spat out.

Xander stretched awkwardly. "Well, I mean, I wouldn't have used that word..."

He might have a problem, but she had no issue with using it. Hannah knew that at the end of the day, Hope wasn't responsible for why she was in this bed right now. Yet, she also knew that Hope was responsible for what drove her to leave home in the first place.

"Xander, thanks for checking on me, but I'm not in a place where I need or want a relationship. Yes, I find you attractive, but I don't think I like your personality."

The blond officer just stood there for a second. "Hannah, I think we should still try talking. You clearly need to speak with someone. Are you seeing a therapist?"

Hannah sighed. "I was up until I moved back to North Pointe. It doesn't matter. She kept giving me the same advice over and over again. I have to quit my job at Jordan Food Store. I did. Clearly, it wasn't great advice."

"I mean, maybe there are deeper issues that you could explore. I'm happy to help you. We can do this as friends. We don't even have to do it as friends. Just think of me as someone to bitch at when you need to."

"You do realize that a lot of my bitching could end up being about you." Hannah pointed out.

Xander shrugged and sat on her bed. "I can handle it. You've met my younger sister. All she does it, bitch to me about everything under the sun: I always listen, though. I'm here for you."

She smiled at him. He smiled back. Hannah had forgotten what an amazing smile he had. "Ok, it's a deal."

NADIA – 1963

Nadia and Brandon had been holding hands for at least ten minutes, but it was only now that they were entering the bar when she realized something shocking- he was taking her to dinner at the bar that his family ran. She had been there with her mother and grandmother a few times. It was decent enough food, and she wasn't going to pass up food not made by her grandmother. She loved her grandmother dearly, but she wasn't much of a cook.

The two sat down at a booth in the back corner. Nadia recognized many of the people, but none of them seemed to acknowledge her. "So, what would you recommend?" She asked Brandon.

"Oh, I don't know... Everything is pretty good. My parents are both really good cooks." Brandon admitted.

Nadia scrolled through the menu. "I'll get the chicken noodle soup."

"That's all you want?" He asked her.

The Latina girl shrugged. "If I'm hungrier, I'll order something more, but that should be enough... Besides, it was nice to have the day off today."

The redhaired boy nodded. "Yeah, definitely. I like school and all, but we needed an extra day off... It would have been a better day had we not run into Rodrick, though."

Nadia sighed. "Brandon, you need not to let people like Rodrick get to you. He isn't worth our time and energy. Besides- this is between us, but he has a really messed up family. His parents both drank. That has to remain between us. My mother told me back when he and his parents moved back to North Pointe." Nadia admitted.

"Well, that doesn't make his own behavior ok. Timmy Hogan's mother shot his father, and he still manages to be pleasant." Brandon explained.

Nadia couldn't help but laugh. "Timmy Hogan sits in the back of the class and draws guns. The boy is going to grow up and have some serious problems. That isn't to say that Rodrick won't. It's just to say that we should let Rodrick deal with his own issues without interfering."

She had known Brandon for years. He was a fixer. That boy always tried to help everyone around him and couldn't help himself. She didn't know how to tell him just to let things be. Nadia knew that he would never listen. He was a typical teenage boy with a complex to fix everyone. She just hoped he realized that she herself didn't need fixing.

As they continued to stare at one another blankly, Ida Fitzpatrick walked over. She was the lone brunette in a sea of red hair. Still, she shared the trademark Fitzpatrick green eyes.

Ida smiled at Nadia but looked at Brandon with squinting eyes and a scowl. "Brandon, why are you only just getting in? Your sister went out tonight. I need your help."

"Where on Earth would Susan have gone? She has no friends." He said that second part under his breath, but both girls could clearly hear him. His mother swatted him on the head. "I was joking..."

"She is at North Pointe having dinner with your teacher and Delia Knight. Your father, of course, told her she had no choice but to go. Either way, I need your help. Your father has been on the phone all night arranging things with one of his smaller investors." She told her son.

The boy frowned at Nadia. "Sorry, I have to help out." He looked at his mother. "Would it be alright if Nadia stayed and had a bowl of soup, though? I already asked her to dinner."

"I could always help out for the night," Nadia suggested.

Ida and Brandon looked at each other. "We more than appreciate it, but we really couldn't pay you at this moment."

The brunette girl stood up. "Pay me with some soup to go at the end of the night. I can clean the tables or the bathrooms. You clearly need help, and I don't really feel like going home." She walked herself into the back before either Fitzpatrick could answer.

The mother looked at her son. "You keep that girl close, boy. She could be good for you."

LUCY – 2018

Lucy casually knocked on Perry's slightly opened office door at the Fitzpatrick Group. She let herself in, as she could see he was on his phone. She didn't know what she was doing here, but she needed to bitch with someone. Holly was too busy bitching at Vivica throughout the morning about things and didn't want to bother either of them. Lucy knew she couldn't talk about her father with Xander or Langley.

It was only now that Lucy realized in the five years she had lived in Grosse Pointe, the closest she had to real friends was Holly, who was more of a frenemy, and Vivica- who had been her employer up until very recently.

Lucy waved at Perry. He waved back.

"Mrs. Templeton, we can talk about what flavors to keep later. I just had an appointment walk-in. Yes, I will consider your proposal, but I think we have to keep chocolate ice cream as a flavor..." He hung the phone. He looked at Lucy. "I've unfortunately had the displeasure of knowing that woman my entire life. The scary thing is there are pictures of her at events from when my grandparents were in grade school, and she looked the same damn age... So, what brings you here?"

"Well, to be honest, I just needed someone's opinion, and I thought you were far enough away from my family where you could give an unbiased opinion. Obviously, Mrs. Templeton or Jackie Costa were my first choices." Lucy admitted.

Perry gestured for her to sit down on the couch in his office. She did. "So, what seems to be on your mind?" He asked as he sat down next to her.

She gave it a second to really sink in. "My father is demanding to see me in New York. I'd rather not go back. At least not for him. They want me to testify for him. At least, that is what I assume. But I'm not a liar. After all, I know he was up to something shady and ran the moment he realized he would probably be caught."

"I can relate to some degree. Margot has gotten herself into some stupid situations in the past."

Perry looked at Lucy in the eyes. She looked back and couldn't help but fall for how amazing they were. "You know, maybe I could come with you for moral support. Would that be ok with you?"

While the blonde wanted Perry to come with her, she did have to admit it did seem a bit odd for him to go along. They had just met and were just new friends. Brand-new friends...

"Definitely!"

Brand new friends... And it might be the only time she got to spend alone with him where Langley, Vivica, or Holly weren't being nosy. That made her think for a long moment. After all, she didn't need Langley knowing that their father wanted to meet up with her. Langley was still under the impression that Alex Kingsley, their father, was getting out of jail sometime soon. Every time the lawyers would call, she practically started packing her bags. The last thing Langley needed was to get her hopes up when she would be starting school in just a few days...

Lucy turned to Perry. "We should keep this between us. In other words, don't tell your mother or cousin..."

"I can promise you my mother doesn't need to know, but even if she did, she doesn't care," Perry assured her.

"I doubt she would care, but Lord knows that the moment she sees Vivica, the two end up going at one another. And I don't need Vivica finding out, because she'll tell Brad, who will then tell Langley. I'm trying to keep this on the down-low right now. I doubt my father is getting out of jail anytime soon, and I don't need my wealth-obsessed sister thinking otherwise."

Lucy sounded a little hostile, saying that, but she needed to be clear. Xander seemed to enjoy his new life. He was away from his own friends, but really, he could be a police officer anywhere, and it wasn't like they were in a dull area for that career path.

LANGLEY – 2018

The blonde was doing her makeup in her bedroom. She hated the Saint Agnes uniform. She was never really fond of her old school uniform, but she had mastered her color pallet around the outfit. She really should have started sooner on matching it. Langley was going to make it known that she was the head bitch in charge in Manhattan- but also in Grosse Pointe. A lack of available funds meant nothing. They might not have had access to any of it, but the Kingsley's had five homes, many cars, and two yachts.

Langley looked at herself in the mirror and thought about her old life. It hadn't really been that long since things went downhill. Langley would never admit it out loud, though, but for the first time ever, she had a group of people who she actually liked being around- Harry and Brad. Brad drove her up a wall with his values, but she still loved him... Well, she wasn't *in love* with him, but she did like him a lot and loved him as a person. In a similar way to how she loved Harry. She just wished that it had been Brad that she slept with instead of Harry. Although Harry had not been having a panic attack, it probably would have been a lot more enjoyable.

There was a knock at the door. It was Harry, of course. She wished it had been Brad. It was fine, though. "Why are you putting so much makeup on?"

"I'm just prepping myself for Monday. I'm just so glad we have classes together." Langley said. She really was. She had no idea how she would have gotten through things if she hadn't had classes with him. She did have one class with Brad and also one with Preston. Which she knew would bother Brad. But as much as Langley was Queen Bitch, it helped knowing someone.

"I don't think I can face everyone after the video," Harry admitted.

Langley turned and looked at him. "Harry, you told me two girls in your class have been pregnant, and I'm sure nudes and videos are circulating among your classmates. In New York, everyone had some sort of sex tape. The only reason yours got traction is because of your last name."

"You are a great motivational speaker..." Harry mumbled.

"Have you noticed my Aunt has been talking a lot about Madonna and Cher since she came back?"

The blonde girl shrugged. "She is of that age... I'd be more concerned about her constant talk about *Xanadu*. That's a movie you watch once, binge the soundtrack for a few weeks at the gym in shame, and never look back at it again."

Harry, as always, looked at her, confused. "What on Earth is *Xanadu?*" Something I hope you never have to endure. Though, the amount that your aunt seems to talk about it does seem a bit off. We might need to get her checked out in general. I'm beginning to think she doesn't like me." Langley crossed her arms.

The curly-haired Knight shrugged. "I don't know. Why would you say that?"

"She thinks my name is Lasagna or Lamppost..." Langley looked at him as if this wasn't obvious. As they were talking, *Dancing Queen* by *ABBA* started to play. It was clearly coming from downstairs. Even so, it was so loud they could hear it perfectly from upstairs.

"Vivica, turn down the God Damn music!" Holly screamed from downstairs.

"What music?" Vivica screamed back, equally as loud.

This was a very weird house, Langley thought... "So, when do you think Vivica and Brad will move into North Pointe?" Langley wondered.

"I hadn't really thought about that," Harry responded. "I assume, closer to the wedding. I wonder what that means for you and your siblings, though?"

The blonde smiled. "Oh, by then, I'm sure Father will be out of jail," Langley explained.

There was another knock at the door. It was Brad. "Why is my mother playing disco music?" He asked the two of them.

Apparently, Langley was going to have to be the one to spell it out for them. "Harry, didn't your father try taking you to that LGBT dance the other day? Oh, and then there were talks of going to a Pride Float... Your loving but clearly not woke parents are trying to appear supportive..."

The young Knight turned pale white. "I really wish they would just leave my sexuality alone. I like guys, but I'm not a neon rainbow.

Brad looked at Langley's face. "You're looking really hot," Brad blurted out.

Langley darted up and gave him a hug. "Oh, really?" She looked at Harry, who was still thinking about something else. Langley sighed; she wanted him to go talk about *The Golden Girls* with his aunt while she spent time alone with Brad. Very alone... His phone went off instead.

"Preston wants to see me." Harry looked up at Brad, immediately regretting saying that.

The Fitzpatrick boy sighed. "Look, I know I've been a little uneasy the last few weeks. I'm just stressed. My dad got engaged again, and I haven't seen him since last spring. My mom is well… being herself again, and I'm so nervous about football." He looked at Harry. "If Preston Costa makes you happy, then be with him. I support whomever you decide to date, but I'd rather you date basically anyone else. But for you, I'll learn to tolerate him/"

"I'm not dating him. Why does everyone think I'm dating him? I've legit only had a few conversations with him. Yeah, he is gay. Yes, I admit he is hot, but that doesn't mean a whole lot."

Langley got in the middle of the two cousins. "We are going to be Juniors a few days from now. We need to look at things with a pair of rose-colored glasses. I'm going in as the new girl who is dating the quarterback. Harry, you are internet famous and Brad, your parents are batshit nuts. But at least, Brad, that means your parents might stay away from family events… Oh, and you both get to be around me practically 24/7!"

Brad looked at his girlfriend. "What's it like to live in your world?"

"Pre-crazy Kanye is president. The original *Beverly Hills, 90210* was never canceled. It's a pretty damn great world." Langley said as she smiled.

VIVICA – 2018

Holly finally was able to find the cord that connected Vivica's speakers in the living room. She yanked off the music and looked at Vivica.

"What on Earth are you doing?"

The redhead shrugged. "I just noticed Harry walked in, and I wanted to lure him down. I have a portfolio of men for him to date." She held a giant book out for Holly to see, and Holly quickly yanked the book away from her.

The maid quickly flipped through the pages. "Half these men are located out-of-state, and the others are all in their mid-twenties. Do you honestly think Cliff or Tiffany would appreciate you setting up their son with a grown man?" She questioned.

Vivica sighed. This was the best she could do on such short notice. There weren't exactly a thousand teenage boys *out and proud* in Grosse Pointe and the surrounding area.

"Holly, my relationship with the Costas is not exactly good. The last thing we need is for them to show up right now, while I'm planning my wedding."

"You don't get along with anyone." Holly rolled her eyes.

"That isn't true. I get along with almost everyone minus Tiffany, Margot, Nial, Mrs. Templeton, Lambie, the GPPD, Australia, Clifton Knight I, Dallas Knight, and a few other people. Jackie Costa, on the other hand? She downright hates women and clings to the men in her life in an unhealthy way..." She could easily tell that Holly was giving her the side-eye. "I'm nothing like the loon! Holly, they are gangsters! Your husband is a cop. I'm sure he could tell you all about them."

Holly sat down on the couch. "Vivica, I grew up here, just like you. I've read everything you have in regard to the family. It doesn't change the fact that your nephew has fallen for the Costa guy."

While Vivica had a response ready, Lucy walked in with a bag. "I have to leave for a few days. I'll be back on Monday to make sure that Langley actually goes to school."

Vivica walked over to her and looked confused. "We have to start prepping the company. I wanted to get a perfume underway that we can launch for the wedding. As well as a makeup palette. Those are in right now. It's perfect, really, you have a pink complexion, I'm pale, and Holly is dark-skinned. We will have three different versions to top any skincare items we might want to include."

Lucy said, "I spent months trying to discuss all of this with you, and you ignored half my calls and asked me how Cliff was doing in the other half... Why on Earth would I have been spending time with your fiancé? The motherfucking CEO of Knight Auto! Hire some damn chemists, and then we can talk! Until then, I'll be out of town. Don't ask where I am. I'll tell you when I get back! Don't worry; I'll actually be back by Monday morning. Unlike when you go away for a few days, and we have to play a game of Where in the Fucking World is Vivica Weston-Fitzpatrick-Knight-Fitzpatrick-Fitzpatrick!" Lucy picked her suitcase up and stormed into the foyer, opening the front door and slamming it behind her.

The Weston woman looked at her maid as she stormed away. "Well, hopefully wherever she is going, she better get laid. That blonde needs some sex in her life..." She looked at Holly, who nodded in total agreement. Just then, Harry walked down the stairs alone. "Hello, Harry. I thought I saw you walk upstairs!"

Harry looked around the room. "Did I hear *ABBA* playing earlier?"

"Well, yes. Are you a fan?" Vivica wondered.

"Eh, I'm more into Taylor Swift and Harry Styles kind of music, if I'm being honest," he admitted to his aunt.

Vivica took note of this. She needed to find out who this *Harry Styles* and *Taylor Swift* were. "Oh, well, are you going to come shopping with Brad and myself tomorrow? We were going to go to the mall in Troy to buy some after-school clothes."

Holly snorted. "Your teenage son agreed to go shopping with you?"

The redhead turned to Holly and gave her a dirty look. "Well, we have done it every year, right before school starts. Why would we stop now?" she wondered.

"I'd love to come along, Aunt Vivica. I'm just going to go hang out with someone right now."

She knew this meant Preston... Holly was staring her down. "Well, have fun." She said as he walked out the front door. Vivica got out her phone and sent a text.

"Did you just text Cliff about what Harry was doing?" Holly asked.

Vivica sat down next to her on the couch. "No. I texted the one person in town I know would not let them have a good evening."

HARRY – 2018

The two boys sat down at a diner in town. Harry had been coming there since birth. He sat across from the Costa son and really looked into his eyes. They were beyond beautiful. He was shocked at the amount of time Preston wanted to spend with him. When Harry was back in the closet, no one ever wanted to spend time with him, other than Brad and his aunt. Then Langley came to town, and she really wouldn't let him decide if he wanted to do things or not.

While the two boys looked at their menus, the front door opened. The diner was half-filled already, and the smell of *Chanel No.5* filled the air. Harry and Preston both turned to look. It was her...

"Get me a table, and don't sit me near any colored people!" She screamed. She then whispered very loudly, "That includes the Jews and Eye-talians!"

Preston giggled. Harry found it cute. "Well, I guess that means we should be safe."

Harry couldn't help but laugh back a little. The racist woman turned and looked at them. "You boys better not be doing anything dirty over there!"

The curly-haired Knight started turning pale white. Preston turned to the old bat. "Hey, Mrs. T., shut the hell up! Everyone in here is trying to enjoy their food, not deal with your old ass!" The restaurant clapped but then went back to their meals. Preston looked at Harry and winked. "Pay her no attention."

"She definitely has some serious issues," Harry whispered.

"We need to work on your self-confidence. It's clear there is a big personality in you, just waiting to get out. I can tell you are more than just a pair of nice eyes." Preston smiled.

The young Knight blushed. "Oh, I don't know about that... I mean, I have pretty bad anxiety. I'm on several medications... Why did I just say that out loud?"

The Italian boy laughed again. "Eh, we could all probably use a few meds if we are being honest. Just look at the Vampire Lady over there."

"So, why did you want to hang out?" Harry realized that sounded stupid the moment he said it. Once again, he wished Langley had been there. She would have come, too, but Brad wanted to spend *personal* time with her, which Langley jumped at. Harry knew very well that nothing was going to happen between him and Preston. Why was he thinking about this right now?

"I mean, I just thought it would be fun. I'd honestly like to spend a lot more time with you," Preston admitted. Harry kept looking at his perfect eyes. He also couldn't help but look at his chest area. His shirt was slightly open. Preston had a little stubble, and it was turning Harry on a bit of bit. "Our first game is this Friday. Would you maybe want to come to watch with me, and then we can go out afterward?"

Go out afterward? Did Preston mean, like- *on a date,* Harry wondered? "I mean, yeah, totally. I know nothing about football, but yeah."

The mobster's son smiled. "Awesome. I'm sure Langley will already be there to keep you company while she lusts after your cousin... Maybe that was too far?"

"That's about accurate," Harry admitted. He looked at his menu for a moment, realizing he still hadn't decided what he wanted.

SUSAN – 1963

Susan sat in a booth at a diner that had just opened up in Grosse Pointe. Delia had invited her. She had also invited Mary, but it was a school day again. It was odd, sitting alone with a Knight in public. It was clear that other people recognized Delia.

"So, what do you think you will get?" Delia asked with a more chipper voice.

When Susan had met Delia the other day, it was very obvious that she had been drinking. Today, however, it was obvious that she had either drank a lot less or was sober. It was probably a good thing that they didn't go to the bar for lunch. Then again, she would not have suggested it regardless. Her father would have ended up driving her insane with a Knight there.

"Oh, probably just a tuna sandwich," Susan said.

Delia laughed. "Tuna sandwich... Oh, we need to work on your pallet. I'm taking you and Mary to the club sometime. We have all these guest passes and never use them. Benton isn't much for golf. Heathcliff was the golfer, but he has bad back." Delia had an evil smirk while saying this.

Susan nodded and continued, "I've never played golf myself. Though, I do admit that I've always wanted to try."

Delia had really nice skin, Susan thought to herself. She couldn't help but notice. *She had nice eyes too, but they weren't as nice as Mary's.* She pinched herself. She shouldn't be thinking about this woman or *any* woman like this.

"Sweetheart, women don't go to the club for golf. They go for the lounging. I mean, we could maybe play a game of tennis. Back when we lived in California, Benton made me take tennis lessons. I don't know why." Delia rolled her eyes.

"Do you miss California?" Susan wondered.

The Knight matriarch shrugged. "I suppose. I know the boys do. Honestly, Clifton was better off back there. He had such a sweet girlfriend. His current girlfriend is trash. He keeps accusing me of being racist towards her. I don't care what her skin color is. I care that she is Trailer Trash."

Susan honestly never knew what was going to come out of Delia's mouth. She clearly was a tiny bit racist, even if she didn't think she was. As she thought this, the front door of the diner opened. In walked a familiar face...

"Oh, wonderful..."

Delia slightly turned to see who had walked in. "Oh, that bitch lives on my street. Just try ignoring her."

It was easier said than done. Mrs. Templeton walked right up to them. "Hello, ladies."

"Mrs. Templeton..." Delia said in response.

"What brings you to lunch with this lesbian?" Mrs. Templeton said.

The Fitzpatrick daughter's face turned pale white. "What do you mean, she's a *lesbian*?"

The Knight wife, Delia, stopped Susan from saying anything further. "Lesbian? Oh, how cute. My Father-in-Law didn't approve of you putting a giant confederate flag on her lawn, so now, you are going around starting rumors."

Mrs. Templeton, the ice cream-obsessed spinster, gave her a dirty look. "There ain't nothing wrong with me showing support for my ancestors."

"For the last time, you now have proof that you were related to Robert E Lee!" Delia screamed at her.

"My Daddy was his cousin!" Mrs. Templeton screamed.

Delia looked at Susan. She couldn't tell what Delia was trying to accomplish with this look, though. "If your Daddy were his first cousin, that would mean either your father had you sometime in his early 100's or you are a lunatic. On top of the fact that you proclaim to be born in Michigan, not the Confederate South. Will you leave us alone?" Delia screamed. Mrs. Templeton slowly walked away. Delia turned back to Susan. "I'm sorry about that. She is the worst type of neighbor. At least I don't live on the same street as all those mobsters. Benton mentioned that there was a property that had partially burnt down over there that they were rebuilding. I don't know what family would be stupid enough to buy it..."

MARGOT – 2018

The mother, Margot, crossed her arms on the staircase of her family home. She had been trying to get her son to explain to her why he was going to New York, all of a sudden.

"Honestly, Perry, I don't care. I just feel like you want me to care. So, it's the only reason I'm asking."

"Mother, what you just said makes no sense," Perry explained.

She never knew how to talk with either of her sons. She could easily talk with men- aside from maybe Nial. Then again, Nial never listened to her.

"Well, have fun, I guess."

Perry shrugged. "I hope you enjoy having the mansion to yourself for the next day or so..." He clearly wanted to say more, so he did. He got in one last dig. "Do you really just want to live in this mansion by yourself the rest of your life?"

Margot took a second to think about this. "Yes." She said. That was the only answer she wanted to give him. Margot had very little consistency throughout her life between parents, who traveled the world while she was a little girl on an adventure. Then, as an adult, she had multiple husbands who mistreated her. Her brother married their damn cousin three times, amongst other idiot women and her two sons felt victimized by her.

So, yes, she wanted to spend the next twenty-forty years in the home she was born in alone.

"Well, too bad. I'll be back on Monday!" Perry screamed as he stormed out the front door. A familiar whore was standing at the door as he stormed out.

The Fitzpatrick matriarch quickly ran to the door and tried to slam it. "Oh, no! I finally got you out of here in January. You aren't coming back!"

"Margot, will you relax. I just want to talk business with you." Vivica explained. The supposed whore went into her purse and pulled out a silver pony. "I bring gifts."

She was reluctant, but it was a pony she had been seeking for a while now. "You have five minutes. What type of business are we talking to?"

"I want to relaunch my cosmetic company, and I just need access to a few former clients and patents. I know you haven't touched the company since I left Nial the second time. I'm willing to pay you for it." Vivica explained.

"The last thing I want to do is help you succeed," Margot reminded her for the billionth time.

Vivica sighed. "Look, I came to you so that we could maybe be a little less hostile. I want to remind you, though, that I do own three percent of the company from my three marriages. Brad owns another ten percent. Nial and I are on speaking terms. It wouldn't be that hard for me just to ask him to get me access."

"You have to promise me one thing," Margot said.

"I feel like I already know what that one thing is... I just wanted to let you know, Cliff and I will be getting married soon. Nial and I will have no chance of getting back together." Vivica explained.

Margot couldn't help but start laughing, at this notion. "You expect me to just take your word for it? Honey, you and Nial are drugs for one another. At some point or another, you will end up together again. Save the whole *Cliff is your Knight in shining armor* nonsense you tell everyone… I know better."

It was obvious that it was taking everything for Vivica not to smack her. Margot couldn't help but laugh a little.

Vivica said, "I'm marrying the love of my life. Why would I go back to your loser brother?"

That was a question everyone in town had asked her a number of times. Margot had no intention of posing it for her again. "You know what, I'll humor you. I'll give you your patents and contacts. That's it, though. On the very likely chance that you become Vivica Weston-Fitzpatrick-KnightFitzpatrick-Fitzpatrick-Knight-Fitzpatrick; you are signing a paper that says you don't get another share of the Fitzpatrick Group. You also will not work with the company ever again as an employee."

The two redhaired women shook hands.

LUCY – 2018

She had been back to New York several times since moving, and yet this was no longer home. She was a stranger to this once-amazing land of hers. She had no idea why her father's lawyer had told her to come to some random building in Brooklyn. She honestly hadn't thought about it at all, because her father was still being held in Pennsylvania somewhere. Lucy was starting to tell that something was clearly going down and she didn't like it. She turned to Perry.

"Maybe we should go back to the hotel."

Perry sighed. "We can do whatever you want. I'm not telling you to give your father anything, but I feel like you have some words to share with him. This might be your only chance." Perry explained.

"It's not like he is dying... Besides, why would he care?" Lucy wondered. That was enough to make her curious. "Let's go inside..."

She walked up the steps of the brownstone and knocked on the door. A short man came opened it a few moments later. He looked to be in his sixties. It was Bruno... Her father's obnoxious lawyer that had legit been there the day she was born. At the time, her father was paranoid that she might not have been his child. Apparently, he was convinced that her mother would have a black or Asian child...

"Why are we here, Bruno?"

Bruno looked at Perry. "Who's the redhead?"

Lucy walked past him and grabbed Perry's arm. "Not your business, Bruno. Where is A-King?"

All of a sudden, a man wearing entirely *Gucci* and *Versace,* walked downstairs, smelling of a designer cologne that cost at least a thousand dollars- but came in the smallest quantity possible. He had the Kingsley eyes and the signature blond hair, but extremely curly. The guy clearly worked out daily for hours on end. "What up, Momma?" He asked.

"A-King, why are you out of jail?" Lucy asked her estranged father. She clearly looked sickened at the sight of him.

Perry got close to her and whispered. "Do you really call your father *A-King*?"

Lucy turned to him. "Oh, my dad doesn't like being referred to as Dad by his children. He doesn't mind when women younger than me refer to him as such, though…"

A-King started to pound his chest. "What took you two so long? I have company coming over, later."

"Once again, I will pose the question. Why the fuck are you out of jail?" The daughter asked her idiot, father.

Bruno walked over. "I got him out on bail, but I did it on the down-low."

Lucy was going to ignore the fact that *downlow* was apparently only extended to his three children. "How are you affording this place?"

"Offshore accounts," A-King explained.

Lucy started to rub her forehead in frustration. "So, what you are saying here is that some moron judge let you off? So, you are now using the money that you stole?"

"Uh, no… You aren't listening. I'm using the money I've been hiding from the IRS. The money that I stole from people is still in a few Swiss bank accounts. I'm not stupid. I know now how to use that money right now. Tell 'em, Bruno, how we are going to get this case all wrapped up, though!" A-King looked at Bruno.

Bruno looked at Lucy. "All we need is for you to be a character witness."

Instead of saying anything this time, she once-again grabbed Perry's hand. "Let's go see what the prices are for tickets to see *Chicago*." They walked out the front door. "I'm really hoping that ankle bracelet can't go outside." They walked down a few blocks. "So, you can now see where Langley gets her personality."

Perry cleared his throat. "He's considered old money?"

Lucy shrugged. "He's the fourth generation... Let's not pretend he worked for a dime he ever made." She tried to move her mind away from this. She then took a moment to realize that her idiot father could have been paying for Langley's school, or for a house the three of them could live in.

But it kept hitting her. That money was all dirty.

"So, I found a few tickets to *Chicago*. They are a little more expensive, but I don't have an issue with paying." Perry explained.

The blonde girl looked at him. "We don't have time to see a musical! I have to deal with A-King!" What on Earth was Perry thinking? She didn't watch musicals. She made business deals. She was all over the place right now. It was a combination of seeing her father and being back in New York. "What has my life become?" She looked at Perry.

He smiled at her. He had a great smile. "I mean, you are pretty successful; it seems back in Grosse Pointe."

"I work with a serial bride supermodel with no business sense. She happens to be my only friend other than her lazy maid, which makes for a very unhealthy friendship. I'm back to raising my siblings, a mini female version of A-King and my brother, who lets two twins fight over him... What on Earth has my life become?" Lucy started to breathe heavily.

VIVICA – 2018

Shopping for after-school clothes at the mall had always been a tradition for Brad and Harry, along with Vivica. This would be the first year in many that Brad wasn't going off to boarding school. The boys had grown so much in such a short amount of time, and Vivica wasn't sure she was prepared for it. She looked at her two boys and smiled. "So, where should we go first?"

Brad was with Langley, which Vivica wasn't thrilled about. She wanted this just to be the three of them, but Langley had overheard their plans and insisted on coming along. Still, Vivica took solace in the fact that Harry hadn't asked for the Costa boy to go as well, though. Her plan to get Mrs. Templeton to ruin their date backfired big time.

"Oh, we should go to *Saks!*" Langley said.

How on Earth was this girl going to afford to shop at a luxury store? She Vivica even sure that she had any money. "Well, we could go there, but we should really see where Brad and Harry want to go first," Vivica told her.

"I don't really care," Brad said, looking bored. He looked at Harry.

"We can go wherever. It's fine with me." Harry whispered.

The mother and aunt sighed. "Well, alright... We can go there first." Vivica said as they walked towards the store. She remembered begging her own mother to take her shopping when she was this age. After all, she was a girl, not a boy. It seemed the only time she got new outfits was when she was modeling them in local fashion shows and later in actual New York fashion shows. She remembered her stepfather DJ always giving into her demands for new clothes. Then she remembered her mother after, screaming at her for letting DJ spend that kind of money on her...

VIVICA – 1984

"We need to hurry up, DJ! I'm expecting a call at the house this afternoon." Vivica explained to her stepfather.

DJ looked at the price tags that Vivica had put into his arms. He looked down at her and gulped. "Are you sure you really need this dress, sweetheart?" He asked his fourteen-year-old stepdaughter.

She grabbed the dress out of his hands and examined it.

"You're right. I don't. I should have gotten the blue one. Redheads should seldom wear green. Good call, DJ." She walked back over to the rack and pulled out the blue version of the same dress.

"When you asked if I would take you shopping, I thought you meant like Hudson's or something." He explained to her.

The young redhead shrugged. "Mom already took me there. You said you wanted to spend more time together. I like to go shopping."

VIVICA – 2018

Vivica smiled as she thought about her late stepfather. She wished that she had been kinder to him back when he was still alive. Vivica knew that DJ would have loved Brad. The redhaired vixen wished that both DJ and her mother Gail had lived longer, just to see their two grandsons. Vivica often wondered how things would have been different had DJ been around when Tiffany moved to town or when she was engaged to Nial. Surely, DJ would have gradually talked her out of marrying her step-cousin. Then again, Brad and Laura never would have existed, and if her bitch of a sister hadn't married Cliff, she wouldn't have Harry, Hannah, or even Hope.

"Oh, this dress is so pretty," Langley said.

Vivica looked at the price on a sign above the rack as Langley swooned over it. "Sweetheart, it's three hundred dollars..."

"I miss the days of being able to have whatever I want." Langley frowned.

Vivica wrinkled her nose. If this girl thought that her son or nephew was going to buy her an outfit, she was nuts. She was about to say something when Langley continued to speak. "One day, when A-King is released from jail, I suppose."

For a moment, Vivica felt bad for her. It was only for a moment, though. She wished that Lucy had been there to scold Lawn Chair, though. It wasn't her responsibility to do so. "Why don't we just get something to eat, and then, I'll just give you boys money while I go look at earrings for a while?" This was becoming overwhelming.

BRANDON – 1963

Last night have been pretty awesome, Brandon thought to himself as he walked down the hall at Saint Agnes. It was his lunch period, and he was planning on sitting with Nadia at lunch if she would let him.

Then a familiar boy walked up to him. "Not today. Rodrick…"

"Fitzpatrick, I just want to talk. It seems like your sister and my mother are becoming quick friends. I was thinking that you and I could be the same." He explained to the redhaired boy.

Brandon didn't buy this act for a moment. Rodrick clearly wanted something. "Look, I have absolutely no idea why my sister is spending time with your mother and our teacher, but that is her business. It doesn't mean we have to be friends."

"I was just hoping to have you and your family over for dinner next week," Rodrick said with a very evil smile.

It didn't take him long to figure out what he was doing. Rodrick clearly knew how obsessed his father was with Knight.

Brandon sighed. "If your mother wanted us all over for dinner, she could've just asked Susan."

Rodrick rolled his eyes. "My mother isn't the only one who can extend invitations to poor white trash."

He wanted to punch the Knight boy in the nose but knew that it wouldn't end well. "I suppose I can ask my parents."

Rodrick patted him on the back and then walked away. As he walked away, Nadia walked over. "Hi." He said to her.

"Last night was really fun. I'd love to come to help out again, sometime soon." Nadia explained.

"Oh, well, I mean, I don't think that would be fair to you. I mean, I really don't think my parents could afford to pay you," Brandon explained.

Nadia giggled. "I already told you, I don't need the money. I mean, I do, but it was just fun spending time with you."

The redhaired teen couldn't figure out if Nadia were flirting with him or not. He hoped that she was, though. Nadia had the best eyes he had ever seen and the most amazing long brown hair. "Yeah, definitely."

"Just think of it as the first of many adventures we will go on. Surviving the drunks of Detroit and Grosse Pointe together!" Nadia winked at him as she walked off.

CLIFF– 2018

It didn't take long for Cliff to realize that soon enough, Vivica and Brad would be returning to North Pointe. He knew that meant getting things in order, which would mean changing rooms. Cliff didn't want them in the same room that he and Tiffany had slept in together as a married couple. Cliff had ordered new *everything* once he came to the realization. The room that had once been his own would also be repainted and remodeled into a Guest Room.

Cliff was taking no chances, this time around. He finally had his Weston back. There was a knock on the door of his new bedroom. He turned around, assuming that it would Hannah or Harry, but instead, he saw someone he never thought he would see again... His father. The gray old man looked worse than when he died before the summer. Yet, he was wearing what looked to be a *Prada* suit. Apparently, the Devil really did wear *Prada*...

"Boy, what are you doing? You think some fresh paint is really all it will take to repair things with your whore?" He asked Cliff in a haunting voice.

"You're a dead old man! Leave me alone, already." Cliff said, still trying to get the image of his father out of his mind.

Rodrick laughed. "I'll never be dead in your mind. I know you all too well. I know you cannot get the truth out of your own mind. As soon as Vivica finds out DJ was your uncle and that I had him killed, she won't want to marry you. And you've known the truth for months... Yet you didn't tell her.

The Knight CEO sat down on his new bed. He knew that Rodrick was right. He just couldn't think of how to tell Vivica.

"Will you just leave me alone?" Cliff practically screamed.

That's when the door burst open again, but this time, a living person entered. It was Holly. "Oh, hi."

"Were you on the phone?" Holly looked around the room and noticed that no one else was in the room.

Cliff nodded. "Yes. The phone. I was on the phone. What exactly are you doing here?"

Holly gave him a look of concern. "I was just moving some of Vivica's Spring and Summer wardrobe over. She told me it would be best to start here. I can't imagine she is going to move any of her furniture out."

"You never know with Vivica. She is always such an open book."

The maid sat down next to Cliff on the bed. "You know, she really loves you. Even when I first started working for her and she was married to Nial, you were all she talked about."

He knew this... Nial used to call him up constantly with threats. Tiffany would scream at him for hours as well because Nial would confront her at work.

"I'm just happy that we will finally be together." Cliff wanted to smack himself sometimes for not realizing how much Vivica meant to him. He loved her so much but never really gave it a chance, before. He had always doubted himself. Cliff never believed that she loved him like he did. It should have become clearer to him that she never wanted to leave him when Tiffany came back to town. Cliff just didn't know how to handle the situation.

He looked at Holly again. "I hope you realize that you will, of course, be extended an invitation to be on staff here at North Pointe."

"Well, no shit! You think I was going to go back to working for Margot?" Holly asked him.

Another person walked in. This time, it was Vivica. "Well, we just got back from the mall. Check your credit card purchases. I think Leonard tricked Harry into buying her a few things…"

"That's fine with me," Cliff said as he stood up to kiss her.

Vivica looked around the room, inspecting the new shades on the walls. "I like it. I'd prefer red to green walls, though." She explained.

The Knight man laughed. "You can have whatever color walls you want. Where are the boys?"

"Brad went to football practice, and Harry is with Langley in his room right now. I don't trust her with the door closed. Yes, I know Harry is gay, but it doesn't change the fact that she is a little loose."

"Weston, you sound like every person who has ever described you in your life. Just give the girl a little slack. She seems to make Brad happy, and I know she is the best thing to happen to Harry in years. How many times do we have to go over this?" Cliff realized he just walked into a pit of fire with that.

Vivica huffed and puffed. "I'm not in the mood to argue about Lockjaw. I started thinking about my uncle at the mall today for some reason. It's been a while since I've thought about him." She admitted.

Cliff's eyes widened. "Oh, really? Well, maybe we should visit his and your mother's graves sometime soon?"

This was far too coincidental. Cliff needed to figure out what was in his father's will. He also needed to speak with a lawyer about a few things.

"I wouldn't mind that, actually. We could go visit your grandmother too." Vivica looked at her phone. "Holly come on. We have to go buy real estate."

Holly and Cliff looked at one another. "Um, Vivica, why on Earth would we need to buy real estate?"

"Well, Lucy and I are going to need a place for our cosmetic company. I'm trying to prove to Lucy that I'm semi-responsible." The redhead smiled.

LUCY – 2018

The eldest Kingsley child banged on the brownstone again.
This time her father answered the door. She came alone, this
time.

"We need to set a few things straight." She shoved a
piece of paper in her father's hand. "That's the price of
Langley's tuition a semester. I want a legal check sent to the
address I wrote down. I also want a grand to put into the
account I wrote down each month. The price will be going up
to ten after you are off house arrest. Your *legit business
dealings* are paying for these things. Do we understand one
another?" Lucy gave him a look that meant she was here to
talk about the family business.

"There's the daughter I raised," A-King said.

"Let's make a few things clear. I raised myself and my
siblings until I had to run away from your idiot business
practices."

A few hours earlier, Lucy had a nervous breakdown
when she checked into her hotel room. She had a separate
room from Perry, and he had no idea she was even here. Lucy
snapped, though. She had spent the last five years living in the
middle-class with a loser fiancé, working for an airhead. Sure,
she had learned to love the airhead for who she was, but it
didn't change the fact that her life was clearly a mess. Lucy
was a rich bitch, not a humble middle-class girl.

A-King looked at the paper. "This money is really only
for Langley?"

Lucy looked around. "We'll see. Also, one more thing-you stay away from Grosse Pointe. Forever. I don't want you anywhere near Langley or Xander. They both have way too many of your personality traits in them. I'll continue watching Langley. If she wants to find you when she turns eighteen, that's her business."

Lucy was going to stay in Grosse Pointe with Langley. Xander was free to leave if he wanted, since he was an adult. Lucy would inform him when she got home that he could technically return to his plan of being on the NYPD. Lucy wasn't going to have Langley waltzing back to New York, though. That was the last thing this girl needed.

"You want to raise a teenage girl?" A-King asked, confused.

"I already raised one." She was referring to herself.

Lucy knew that she was essentially signing herself up for with this. This meant she was embracing her Kingsley upbringing, but the reality was that she had no choice in the matter. It was either be a wealthy Kingsley or hope and pray that Vivica didn't completely fuck up a cosmetic company. A field in which neither of them knew anything about.

The father looked at his eldest child. "So, this means that you will say positive things about me in court?"

This was going to take going back into her early childhood, but she could probably find a few positive things to say about him. He did donate to charities. She wasn't exactly sure how many of them were legit- so, there was that. But she was far enough removed from the family at this point that she could be believable on the stand. Something that Bruno and A-King probably realized.

"Yes. I will. I've got you, Dad."

HANNAH – 2018

Hannah had no idea why, but for whatever reason, she was allowed Xander to drive her home from the hospital. Even though she only lived ten minutes from GPGH, they were still in Royal Oak. She was starting to catch on to what Xander was trying to do.

"Turn this car around already!" Hannah started screaming. She realized she sounded a bit crazy, but she honestly didn't care. The Knight daughter would not be going back to that godforsaken grocery store.

Xander glanced at Hannah from the driver's seat. "The only way you can move on is if you actually confront these people."

Had Hannah been confronting her mother or Hope, it would have been one thing. Instead, she was going to be confronting a sexist and a male Mrs. Templeton. "Please, don't make me do this."

The car stopped, and they were in the parking lot of the grocery chain. "I'm going to take a page out of Langley's playbook for a moment. You are going to walk in there and inform them that you are THE one and ONLY Hannah Knight!"

Hannah looked at Xander. "Well, then, why don't you come along with me?"

"I will come in. I just want you to go alone, first. You know exactly what you want to tell them. Don't act like you haven't held this in for a while. If I go in with you, I'm going to be the man protecting you. You need to be the woman that we both know you are." Xander smiled at her.

While it was nice to see a feminist side of Xander. She really didn't think that now was the time to start spelling woman with a Y and burning bras. Xander continued gesturing for her to get out of the car. Hannah huffed and puffed. The brunette unbuckled her seat belt. It took her a minute to realize that she wasn't an employee at the store anymore. It wasn't her responsibility to get the carts. It shouldn't have been her responsibility to get the carts when it was negative seven degrees outside or when it was pouring rain. Especially when her two idiot managers were sitting around on their phones, gossiping about other stores.

Hannah saw a few old co-workers but ignored them. She had no ill will towards them, but after a year of being out of the hellhole, she realized it wasn't their fault that they settled with the culture the two egotistical managers created. She spotted them sitting at the Customer Service Center. A space where all the employees were technically supposed to have access to, but the assistant manager camped out at. "You two!" She looked back at her former employers.

"Why, Hannah! How the heck are you? We didn't think you would ever come back to visit." The male assistant manager said.

"It's nice to see you with your figure being the same." The store manager joked. He nudged her ex-assistant manager.

"So, what the hell brings you back?"

Hannah noticed that Xander was walking in, wearing his Deputy Uniform.

She smiled. "What the hell brings me back? Oh, I don't know... I was just wondering how many women you had on staff. Are black employees or any of my old friends allowed to take breaks? No? How is your employee of the year?" For some reason, she was acting like her normal Hannah-self that let everyone else around her get the last word in. She almost felt as if she were some strange cross between Langley, her aunt, and even Hope...

The assistant manager looked confused. "I'm not sure what you're talking about. Do we have a problem?"

"No, dimwit... We had a problem when I fell in the freezer and almost cracked my skull open. We had a problem when you had me under a microscope because you weren't comfortable having a fucking Latina or woman or any combination of the two working in this store. I know we have been over this before, but do you know who my father is?" Hannah hated pulling the father card. "You both happen to drive Knight vehicles. I now work as a VP of the company. You know, with the degree that I earned just barely while the two of you refused to let me have a damn day off."

Xander walked over. Hannah realized that her confrontation was getting a little bit loud. "Is there a problem here, Ma'am?"

Hannah looked at him. "Oh, nothing really, This man..." She pointed to the assistant manager. "Was just being racist towards customers, and I thought I'd confront him. Meanwhile, his boss, not co-worker, was too busy texting his sidepiece to notice..." She stormed out.

Xander waited a few minutes before exiting himself. He looked at her and started laughing. "They wanted to press charges on you for disturbing the peace. I asked for proof. They showed me about five minutes of video footage of them being on their phones..."

"Sounds about right," Hannah admitted.

"So, do you think you feel better?" Xander wondered.

While, yes, she did feel better, she wasn't exactly cured of the insanity that job had caused her. Really, it was just one stop on a road of confrontations she probably would never get to have.

"I've decided that I'm breaking the Knight streak of not speaking up for myself."

LUCY – 2018

Perry looked at Lucy, and Lucy knew he could tell that something was off. She was starting to regret making a deal with her father.

"I might need to go see my father again…" Lucy explained.

"Well, ok. We can, if you want." Perry said, grabbing his jacket from the chair in her room. They had been watching TV together.

"I made a really stupid mistake," Lucy admitted out loud.

The redhaired Fitzpatrick boy looked at her. "What kind of a mistake?"

Lucy sighed. "When we got back to the hotel earlier, I went back to see my father. I had a momentary lapse of judgment. I thought I wanted to be rich again and told him that I would give him a positive testimony. Let's be honest. He isn't going to jail anytime soon… He will get a slap on the wrist, and that will be the end of that. Sure, he has mob connections, but so did every fifth man in my building back in the day."

She waited for Perry to storm out and never speak with her again. She, for some reason, thought about what Austin would have done, had he been here. They most definitely would be helping A-King out.

"Did you sign any papers?" Perry wondered.

She looked back at him, befuddled. "Um, no… No, I didn't."

Perry put his jacket back down. "Well, then I don't think we need to worry." He sat back down next to her in bed. "We all have those temporary lapses in judgment. I used to stand over my mother's bed with a pillow in my hands as a child." He looked at her, and Lucy couldn't tell if he was joking or not. Then he started laughing. "Ok, not really, but you get what I mean. You didn't sign anything. If you want to make more money and I *mean a lot more money*, then I can set you up at the Fitzpatrick Group."

Lucy smiled. "I appreciate the offer, but really, it was just the stress of getting my new company off the ground. I might not have made a billion dollars off of being assistant to an Event Planner. Imagine if I own a cosmetic company. It's just a matter of finding the right people to work for us." Perry nodded. Lucy continued with a bright laugh. "If in six months, I'm still living with your Ex-Aunt, though, feel free to hold a pillow over me while I sleep."

At the very end of the day, Lucy knew that Vivica's name could get the brand out there. It was just a matter of having semi-decent products. This didn't need to be a luxury brand.

It just needed to be a selling brand.

Her phone rang. It was A-King. She looked at Perry. "Should I just ignore it?"

"Well, it's up to you," he explained.

She silenced the phone and took a sigh of relief.

DELIA – 1968

The last week had been much calmer for the housewife. She had not drunken anywhere near as much as she normally did. She walked down the staircase to the foyer of North Pointe and smiled. Then, the front door opened. It was Benton... He was finally coming back from all his meetings. Delia kept the smile on her face. She had missed her husband. At least the loving husband that he used to be, and she wanted to get him back at all costs.

"Hello, darling!" She practically skipped in her heels as she walked over to him.

Benton gave her a look. He didn't seem to be drunk himself, and if he was, then he was doing a very good job at hiding it for once. "What has you in such a good mood?"

"I just didn't realize how much I missed you." Delia smiled. She really hadn't. Normally, she dreaded thinking about Benton coming back home. At least, since they had been in Grosse Pointe. Back when they lived in California, things were so much calmer.

"It was a long week, Delia. You remember Tadd Weston? Well, apparently his son Drake isn't doing so well in school. He wouldn't shut up about it. He was trying to seek advice from me. Drake's around Rodrick's age. It got to the point where I told him just to send the boy to a boarding school. Let proper discipline take over him. I suggested that school out here. Who knows if it would do any good for him? Who honestly cares? It got me thinking about Rodrick and Clifton, though."

The wife could see where he was going with this. She said softly, "I don't think that boarding school is the way to go. Clifton's only real issue is that girl he insists on spending time with. If I get accused of being racist one more time by him... And Rodrick just needs actual friends. You know, Susan Fitzpatrick has a brother around his age." Delia knew they got into a fight, but most boys their age got into scraps.

The husband looked at his wife. "You want Rodrick to spend time with a bartender's son? Why on earth are you spending time with Susan Fitzpatrick? Isn't she about fifteen years younger than you?"

"Well, I ran into her, along with Rodrick's teacher, while you were out of town. It's just some friends for me to be around while you are at work," the Latina woman explained.

Benton nodded. "Well, I guess that's harmless. Just don't bring them to the yacht club."

He said *yacht club,* not a country club, so Delia took that as an all-clear. She couldn't wait to take the girls to the country club! Delia smiled at her husband. "Really, though, I do think the boys should get along."

Rodrick himself walked downstairs. "Oh, I couldn't agree more, mother. Which is why I have taken it upon myself to invite the Fitzpatrick's over for dinner." Rodrick crossed his arms and smiled.

The husband and wife both looked at one another, confused. "Boy, why would you invite an entire family over for dinner?"

Rodrick laughed a little bit. "I know you and Grandfather want to get as much steal from Seamus or whatever his name is... So, why not speed things along a little bit?"

Benton thought about it for a second. "Well, boy, you might have done good, for once. Now get to school, or you will be attending a boarding school along with Drake Weston." Rodrick hurried along out the front door.

Delia had wished that Benton and Heathcliff were off that idea. It wasn't right to go after the Fitzpatricks like this. She knew that her opinion meant very little in terms of the company, though.

***

Later that day, Delia showed up to Saint Agnes, her husband and father-in-law's plan still weighed on her. She couldn't believe what they had in store for the Fitzpatrick family. She knew that she couldn't speak about it with Susan, though. Instead, she decided to turn to Sister Mary. She knocked on her classroom door.

"Hello, Marry," Delia said.

Sister Mary Newman smiled. "Delia, so good to see you! Come in, please. So, what brings you by?"

Delia looked around to make sure no one was around. "I need to speak with you about a concern of mine. Nuns are like priests, right? They can't tell secrets?"

"Well, no. However, we are friends, so your secret is safe with me." Mary gestured for her to take a seat in a chair that was next to her desk.

"You see, my secret is about the Fitzpatrick family... I'm sure you know all about Seamus. Susan and Brandon's father? Well, it's a well-kept secret within my circle that the man practically goes door-to-door, looking for people who will invest in his steel business. I know of people who have actually slammed the door on him before." Saying it out loud, she knew that Seamus was on the annoying side. He didn't seem to understand the class system very well. He was an Irish immigrant with a hard-to-understand accent. Seamus would go to strange people and present his plans, only to be relentless with getting people to agree. It seemed the man was under the impression that the people with money owed him something. They didn't... At least not him alone.

Mary nodded. "Yes. Mr. Fitzpatrick is an interesting man.

I've met him a few times in passing and a little bit more socially the other week. He isn't a bad person. It just doesn't seem that he has his priorities in order."

It was a sigh of relief to know that Mary seemed to understand where she was coming from. Delia continued, "I understand wanting to do good for your family, but the way he goes about it just isn't practical. My husband and father-in-law have decided to humor him, however, and I don't think it will go over very well. Especially, now that I've struck a friendship with you and Susan."

"What exactly do they plan on doing?" Mary wondered.

"My husband wants to offer him a deal at a formal dinner thrown by my son, for some odd reason... They aren't going to give him a good deal, though. He more than likely will end up losing money rather than making any in the long run. Essentially, they are trying to shut him up once and for all. I'm not sure if any of the other car companies are in on it. I just know that the man isn't exactly in a place to be giving Knight the deal that they are going to set up for him. Though, I also know that he will take it, regardless of what anyone says to him."

The nun rubbed her forehead. "I see the dilemma. Well, why not invite me over as well? Also, maybe a few other people. That way, it becomes a little less intimate. It might throw off Benton and Heathcliff a little bit to have other people there. We can't stop the deal from going through, but we can at least prolong it."

That wasn't exactly the advice she was hoping that Mary would give her. "Shouldn't we try to stop the deal altogether?"

"Have you ever been able to change your husband's mind about anything? I know that Susan and Brandon have attempted to get through to their father with no success. I'm not sure how his wife plays into things. We as women know that men don't listen unless other men give them advice."

"Thank you, Sister," Delia sighed.

HARRY – 2018

"So, Preston wants me to watch him play football on Friday, during the game," Harry whispered to Langley as they watched *Dallas* reruns on TV.

Langley turned to him. "Why are you only telling me this now?" She got up and walked over to his closet. "This was the information to share before or during our trip to the mall. We will be far too busy to shop this week. We could express-order an outfit, but no... Those things never fit the way they are supposed to." She groaned and turned to him. "Harry, this is essentially your first real date with him."

Harry was a little confused. "How is it a date if he will be on the field, while I'm watching from the stands?"

"Didn't you learn anything from when we binged on *Friday Night Lights*? Damn, that was a good show. I don't even know a flying fuck about football... Anyway, football is an intimate sport where people get together and scream. A touchdown can be a turn-on for many people, though."

"I'm not looking to have sex with him..."

"I'm not saying you will. At least not right now. I'm just saying that after he plays and the team wins, you go to a diner with him, or to some party where the only liquor is cheap beer and vodka. It's where you will sneak a kiss for the first time. Then on

Monday after not saying anything about it for two days, you confront one another and ignite a hot make-out session behind the bleachers before he goes off to football practice."

Langley looked through her purse. "Damn, I need a cigarette, and I don't even smoke!"

This sounded nice and also filthy in theory, but it also seemed like Langley watched way too many prime-time soap operas. "I don't know. I mean, I know how literally everyone in my family feels about the Costas. I can't imagine Aunt Vivica and Jackie Costa sitting down together and not trying to kill one another. The same goes for my dad and Anthony Costa."

The blonde girl nodded. "I see what you are saying, but the most important question right now is, do you want?"

He wanted Preston. There was no doubt about it. He was beyond beautiful, and he treated Harry well when they spoke. The boy listened to him and clearly was interested in what he was saying. The only other people who did that were Langley and Brad. Also, his aunt and Hannah, but they were more closely related.

Harry said, "I mean, I'm going regardless. Brad is playing, obviously."

Langley blurted out, "Your cousin is a little too obsessed with football... I'm just going to say it out loud. He has far too much money for him to be this obsessed with football as a possible career move."

Harry had been waiting for Langley to finally question this. "Yeah, Brad uses sports as a way to calm himself down when he is stressed. He always has." Everyone thought it was unhealthy. One weekend a few years ago, Brad had made playoffs in baseball for his team at boarding school. His aunt was able to convince his mom to let him go with her to watch the final game. Brad was using that bat in a rather dangerous way; it seemed. He didn't think that his aunt suffered from anxiety, and yet she seemed to be just as nervous as he was. This was during a time in which his aunt and uncle were fighting with Laura, his other cousin. Brad hadn't been taking it very well.

The Kingsley girl rolled her eyes. "That boy is going to need some serious deprogramming one of these days. I don't think it would be very practical for it to be done by me, though. Brad needs to grasp that he isn't anything like his parents. He is far calmer and far more practical." Langley let out a deep sigh. "I just want to spend more time with him. Where he isn't speaking about sports or school."

If he had to guess, Harry also assumed that Brad spoke a lot about Preston as of the last few weeks. "Well, I'm sure that things will be a little different now. I mean, this will be his first full semester back to school. My dad and aunt are getting married again, and he always seemed to like them as a couple. It will be nice for the two of us to be under the same roof again. You know, at one point, we shared this room." Harry laughed.

"Why on Earth would you share a room in a giant mansion?" Langley sat back down on the bed.

He shrugged. "We were younger. Brad liked protecting me at night when I would have nightmares. He really is my brother, more than he's my cousin."

Harry knew that Brad would say that all the time, but he just thought that he was nice. The two had been close, and he wanted them to be close again. Harry just wasn't sure how it would be possible if he dated Preston.

"So, do I address the fact that my sister has been in New York the past two days when she gets home? Or should I use it as leverage later on?" Langley asked, changing the subject. She looked down at her phone.

"How do you know she is in New York?" Harry wondered.

The blonde pouted. "When I first moved to town, Xander and Lucy put a tracking device on my phone. So, I put ones on their phones, just to get back at them. Neither of them go anywhere interesting, mind you. Until now."

"Well, maybe she is just doing something for the company. I mean, be honest with yourself. Had you known she was going, you would have wanted to go as well." Harry pointed out.

"Just because you are right doesn't mean that I shouldn't have gotten to go along. I miss the city so much." She stopped for a minute and covered his mouth. "Don't mention how Detroit is becoming vibrant. It doesn't compare to Manhattan in the slightest. There is something about getting an overpriced piece of pizza in a dump that has been there twenty years. That great feeling... It'll never compare to getting one in Detroit in a brand-new show ran by white hipsters."

VIVICA – 2018

The last time Vivica had been to this house was after finding out that Lucy had called it home for a while herself. She knew that the Martin family had bought it right after her mother Gail had passed. It was just that Vivica hadn't been in the right state of mind at the time. She had regretted selling the DJ's childhood home and the home that she herself had lived in for much of her own childhood. It was just a matter of it not being practical at the time. Vivica owned her current house with Luke Knight and had just started to date Cliff again, who was moving into North Pointe. What would have been the point in keeping the home empty?

It seemed she had the perfect opportunity, here. She knew that Lucy wanted to move out. But Vivica also knew that right now, it was not practical for her to buy a house. Vivica wanted Lucy close-enough by, though, because their new offices would be just around the corner from this address. She knew that Lucy had already lived here once, so why shouldn't she want to live here again? Obviously, if she wanted to stay at her mansion, she was welcome. It just didn't seem practical though to have all of them move into North Pointe, though– even if Cliff probably would have said yes.

The same real estate agent happened to be in charge of this listing, so Vivica forced Holly to drive with her to the house. She already knew that regardless; it was her duty to buy this home back. Vivica had no idea why DJ had been on her mind lately, but he was, and she felt some form of guilt.

The redhead wasn't particularly sure why. She had made her peace years ago with Gail and Nadia, in terms of her resentment towards DJ.

DJ had been the father figure that her own father, Drake, refused to be towards her. Vivica wasn't exactly sure why her father had always been so distant. She had ruled out him not being her father years ago. He had a great relationship with Tiffany. Her mother had a great relationship with Tiffany, even if Tiffany never was around when she was growing up. Drake would come to see her every few months for a few days and then turned into every nine months to once a year as time went on. Even so, Tiffany never came to see Gail. The two sisters would write to one another every so often, and on occasion, they would talk on the phone, but they grew up as strangers. DJ made sure that she was part of the Brash-Bloom family, which had at that point extended to the Fitzpatrick's as well. Brandon and Nadia were welcoming towards her but never really her mother until after DJ's death.

Vivica remembered family nights and how she tried so hard to get herself out of them. She would beg to be invited to spend time with her friend Brianna Bell or if she was really lucky, Cliff. DJ always made sure that the Fitzpatrick-Knight feud never got in the way of her friendship with Cliff. They had only just started dating when DJ was tragically killed in an accident at the construction site of a Knight dealership.

DJ had been so proud to be heading the dealership for a division of The Fitzpatrick Group. He was so proud, in fact, that he had been working much longer hours than he really should have. The police reports put *stress and lack of sleep* as the cause of his accident. Luckily, he had been the only one injured.

The two friends opened the front door. It was empty for the first time in her life. The carpets had been removed and solid wood floors glistened in its place. Vivica assumed that they had always been there were just covered by some very ugly carpet. The once-red walls had been painted a dull white color, and there were no curtains or blinds up as of yet.

"Well, it needs some work, but I think it will be nice for Lucy and her siblings."

"Do you really think that buying Lucy a house is going to convince her you have any business sense?" Holly asked, looking around the living room.

Vivica closed the door behind her. "I'm not buying the house for her. I'm buying the house for myself. I'm planning on letting Lucy rent the house, though." She probably wouldn't charge Lucy much a month, other than utilities. She had enough that could just outright purchase the home. It wasn't exactly going for much, considering the location and the fact that Austin had killed himself here.

"Will she really want to live in the home that Austin shot himself in?" Holly pointed out.

"Again, we will work on it a little bit before they move in. Plus, it's not as if we all haven't lived in houses where people have died. Benton Knight was shot on the foyer of North Pointe; several people have been shot at the Fitzpatrick estate. On top of the fact that mobsters owned the original property. Oh, and that crazy woman who wanted to be me killed herself at my house." Vivica said all this, practically unaffected.

Holly looked at her friend. "I'm not really sure how to respond to you."

The Weston daughter didn't, either. She just wanted her family home back. She walked upstairs and to the room at the end of the hall on the left. Her childhood bedroom. "This is where the magic happened."

The maid cringed. "I don't need to know where you lost your virginity."

"That was in Hannah's room at North Pointe…" Vivica mumbled. That night itself brought back terrible memories. Rodrick and Margot were walking in on them. Then DJ died… She walked over the window. Vivica remembered Cliff showing up practically every morning to take her to school… Everything had been much easier before Tiffany came in and ruined it. They were happy. She reminded herself, though. Harry, Hannah, and Hope. As well as Brad and Laura. None of them would probably exist, had things not turned out the way they did…

DELIA – 1963

The dining room at North Pointe had been decorated for the evening. One of the staff would be in charge of keeping classical music playing throughout the night on their record player. Lana, the maid, had been instructed to cook an extravagant dinner. She was also given instructions to make homemade ice cream for dessert.

Delia's plan was underway. She didn't really know if things would work out for the better or not, though. Benton wasn't keen on having other people come to dinner, but he reluctantly agreed after she insisted.

The doorbell rang. It took everything for Delia not to answer it. It was the job of the staff to open the door, though.

Rodrick walked into the dining room. "What are you up to, Mother?" he spat out.

"I have no idea what you are talking about, Rodrick..." Delia proclaimed. She continued to make sure the dining room was set up properly.

"You better not be ruining any of our plans." Rodrick threatened.

The mother looked up at her son. "I suggest not speaking with me like that again." She turned around, where the Fitzpatricks stood. "Welcome to our home! Dinner will be served soon. Until then though, why don't we go to the drawing-room for drinks? Dessert and after-dinner cocktails will be in the library." Delia wanted to give these people the evening of their life. She winked at Susan, who blushed for some reason.

They all went into the drawing-room, where Clifton was on the phone. Delia quickly walked over and ripped it out of his hands. She hung it up. "You can talk to the trailer trash later." Delia scolded him. Clifton rolled his eyes at her.

"This home is so beautiful," Ida admitted aloud.

"One day, we are going to have one just as grand," Seamus said. Delia could tell that the entire family, including his wife, looked a bit annoyed by this proclamation.

The doorbell rang again. It took a few moments, but a few more friends of the family had shown up. Brandon Fitzpatrick noticeably looked confused. Rodrick looked pissed off. Delia paid him no attention. The bell rang again, and this time it was Mrs. Templeton. Quickly, Delia walked over. "Lady, I didn't invite you here!" Delia lied.

"Well, I'm not leaving." Mrs. Templeton sat down on the couch next to Clifton. "You're the one into chocolate? There is something wrong with you, kid." She held her purse as if someone in the room was going to steal it.

Finally, the doorbell rang one last time. This time it was Mary. "Hello, Delia! Thank you so much for inviting me this evening."

Rodrick stomped over to his mother. He looked at her. "What the hell are you up to?"

"Either behave yourself, Rodrick, or you are going to your room. Do you really want to embarrass yourself in front of your friend Brandon?" She asked him.

"Brandon Fitzpatrick is not my friend." He stomped his foot on the ground.

Delia patted her son on the head. "Oh, honey, I know."

The door to the drawing-room opened again. It was Benton. He was holding a glass of something. Probably whiskey. "Hello, everyone!" He looked around the room. He got close to Delia. "I thought you said just a few more guests, dear..." He whispered.

The Knight matriarch shrugged. "I couldn't help myself. It's been so long since I've gotten to entertain.:"

She knew her husband was drunk enough that he didn't suspect anything. She only had to worry about her son and Heathcliff. Heathcliff didn't drink. He, however, could be easily distracted, which is why she made Lana wear something a little bit nicer to work that evening. It would be the perfect distraction.

At the moment, Lana walked over, wearing a highly-starched maid dress, which barely grazed over her kneecap. Heathcliff was trying not to oogle, and snuck a few glances behind the other guests, checking her out in silence.

Susan walked over. "So, how are you doing this evening?" Delia asked her new friend.

"Oh, pretty good. It was so nice of you to invite all of us over for dinner. I mean, getting to dine here twice in one week is crazy." Susan admitted.

Delia felt bad. Susan was such a good friend, and at the end of the day, this dinner was just going to prolong her husband's business deal. It wouldn't stop him from going after the Fitzpatricks forever.

"Oh, yes. It's a fantastic business model. I've been working on it for years." Seamus was telling a few people about his plan for his steel company. The Latina woman could easily tell that his wife and son were getting ready to yell at him later on.

Then Benton walked over... Seamus turned around. "Mr. Knight! It's an honor to be invited into your home. I have a business proposition to discuss with you."

Benton patted him on the back. "Oh, yes. I know you do. Don't worry. We will have plenty of time to discuss it. I might actually have an offer for you." He said as he walked away with a smirk on his face.

Seamus gasped into the open air, with his rosy-colored cheeks and his entire face brightening. In that very moment, he looked speechless with anticipation.

BRANDON – 1963

Brandon didn't trust the Knights. He knew that his sister had weirdly become close with Rodrick's mother. Still, this didn't change his opinion. It was obvious by the way that things were set up that Delia wasn't in charge of this evening. It was all on Benton and oddly enough, Rodrick. Yet, at the same time, it seemed as if they were both thrown off. Brandon knew that he needed to keep his father from completely embarrassing them, though. He was going up to every person in the room, giving the same pitch to them. It wasn't going to work. It never worked, and yet it wasn't stopping his father.

Brandon sighed and walked up to his father. "Dad, why don't you just sit down for a minute and enjoy yourself?" He crossed his arms.

"Son, this is an opportunity of a lifetime. We can't just turn it down." Seamus looked offended that his son was saying this to him. "Really, though, Brandon. You need to let the adults do the talking."

The redhaired boy wanted to be nice. He really did. It just was extremely difficult when his father was making a fool out of himself in front of several wealthy people. "Dad, you need to chill the hell out." He said loudly enough that his teacher Sister Mary Newman heard.

Seamus looked at his son. No one else had heard, it seemed Brandon noticed. At least no one else really seemed to give a damn. "We will talk about this later. You need to think about our future instead of being so selfish." He stormed off to go talk with another man in the room.

"You just have to let him do what he thinks is right," Mary explained to him.

Brandon sighed, taking a deep breath. "Yes, I know, obey my parents and be respectful. Sister Mary Newman, it isn't that easy. We could have a thriving family business. A bar isn't good enough for him, though. Seamus needs us to be as wealthy as these jackasses!" He realized that he had just sworn in front of a nun. He looked up at her.

She rubbed her forehead. "Why don't you just say a hundred hail Mary's and ten Our Father's later... Just take a deep breath, child. It will be fine." Mary walked away.

Brandon knew something was up that night. He wasn't going to let his family be made fools of. He spotted Rodrick leaving the room and quickly followed him...

LUCY – 2018

Lucy and Perry took a late flight that Sunday. She had to block her father's number. He and Bruno wouldn't stop calling her. Perry was about five minutes from Vivica's house. She still felt guilty after her temporary lapse in judgment.

"I know he is going to try getting a hold of Langley," Lucy murmured.

Perry looked at her for a brief second as he drove. "Well, maybe you should try thinking about something else for a moment. Do you maybe want to stay at the Fitzpatrick estate tonight? In your own room, of course. Just to have a little bit longer to think about things."

What was there to think about? She just gave up millions of dollars to be the middle class in a wealthy town. "No, I need to be there in the morning. Brad or Harry will probably be driving Langley to school, but I'm still following her. She went to class for only a week last semester once she moved here. I don't need a truancy officer coming after us."

"In all fairness, I should probably admit that I ditched classes a lot back when I went to Saint Agnes." Perry laughed.

"I ditched all the time back when I was in high school as well. It's not like Langley doesn't do well in school. It's just a matter of taming the girl. You can't trust her." Lucy giggled.

She loved her sister; she really did. That's why she made this decision. It had only been less than two days, but Lucy honestly did miss Grosse Pointe. She was ready to get back to her life. Vivica and Lucy would finally be able to sit down and get business taken care of. Things would be good, she thought.

Then Perry pulled down Vivica's street... "What on Earth?" "I'm keeping this flag up!" Mrs. Templeton screamed.

"Bitch, you aren't putting up that racist flag!" Holly screamed back.

Vivica was filming while Cliff watched from the porch of North Pointe. Langley, of course, also filmed everything from her own phone with Brad and Harry just looking at one another.

Lucy got out of the car along with Perry. "Um, Vivica, what exactly is going on?"

Vivica turned to the blonde. "Oh, good, you are home! I have so much to talk about with you! We just have to wait and see how this turns out. Holly might sucker punch Mrs. Templeton." She said this with a smile on her face.

Lucy told herself she had no regrets. She kept saying it over and over again in her head. Things would be fine. She had no regrets!

Perry walked up to Mrs. Templeton. "Why don't we go inside and discuss things over some ice cream? You like ice cream." Mrs. Templeton looked at the red-haired man and nodded. Perry winked at Lucy, and Lucy smiled back at him. He walked inside with Mrs. Templeton.

"I'm burning that flag tonight while she is asleep," Holly explained.

"Oh, just give it a few days, and we will get some local children to steal it from her. It happens all the time." Vivica said.

The eldest Kingsley looked around... "I see that things went on without me?"

The redhaired vixen laughed. "You weren't exactly gone long. I have great news, though! We have an office building to work out of. We also have all the patents for my previous companies' cosmetics."

This sounded promising. Lucy emphasized in her mind that it sounded promising. So far, this business venture was causing her more stress than anything else. She remembered though that this was the life that she had chosen, and she needed to move on.

BRANDON – 1963

Brandon marched himself down the hall of North Pointe, where he followed Rodrick. He went into a room where Brandon could hear voices. One voice was Rodrick obviously, but the other sounded like an older man.

"I think that things will work out just fine, Grandfather."

"They better. This would be an excellent deal if it actually works out. At least on our end."

Brandon was confused. Why were Rodrick and his grandfather trying to set up a deal? He assumed it was meant for his family. Why else would they have been invited over to the wealthiest family in town's house for dinner?

Brandon was still confused as to why his teacher was there, though. Mrs. Templeton was their neighbor, and the other people were clearly friends of some sort. Brandon knew something was up. He heard footsteps and quickly ran in the opposite direction. He accidentally found himself into the kitchen.

"Oh, hi, Mrs. Bloom."

Lana looked at Brandon and smiled. "Oh, Brandon. It's nice to see you. Nadia was talking about your little date the other night."

"Date? I mean, we were just hanging out..." Did Nadia consider it a date? He started to blush at the thought. Brandon quickly got back on the topic of what was going on this evening. "How can you work for these people?" Brandon blurted out.

"Heathcliff has always been good to me," Lana said as she stirred a pot.

Brandon walked over to the counter. "Yes, but I mean, come on... The rest of them? You really like dealing with the rest of them?"

The maid shrugged. "Brandon dear, when you are older, you will understand that you do what you have to in order to put bread on the table. I have Nadia and my mother-in-law to think about."

He felt bad having asked when she put it into that kind of a perspective. He heard footsteps again.

Rodrick walked in. In a moment, he was sneering at them. "Well, this looks about right. You in the kitchen with the help."

"Hey, Mrs. Bloom is a good woman. Don't call her the help." Brandon screamed at him.

Rodrick rolled his eyes. "Yeah, whatever... Why are you in my kitchen, Fitzpatrick?" He crossed his arms.

Lana looked at Rodrick. "I asked if he could help me for a moment."

"Are you not capable of doing your job?" Rodrick looked her right in the eye. "If you aren't, I'll have no issue with telling Grandfather about this."

Brandon groaned. "Why don't we go back to your living room, Rodrick?"

"Commoner... It's the drawing-room." He started to walk towards the kitchen entrance. "Well, come on..."

The Fitzpatrick son followed him, reluctantly. Rodrick and his family were up to something. The worst part is that Brandon knew that there was nothing he could do about it. They walked back into the poorly named drawing room where everyone was mingling

Brandon walked over to Susan. "These people are up to something."

Susan looked at him. "What do you mean?"

"They are trying to set Dad up for failure, I think. Susan, we need to get out of here before Dad does something asinine."

SUSAN – 1963

"They are trying to set Dad up for failure, I think. Susan, we need to get out of here before Dad does something asinine."

The strawberry-blonde Fitzpatrick looked at her brother.

She wasn't sure who to believe. She knew one thing, though.

Delia would know the truth.

"I'll be right back," she told Brandon. With that, Susan walked over to Delia, who had been eyeing a bottle of wine for a few moments. "Can we please speak?" She asked. She grabbed Delia's hand, and they walked into the foyer.

"What did you need to speak about, dear?" Delia wondered.

"Delia, what is your husband up to?" She asked.

Delia turned around. "Who told you?"

Susan's body turned cold. She knew something. "Delia, why would you let your husband do this to my family?"

The Latina woman turned back around. "You don't seem to understand. I have no control over any of this. The reason that Mary and many other people are here tonight is so that Benton gets nervous. I don't want him to go after your family. We obviously haven't been friends long, but you and Mary have been the only friends I've had since moving to this town."

Susan took a deep breath. She considered Delia's words. She was loving having Delia and Mary in her life as well.

"Is there anything we can do to stop him?" She asked.

"The only thing would be convincing your father otherwise. This deal sounds amazing on the surface, Susan. But as time went on, he'd essentially be giving away steel to KMC." Delia explained.

It only took a moment to realize that Seamus would make the deal instantly. He wanted to be part of the world of the Knight family, as well as others like them. He wanted it so desperately.

"I believe you. You should have been honest from the start, though."

"Aren't you going to go and tell your father what is going on?" Delia asked, confused.

"No. He won't listen to me. Brandon already tried warning him tonight. We all have tried to get him to stop being so obsessed with your family for years. There is no convincing him." Susan explained. She thought for a moment. "Are they planning on having him sign tonight?"

"I'm not entirely sure," Delia admitted.

There might still be a way out of this, Susan thought. "Do you know anything about the business?" She asked.

Delia nodded. "I worked for Knight before I married Benton. I was just a secretary, but enough documents passed my way. Plus, I always read through Benton's work papers at night when I couldn't sleep."

Susan thought again. Could there be a way to get everyone what they wanted? At the end of the day, she wanted her father to get a good deal. She knew he wouldn't, but she wondered if there was a way that he could at least break even.

"Is there any way you could get access to the documents before my father was to sign them?"

"I have a key to Benton's office. Ripping the papers up won't do anything, Susan." Delia pointed out.

"We aren't going to rip them up. We are just going to change a few numbers. Only slightly, mind you. I've done the book work for the bar and dealt with my father's dream of a business for years. So, long as our bills are paid normally, people don't look around to see what is going on. We just need to fix the wording enough, and a few numbers, so that my father can make a profit. It might not be a quick profit- but a profit nonetheless. Also, how quick do you think we can spread a rumor?" Susan asked.

The Knight matriarch thought for a moment. "Well, a good rumor only takes a few days to circulate properly. What does that have to do with anything?"

Susan wasn't entirely sure if she was being greedy with this, but she was thinking pretty quickly, here. "I'm going to need you to spread a rumor that KMC will be working with Fitzpatrick Steel. Add in that Benton and Heathcliff couldn't wait to work with my father and his company."

It took Delia a second, but she clearly got where Susan was going. "If all the wives in town tell their husbands that my husband is working with your father, they will think that they are giving him the Knight seal of approval." Delia smiled. "I like it!"

"Now, let's allow the evening to play out." Susan smiled.

"I have to be honest. I'm a little excited now." Delia said.

"Oh, me too."

LANGLEY – 2018

The mistress of Manhattan was about to show the whole Saint Agnes school that she was the Princess of Grosse Pointe, Michigan. She would ignore the entirety of her last semester. Langley signed and looked at Harry. He was still all freaked out that today would be a disaster. He had driven her to school that day. After all, Brad had a morning workout with the football team. Langley knew that Lucy was somewhere in the parking lot, watching to make sure she actually went into the building and stayed until the final bell.

"Are you ready?" Langley asked her best friend.

"Not even slightly," Harry admitted.

She grabbed his hand. "Oh, come on."

Finally, she opened the doors to Saint Agnes- the school that apparently all the Knight's and Fitzpatrick's had attended for decades at one point or another. Here they were. Langley looked at her new surroundings. It was ok, she supposed. It was a school, after all. In comparison to the day school she went to in Manhattan; it looked pretty similar. The uniforms were just as dreadful. Langley knew how to put a spin on it, though, and that would be sure to help cement herself.

She looked down at her schedule. "Which hall are our lockers supposed to be down?" The blonde asked.

Harry shrugged. "Everyone is looking at us," he pointed out.

"Well, considering the amount of time I spent on my hair and makeup this morning, Harry, I would sure as hell hope so." Langley wondered if she was going to go to hell for saying hell. She wasn't Catholic, so who even knew...

Harry looked at her. "Langley, I don't know if I'll be able to do this."

Langley grabbed her friend and took him into a less crowded hall. "You need to calm down. Harry, your sex video can't possibly still be on these idiot's minds. If anyone gives you shit, I've got sixty thousand social media followers." She grabbed his hand, and they went back into the main hall.

Meanwhile, tthe blonde scoped out her classmates. Some clearly had money, based on the accessories and shoes they were wearing. Some clearly were on the poorer side. Langley purposefully brought one of her more expensive bags to school. She tied her hair back with an expensive silk scarf and wore a pair of stilettos that cost about as much as a new car. Albeit, they were from last season. Hopefully, no one noticed.

Langley spotted Brad talking with a few people by the lockers. She knew that her locker was near his. She waved, and he looked up. His eyes widened.

"Hey, Brad! Who are your friends?" She kissed him.

He quickly moved away from her. "Uh, Langley... Can I see you for a second?" He took her hand and walked over to another corner.

"What's wrong?" She asked him.

Brad looked about both sides of them. "You aren't wearing a blouse under your blazer..." He pointed out.

Langley smiled. "Oh, I know! It's part of the style I'm going for. "

The Fitzpatrick boy rubbed his forehead. "Langley, you can't go around school without wearing a top."

"I am wearing a top. I'm just not wearing a blouse." She reminded him.

"You are going to get in trouble," Brad told her.

She was hoping. It would help cement her place. She honestly thought that Brad was overreacting. She still had a shirt on, and there were no specifics in the dress code.

"Just relax," Langley told her boyfriend.

Brad gave her a dirty look. "Fine, just don't say I didn't warn you." He said as he stormed off.

This was getting ridiculous. She wasn't some pure angel. Yet, Brad, for some reason, expected her to be. It wasn't Langley's fault that Vivica had a colorful past. If Brad wanted a saintly nutcase, she was sure that at least one of these girls would be perfect for him. It wouldn't be her.

Langley looked around, and she couldn't find Brad or Harry. "Oh, for fuck's sake…"

HARRY – 2018

He could do this. Harry knew that it would be all right. Langley tended to know what she was talking about even if it sometimes didn't seem like it made any sense. The boy found his locker and put his backpack away. He was still looking at his first class. Langley and Preston were also going to be in it. That would be just fine. But he still had no clue where the heck Langley was at the moment. Which wasn't looking goof, he thought, but still.

The curly-haired Knight was going to have an anxiety attack. He knew it. This wasn't going to go over well. Harry knew it wouldn't.

"Take a deep breath," he told himself. Why did he just say that out loud? Why was he acting like a weirdo in front of all the people he went to school with? God could see him. God could always see him. Was Harry being judged constantly? He was sure that was the case. He had bought new shoes and wasn't sure if they were in the dress code. Brad and Aunt Vivica told him they were, but still, he wasn't sure. He kept waiting to get called down to the office. He looked at his watch. Was he even going to have enough time to get to his classroom? Harry started freaking out even more. Was this the right wing? Where the heck was his English classroom?

"Langley?" He called out. Harry needed his friend.

Someone patted him on the back. Harry was sure that it would a teacher or someone to take him to the office for being out of dress code. He felt his face. He was sure that he had shaved. He did, but there could still maybe be a little stubble. Oh, fuck, he thought, his hair. Harry hadn't had a haircut in over three weeks. It might have been too long. He felt it, but it was just above his ears.

The boy turned around, and his heart skipped another beat. "Preston!" He gasped.

Preston took his hand and yanked him into the nearest bathroom. "Man, what's wrong?" He asked Harry.

Was it that obvious that he was freaking out? Harry looked around. The lights were so bright but yet not bright enough. Where was Harry's phone? He didn't remember if he had turned it off or not. This wasn't going to turn out well...

"I... I don't think I... Can... Can do this." Harry started to shake, violently.

The Italian boy put his hands-on Harry's shoulders. He leant close to Harry and hugged him tightly. It only lasted a second, but Harry went from having the *Energizer Bunny* pounding a drum in his stomach to having a billion butterflies trying to get out of him.

"That seemed to calm you down at least for a second. Just take a few deep breaths." Preston smiled.

How on Earth was that supposed to calm him down? Now he was going to spend the rest of the day wondering if Preston hugged him because he liked him or because it calmed him down. Why was it that whenever Harry had an anxiety attack, people started doing romantic and sexual things to him? Why did it always seem to work? Was he a slut? Considering the title of his sex tape, he probably was.

"I'm sorry," Harry said.

"Why on Earth are you sorry?" Preston asked him.

"I totally freaked out right in front of you. I didn't mean to. I completely lost track of Langley after she had another fight with Brad," he admitted.

Preston laughed. "I'm assuming due to the fact that she isn't wearing a top under her blazer?"

Harry nodded. "So, you've seen her?"

The Mobster's son nodded. "Yes. I've seen Langley and your uptight cousin." He crossed his arms. "Oh, boy, what am I going to do with you? Don't worry; we'll get through the day together."

"Together? What do you have to worry about?" Harry wondered.

"I'm Anthony Costa's son, Harry. There are enough people at this school who want nothing to do with me," he pointed out.

Harry guessed that made sense. It didn't feel right, though. Preston was the, nicest, most helpful guy ever. He was so amazing and so perfect. All one had to do was look into his beautiful eyes.

"Ok, we can do this together, then." Preston took Harry's hand, and he navigated them to class. It was only when they finally got to the classroom that he realized they were holding hands the entire way. Langley was sitting in the back row and looked annoyed.

"Sorry," Harry said. He noticed she was wearing a sweater under her blazer.

"Some bitchy guidance counselor loaned it to me... I get to talk with her about my apparent low-self-esteem for the next month." Langley rolled her eyes and let out a long laugh. "Where did you even go?" Langley asked.

"I was at my locker. It's right next to yours." Harry pointed out. He looked down. "You know you can't bring your backpack to class, right?"

The blonde buried her head on her desk. "I haven't even been here for an hour! Can we wait a little longer before I'm prosecuted for another rule I've apparently broken?"

The Knight boy shrugged. "Sorry." He turned to his right, and Preston was sitting next to him. He had been looking at him. "Oh, you don't have to sit next to me. I'm sure you'd rather be sitting with your teammates over there."

"Eh, I see them all the time. I'd rather sit next to you if we have classes together. I mean, as it's ok with you." Preston asked.

Harry nodded. It was perfectly all right with him.

Then, the class started, and the teacher walked in. To Harry's surprise, it was Sister Mary Newman.

"Hello, class. Your regular teacher went into labor. So, I've been asked to come out of retirement for the semester. I recognize a lot of you from Mass and the library. This will be a mix of fun and learning." Mary looked at Langley. "Miss Kingsley, we don't chew gum in class." The Kingsley girl stood up and spat it out. She sat back down and gave Harry a dirty look. "Now then. Why don't we start looking over the syllabus?"

VIVICA – 2018

Vivica, Holly, and Lucy finally got the lock on their new office space to open. Holly was about to call a locksmith when Vivica finally realized that she had been putting it in wrong. This was after about fifteen minutes of insisting that she was doing it the right way. They all looked around at the expansive, lonely place in front of them.

Vivica sighed. "Well, it needs furniture, but I think that it will work out."

"I guess an office space is a nice start," Lucy said with her arms crossed. "A business plan would have been better..." She said under her breath.

Vivica knew that this place was still a work in progress, but she needed this to succeed. She stupid. She knew that Lucy was just starting to slip away, and Vivica didn't want to lose one of her only friends. Sure, they could be friends working together, but if they didn't, Vivica was sure that they would never see one another again. "

Well, hire a few chemists and marketing people. You and me, Lucy- we can do this!" Vivica explained.

Holly gave her a dirty look. "I guess I don't count?"

"You're my maid and driver..." Vivica reminded her. She knew that was stepping into dangerous territory, but it was the truth...

Lucy looked over to the window. "You can see Austin's house from here. Isn't that a little morbid? After all, he did kill himself."

Holly gave her employer a dirty look. "I think it adds character." She rolled her eyes at Vivica.

Vivica walked over to Lucy. "Don't pay any attention to her. We can get drapes or blinds. I realize this isn't as big as our offices at The Fitzpatrick Group, but still. I think that it's nice." She got a text, looked down, and smiled. "Perfect! I've got good news. My friend Bridget Madwell has agreed to let us do a photo shoot for publicity. It won't be until we get closer to the actual date of our launch, of course."

"We need to have an actual product to sell." Lucy once again reminded her, now sounding frustrated. "I'm happy that you found us some office space. I'm just concerned about the lack of product that we have to sell."

Holly supposed it was different for Lucy than Vivica. After all, Vivica didn't have to work. Vivica wanted to, and she wanted to keep Lucy close by. This business venture was the best way.

Vivica murmured, "Well, what about *Weston Wash*? My makeup wipes that got your makeup off almost immediately. I've yet to see anything that could compete with it. I have the patent for the product."

Lucy thought for a second. "It'll sell, but a beauty wipe is far from enough. Who was the chemist on your team back then?"

Holly looked at Vivica. "I don't think it'll work out."
"Why?" Lucy asked.

"Luke Knight was my chemist..." Vivica frowned.

BRANDON – 1963

Brandon's father accepted the offer and would be signing at the end of the next day. Brandon couldn't believe that Seamus was so obsessed with wealth that he would put his family into debt. Brandon knew that when he had a family someday, that he would always put them first. He would never be anything like his father.

Brandon sighed, sitting down at a table in a local park. Nadia happened to walk over. He looked over at her as she sat down.

"I'm beginning to think you are following me around town," he stated.

"I have one of those futuristic tracking devices on you. You caught me!" Nadia laughed.

"Is your mother, all right?" Brandon asked. He knew that Rodrick was being threatening towards her last night.

Nadia looked confused. "My mother? I guess she's fine. Why?"

Brandon felt guilty. "Last night, Rodrick invited my family over for dinner. I was talking to your mom when Rodrick walked in. He was being a complete asshole to her."

The Latina teen shrugged. "That doesn't really shock me, to be honest. He's always been like that." She smiled. "Oh, Brandon, don't worry. Heathcliff makes all the final choices in that household."

"I just don't like that family at all," Brandon admitted. "Plus, my father is going to sign a deal today that will completely destroy us."

"What do you mean?" Nadia asked, concerned.

He sighed. "My father was given a deal last night that would allow him to work with Knight. It sounds great on the surface, but even as it was being described to him directly, it was clearly a scam. My mother finally had enough last night. She screamed at him all the way home and halfway through the night. He still wouldn't listen."

Brandon never thought he'd see the day where his mother would give her true opinion of his schemes. It was nice to know that she wasn't completely oblivious to the fact that his father was going to run them bankrupt with this. Still, it didn't change anything. Seamus was still going to sign the deal.

Nadia put her hand on Brandon's arm. "I'm sure things will work out for the best." They smiled at one another. Brandon looked into her beautiful eyes. "Brandon, where do you see yourself in the future?"

"What do you mean exactly?" Brandon asked, confused.

"Well, do you ever see yourself having a family of your own one day? Any idea what kind of career you would want?" She asked him.

Brandon shrugged. "Well, I do want a family and a career. I mean, I like Grosse Pointe. It would be nice to move there as opposed to Detroit. What about yourself?"

The brunette girl looked into the sky. "I want to have a million adventures the moment I turn eighteen." She smiled at him. "Then, I'll have children if the right man can ever tame me."

For some reason, Brandon wanted to be that man. He smiled, but then quickly remembered that his father was going to be further sinking them into the poor house within the next few hours. A while back, Brandon honestly thought that things would improve. They weren't, though. It was worse than before.

"I suppose that sounds nice," Brandon muttered, distracted.

She giggled. "You need to get out of your head, Red. The world is a giant place, and you don't have to worry and protect everyone around you." She smiled.

Brandon shrugged. Someone had to do it. Why shouldn't it be him?

HANNAH – 2018

After several days of rest, Hannah finally returned to work. It honestly didn't shock her one bit that her mother and sister never reached out to see if she was all right. Supposedly, her father was unable to get ahold of Tiffany, but he did leave messages. Hope did pick up the phone but apparently had nothing to say. But still, it was nothing for her to lose sleep over. She gave up on the notion that her sister and mother really cared for her years ago. Hannah would survive.

There was a knock on her office door. "Come in." Hannah said as she logged on to her computer. Her father walked in.

Hannah turned to him. "Oh, hi, dad."

Cliff looked at her, confused. "Hannah, sweetheart. Are you really sure that you want to return to work this soon after...?"

They already had the same conversation this morning. Hannah sighed. "Yes. For the last time, I'm sure. It was just some built-up stress that I had been holding in for a while. I should be fine now."

Cliff frowned at her. "I want the two of us to be more honest with one another going forward. I know we've had our issues in the past. I feel bad about it."

"You aren't anything like Grandpa." Hannah frowned, herself. She knew exactly what he was worried about.

The CEO blinked. "I honestly wasn't thinking about him." Cliff clearly was lying.

Hannah sighed. She could still remember when her grandfather had lived with them, back when she was younger. Hannah remembered that they hadn't always lived in North Pointe. When she was born, they had lived in a home on the other side of town. Hannah remembered a point in time when her parents argued over where they would live. Tiffany desperately wanted to live at North Pointe. Cliff, not so much, because it meant having to see Rodrick on a daily basis. He hadn't been forced to move until after Tiffany had gone missing. It was mainly because of the comments he made toward the situation. Her great-grandmother had still been alive at that point and was fed up. The family home had technically been left to her to pass on to any grandchildren that she would one day have. Rodrick never grasped that even in his final days. Hannah had been shocked to find out that he was moving back home. She felt horrible in thinking it, but she was glad he hadn't lived long enough to cause any real drama.

"Why don't you take a day off?" Cliff suggested.

Hannah rolled her eyes. "Why don't you join Mrs. Templeton's book club?" The daughter suggested to her father, annoyed.

Cliff scratched his head. "I hear it is a damn good book club."

"Dad, I promise you, I will be fine. I might leave a little early but I do have a lot to go over. I'm still trying to track down the missing money," Hannah reminded him.

"I'm sure the money is there. The files are always getting mismanaged. Just don't overwork yourself." Cliff said as he left her.

Hannah sighed, as she finally got back to work.

HARRY – 2018

Lunch finally came, and for the first time ever, Harry was looking forward to it. He was actually going to have people to sit with who would allow him to talk to them. As he entered the lunchroom, he passed a table, and he overheard their conversation.

"I can't believe he is showing his face." One girl said.

"Supposedly, that was his first time. I don't buy it for a second," a guy at the table said.

"He was totally enjoying himself in the vid." Another voice said.

Harry's heart started pounding. A hand touched his shoulder. It was Brad. "How's being rich and having enough money to enjoy gossiping about others?" The blond boy looked at the table. "If you have anything further to say about my brother, please tell it to my face." He pulled up his sleeves, revealing his biceps.

Harry and Brad walked towards the line. "You didn't have to do that."

"Yeah, I did. I'm not having people talking about you. They can talk about me all they want, but you're off-limits." Brad explained.

The curly-haired cousin looked confused. "What would they possibly have to say about you?"

Brad rolled his eyes. "Harry, my mother is known as the whore from Beverly Hills. My dad has more ex-wives than anyone else in town. My sister and half-brother have been

MIA for years. Oh, and I have an aunt whose ex-husband was a serial killer."

"Your grandparents are Nadia and Brandon, though. The entire town is in love with them," Harry pointed out.

The blond laughed. "Your point? Nadia and Brandon are my grandparents. I'm not them. My parents aren't them. You aren't your parents or grandparents. We make up our own actions."

"Which is why I feel like such an idiot," Harry admitted. He knew that Brad wanted to wait until marriage to have sex. Why couldn't he have waited as well?

Brad put his hand on Harry's shoulder as they continued to make their way up the line. "You did what you thought was right at the moment, as a teenage boy. You know now what is more right for you. That could change at any moment, and that is ok. For me, yeah, I'm more than likely waiting for marriage to have sex, but I don't judge you whatsoever for experimenting. Besides, no one else in this room has any right to judge you, either." They paid for their food and found Langley sitting there. Brad looked at her, calmly. "I see you found an undershirt?"

"I don't want to keep talking about it," Langley mumbled as she played with her salad. "I thought that being Queen Bee would be a whole lot easier than this. So, far I'm just the new girl..."

"That's not a bad thing," Harry said, thinking of the minute before. It was better Langley stay invisible, rather than be the topic of conversation around here. Nobody liked getting judged. Harry looked around, and that's when Preston walked towards them. He was looking right at Brad, though.

Brad looked over at Harry. "If he wants to sit here, we can't force him not to..." He sighed.

Langley stood up. "Preston, come sit with us! My boyfriend took the stick out of his ass for five minutes."

"Was that really needed?" Brad asked.

Langley nodded. "Are you going to continue critiquing my every move?" She wondered.

Preston sat down before Brad could answer. "Hey, guys. How's everyone's first day going?"

"I've never felt so invisible in my life!" Langley screamed.

Harry often was so confused with Langley. He himself might have never been popular, but he couldn't understand the concept of wanting to be famous and well-known, either. It just didn't seem to appeal to him.

"I think you just need to get to know people a little bit better," Harry said, quietly.

The blonde girl huffed and puffed. "I suppose. When is the first dance around here?" She wondered.

"Well, homecoming isn't until October," Harry told them. "But the back-to-school dance is the third week, normally"

Langley looked at Brad with big eyes, and Brad rolled his own. "Yes, Langley, I will take you. If you can behave yourself..."

This was another thing that Harry couldn't understand: the overall appeal of going to a dance. He had never gone to any in his life. He doubted he would start now. The curly-haired boy looked up at Preston, who was staring at him from across the table. Harry wondered if Preston would go to any of the dances. He was sure that Preston would find some girl to take as a friend. He knew better than to assume that Preston would want to go with him. Even with that kiss from earlier. Harry's head was going to start hurting from all will we won't we date, but Harry wasn't going to be asking Preston any embarrassing questions.

"Do you like dances, Harry?" Preston asked him.

Harry immediately looked at him. "Oh, um... I've never been to one."

"What do you mean, you've never been to one?" Langley's jaw dropped. "Oh, honey, you have to go to dances in high school. As trashy as they can be, it's a rite of passage," she declared.

His blond cousin gave Langley a dirty look. "If Harry doesn't want to go to a dance, then he doesn't have to go," Brad told his girlfriend.

As much as Harry appreciated Brad for always sticking up for him, right now might not be the right time. Harry honestly wasn't sure if he wanted to go. He did have to admit to himself that dancing with Preston would probably be fantastic. Not that he really knew how to dance...

"I have a feeling that a gay guy going to a school dance probably wouldn't go over very well," Harry pointed out.

Langley said, "Oh, trust me, I'll get into far more trouble than you at a dance, even if you brought a guy... I have my ways." She immediately turned to Brad. "Only to ensure that Harry doesn't get singled out darling." Brad rolled his eyes at her.

MARGOT – 2018

Margot's weekend had been boring, which is how she liked it. After five years of dealing with her idiot brother and his whore, it was nice to work at home with no fires to put out. It was far more fun to read about them from afar than deal with them spot-on. That day, she had lunch with Jackie Costa, who yammered on and on about her own idiot husband. Margot often wondered if she should be worried that she happened to be the only female that Jackie liked. The redhead woman brushed it off. The Fitzpatricks had been friends with the Costa family for ages.

Margot walked into the foyer of her mansion, only to find Perry working in the living room. "Well, good, you're working," she said. "Where have you been?

Perry looked up. "Yes, I got in late last night. I decided to just work from here instead. Mrs. Templeton is getting on my very last nerve."

"Did you honestly expect her to be easy? She's batshit crazy." Margot said. Out of all the women in town she hated, she hated Mrs. Templeton almost as much as Vivica. Margot sat down on the armchair across from her son. "So, how was your weekend away with Lucy?"

"I'm not telling you that, out of fear you'll say something rude," Perry said.

Margot laughed. "Oh, please… You might have found the one woman in the world that I'd actually approve of you dating. I can't stand the people she associates herself with, obviously. But Lucy herself is actually a good businesswoman. She doesn't fight hard enough, though, for what she wants."

Her son looked at her. "What on Earth are you talking about?"

"Five or so years ago, she came knocking on my door. I claimed I didn't have any jobs available for her. A tactic I'd use on any person who came seeking employment from me directly. I wanted her to fight harder. She didn't fight hard enough. She could be working in the office next to yours right now if she had just fought a little harder. Instead, she is going to be in a failed business venture with the whore," Margot explained. She had her people run the numbers. Vivica had the money, but she had no drive. Nial gave her the party-planning business as a way to sweeten the marriage proposal. Vivica had been the face of her previous cosmetic company. Other people ran it for her.

Perry looked at her. "So, what you are saying is you didn't hire her because she didn't beg you for a job?"

The mother thought for a second. "No. She didn't need to beg. She just needed to try harder."

She knew her son was trying to make a point, but the issue was that she actually had to beg for her job, at her own family's company. If she hadn't forced Nial to speak in her favor, she probably would still be a secretary or working for a rival company. People didn't understand that about her. Everyone assumed that Nadia and Brandon obviously gave their own daughter a CEO position at the company once Brandon retired. This was far from the case. Margot had spent most of the mid-to-late '90s running the damn company for them. Her family had been too busy playing volunteer spies with their friends. Just like when she had been a little girl, and they left her with her grandmother's while they traveled the world. Her family would go off, playing super spies and going after their self-made enemies. They only settled down once Nial was born, and that lasted all of seven or eight years, until he was finally put into boarding school. Everyone assumed that Nial was in a boarding school because of his behavioral issues. While Margot could readily admit to herself that Nial was never well-behaved. Even now, he had clearly never grown up. She thought it was ridiculous that he got to go to boarding school while she was forced to attend Saint Agnes like a commoner. Margot could have gotten into any school she wanted with her IQ, had she gone to boarding school. It was something she often lamented about. Instead, she went to *U of M* and *Columbia* for Graduate school.

Perry rubbed his forehead. "I get that you want to create a world of strong women, but what I don't get is why you think you need to build up women by breaking them down."

Why shouldn't she? Margot was broken down by all her mentors. All of which were male. She never added that in when people brought this up, though. Margot knew better. She couldn't be better than a man by talking ill of them. If Vivica were a smarter whore, she would see that she could have used her body to get ahead. Margot had done so with several men, including Rodrick Knight. Her parents never forgave her for that short-lived affair. They didn't get it, though. That affair earned her a colleague and a better business deal. Sure, Rodrick was an egotistical sexist pig. She knew deep down, though; she was probably one of the only women he ever came close to respecting, which included all of his own wives, his own mother, and daughter.

That's why Margot respected Tiffany over Vivica- Tiffany was a sought-after doctor in a cutthroat world. Some people preferred Tiffany to any man in her field. Meanwhile, Vivica posed in lingerie while she sat back and allowed her sister to steal the man she claimed to love. Margot realized that if

Tiffany never came into the picture, Vivica probably wouldn't have married Nial. After all, Margot figured that Vivica and Cliff probably wouldn't have worked out. They were mismatched, and everyone in town could see it. There was a considerable difference between Vivica Weston and Clifton Knight II and Margot's own parents, Nadia Bloom and Brandon Fitzpatrick. Nadia and Brandon had both been selfless people. Something that Margot could never understand, but she had to respect it. Well, maybe not actually respect, but she told other people that she did.

It frustrated her, really. They owned one of the most profitable companies in the world, and yet Nadia and Brandon didn't seem to care. It wasn't until her mother was pregnant with Nial that her father decided to settle down and actually take an interest in the company. Up until that point, some random cousin of her father's had been running it after her grandfather passed away. She actually respected her grandfather. He had a dream, and he didn't step down from it.

SUSAN – 1963

KMC's office map made no damn sense. It took Susan and Delia an hour just to find her husband's office. Susan had assumed she knew where her own husband's office was located. Apparently, with a lack of wine in her system, Delia didn't remember anything. After an eternity, they were finally outside the door.

Susan looked at Delia. "Are you sure you are up for this? You can wait in the lobby or something if you want."

Delia opened the office door. "I love my husband, but I don't agree with this deal at all. Let's do this," Delia explained to her friend.

Taking deep breaths, the two women walked into Benton Knight's office. It was not much larger than the Fitzpatrick family apartment... The desk, of course, was in the middle of the room, and a filing cabinet was behind it.

"Are you sure that the meeting is going to be in here? I mean, it's in an hour."

"Trust me... Benton probably looked over the contract all night. All we're going to do is replace it with the one we retyped up from the draft I found at the home office." Delia explained. She walked over to his desk and sat down. She noticed a picture of her on the counter. Delia smiled. "Well, isn't that sweet? Now, start looking. We don't have much time."

Susan looked around the room. She spotted a couch near the window with a coffee table. Finally, she walked over and looked at some of the papers. One happened to be a thick, full document entitled *Fitzpatrick Steel.* "

I found it." Delia quickly walked over, and Susan handed it to her. "It's the right paper, right?"

The Latina woman looked at the contract in comparison to the one they had made up, in her hand. Delia nodded. "We should be good. Your father will be the only one reading it in the meeting. I've sat through enough of them to know what goes on. All Benton and Heathcliff will be doing is insisting that it's the world's best deal while their lawyers are present."

Lawyers? Susan sighed. "Well, this is going to be a little bit different then. My father doesn't have a lawyer. I'd be shocked if he thought to find one. We were all trying to convince him last night after dinner not to take the deal. So, the thought of suggesting a lawyer never came up."

Susan wished she had thought of that herself or her mother and brother had brought it up. But honestly, it probably wouldn't have helped. A lawyer would have read the contract and insisted it was a bad idea. He would have been fired by her father, who he would still have signed the deal.

There was a shuffling outside the door. The two women looked at each another in fear. Delia pointed towards a closet, and they quickly dove inside of it.

Just in time, the door opened. "I promise you, Father. We will come out as the winners today."

Heathcliff groaned. "I'm just telling you. You better not make a fool of me today, boy. This deal is going to save us millions."

Susan and Delia listened in as the two men continued to speak. They gasped.

Heathcliff lamented, "I hated having to open my home to those people last night. I'm still confused about why your wife invited Templeton. That old bat was an old bat when I was Rodrick's age, it seems!"

Benton turned to him. "You do realize that the maid's daughter is friends with Rodrick? That's what he told me, at least. Yet, that Fitzpatrick boy Brennon or whatever his name is doesn't approve of Rodrick, so he punched him in the face. What a fucked-up family."

As much as she wanted to burst out of the closet, Delia stopped her. Susan knew that she shouldn't leave. She wanted out so badly, but she knew that it would be the end of their plan.

"Grab the contract, and let's go. I don't want to be here all day. Lana or the maid, as you call her, is making meatloaf for dinner. She makes the best meatloaf."

Benton rolled his eyes as he went over to his desk and grabbed the contract. He looked at it for a long moment. Susan started to turn cold. That's when Benton put it in his briefcase, though, and the father and son exited the room.

LUCY – 2018

Housing in Grosse Pointe wasn't cheap, and Saint Clair Shores didn't look much better. Lucy was highly considering renting a place in Roseville or Warren. She had started out looking in Warren when she first moved here. The only issue was that Langley would never go for it, and the school system in Warren was horrible. Langley's transcripts would sure to be screwed-up or ignored. There was also the issue that Langley was finally going to school, now. Lucy had not received one call all week long. It also helped her believe Langley was going to school because Lucy saw her younger sister studying with Brad and Harry.

Lucy sat down in Vivica's living room and sighed. Where on Earth were, they going to go? Lucy wasn't stupid. She knew that Vivica would soon move across the street with Brad. She had a feeling Vivica would let her stay here, but she didn't want to impose like that. Xander's paychecks just weren't the same since he joined the force. Xander had savings, but Lucy didn't want him losing it all now. She knew that when Xander had envisioned being an officer, it was under the idea that he would still have family money to keep him going. Yes, he had a trust fund, but still.

"I made the right choice," she sighed. Lucy's phone continued to be hassled with phone calls by her father and his lawyer, all day and night. It was getting to the point where she considered changing her number.

Holly walked in and sat next to her. "Hi," Lucy said as she continued to look at her computer.

"You can't quit." Holly sighed.

Lucy looked up at her in confusion. "Quit? What are you talking about?"

Holly gave her a look as if she knew exactly what she was talking about. "I'm not stupid. Vivica's not a businesswoman. She's a semi-retired model more interested in Cliff than anything else. That said, you are important to her. The only reason she wants to open a cosmetic company is because of you."

The eldest Kingsley took a moment to respond. "Why on Earth would she open a cosmetic company, then? I worked in hotel management before Vivica."

"Can you honestly imagine Vivica owning a hotel?" Holly rolled her eyes.

"Well, you can tell her I'm not quitting. I just need this to get off the ground. Look, call me a spoiled rich bitch. That's just it, though. I am or was, and it isn't as easy as you would think just to ignore my past." Lucy was still waiting for Holy to bitch her out.

The maid nodded her head. "I understand. A lifestyle isn't something you can easily quit. That said, we still need to find a chemist. Luke and Vivica can't work together again. Cliff will never allow it."

Lucy had heard of Vivica and Luke's life together. She had heard that it was probably her most normal marriage. Yet, Vivica didn't want normal. She wanted Cliff. Vivica always wanted Cliff. Cliff seemed like a nice enough guy; Lucy just didn't understand why Vivica would continue to go after a clearly married man. That didn't mean she wasn't happy for Vivica and Cliff right now. It just seemed like Vivica could have had a good guy and passed up on the opportunity, to continue setting herself up for failure.

Lucy said, "I don't know any chem, and even so, Holly, she wants to launch a full-on business in a matter of months. Can her name alone really do that?"

***

The Kingsley daughter appreciated the conversation that she had with Holly. It just wasn't really enough. Lucy needed to start making real money if she wanted to live a semi-normal (to her) lifestyle again. Lucy sat down at the local diner in town, and Perry walked in.

She waved to him, and he walked over. "Hey, thanks for coming."

"Oh, of course. I needed to get out of the office. Mrs. Templeton's lawyer might actually be even older and more racist than she is." Perry explained as he sat.

Lucy took a deep breath. "I need your help. I don't know how to get Vivica's crazy cosmetic company off the ground. I have a business degree, but I know nothing about the chemistry side of cosmetics. It seems like she just wants to be the face of a brand again. I had no issue with that during our event=planning company. I did everything while she just moaned about being married to your uncle. I could deal with it. I made more money than I did running the East Coast Division of a hotel chain."

Lucy was her damn assistant, for crying out loud. The few friends that she had kept from her old life would judge her. Until they heard she was making the amount she did.

Perry thought for a few minutes. Lucy thought he had the most amazing eyes. She wanted to tell him that, but she knew it wasn't the right time to get into a relationship. Austin had only died a few months ago, and Perry was a Fitzpatrick. Did she realty want to be connected to the crazy family any more than she already was? Langley dating Brad was crazy enough.

Perry murmured, "I could look into a few things. I have another suggestion, though."

"What kind of suggestion?" She asked.

"Why not come work for the Fitzpatrick Group again?" He asked back.

If Lucy didn't want to get into a relationship with Perry, could she really see herself working with him?

Lucy said, "I mean, no offense, but your mother already turned me down once and Vivica would go batshit."

The redhaired boy shrugged. "I adore Vivica even when she isn't married to my uncle. That said, can you really see yourself being happy otherwise? Lucy, I looked into a few things after we got back from New York. You could probably find a job that would put you back into your previous lifestyle. You could probably do so with the cosmetic company, but not in the way Vivica wants it run. Is working with Vivica really that important?"

Was it? Lucy wasn't really sure if she could be completely honest with herself. She liked Vivica as a person, but she was a model, which wasn't a bad thing. It just wasn't enough to convince Lucy that any business venture they would have together would work out.

Lucy sighed. "I'd have to honestly think about this. I don't want to string Vivica along, but I don't want to be indebted to her forever... Even if she would be happy to let me live with her forever."

LANGLEY – 2018

High school football only mattered so much at her old school. Langley only knew of a handful of boys who went to college from football scholarships. Most of the time, it was academic scholarships mixed with some sort of sport like tennis, Cross Country, or Lacrosse. Langley had gone to a small Day School where she would have been one of maybe a hundred in a graduating class. If she really thought about it, the number was probably more likely around seventy.

Saint Agnes wasn't much larger; however, football was a much bigger thing. Sure, in the New York suburbs, football was massive. At a prep school, you had parties and fundraisers on Fridays. But here, football was everything.

This all being said, Langley had no idea how to dress. The weather still hadn't changed enough where she felt justified to wear a sweater. Brad had been not very subtle by telling her not to dress slutty. She sort of assumed they wouldn't let her into the stadium if she did. They played at a local university field that didn't have their own football team in Detroit.

Which also concerned Langley. The blonde knew how to deal with Manhattan, Brooklyn, Queens, and even occasionally Stanton Island, which even her own father told her to stay away from. Detroit, to her, was a new battlefield. She had gone to the city of Detroit several times during the summer, and while she couldn't give directions, she knew where this stadium was located. It had been during the day.

Harry and Brad had taken her to the *DIA, Detroit Science Center,* and Brad himself dragged Harry and Langley to *Tiger's* games, which she slept through. There was still an element of being freaked out though, especially at nighttime.

Harry walked into her room. "Are you ready to leave yet?" he asked her.

She turned to look at him. He was dressed head to toe in Saint Agnes spirit wear. "I didn't realize you had that much school spirit?"

"I just want to fit in as much as possible. This isn't a public school where the alum only come back for homecoming. They are here at every single game of the season..." Harry pointed out.

She couldn't figure out the appeal of watching men tackle each other. There was nothing sexy about how they dressed. However, she felt, Harry agreed that a basketball uniform was still somehow hotter.

"Brad better win this and every other game of the season. I'm going to be fucking miserable." Langley sat down on her bed. The first Friday of the first week at her old school would be filled with parties, with after-parties and crashing in someone's loft. Yet here it meant football and diner food.

Langley liked Brad. There were elements of him that she loved. The blonde girl very much respected that he had a set of values that he was staunch stuck with. She had no issue with supporting him in whatever he wanted to do. She just had yet to see him do the same for her. Yes, she wanted sex, but there were hundreds of other things that she would have been just as happy with, if not more. Such as going to concerts she would actually like. Harry had no issue with going to Rap and Metal concerts, even though he had horrible anxiety attacks halfway through. Brad got her tickets to see some boy band...

It was a nice thought, but they had been together long enough for her to know he wasn't into it.

It also didn't help that his mother clearly disliked her, which made no sense. They had a lot in common, and Vivica liked her sister. Langley would have understood her disapproving of Xander. He did screw over her clearly favorite niece for the other one.

"I suppose I'm ready to go." Langley stated. She looked him up and down again. "Harry, we are stopping back at your house. You can't wear all of that." The teenage girl crossed her arms.

Harry looked at her with his puppy dog eyes. "What do you mean? I think I look good."

"I'm trying not to laugh..." She started laughing. "Sorry, force of habit." She grabbed his arm and went towards her door.

***

It took all of five minutes to realize that Harry had no appropriate outfits to wear and they were now pressed for time. "Harry, what is the likelihood that your father has any of his childhood clothes?"

The Knight boy looked confused. "I mean, maybe... Why?"

She thought for a second. "Well, the 90's are really where it is at right now. However, late 80's apparel might work with the look I'm going for."

"What look? Don't you like the way I dress, Langley?" Harry asked.

It wasn't that she didn't like the way he dressed. It was just that he dressed very low-key obviously, on purpose. If Langley had to guess, it was because he didn't like clothing-shopping and just continued to get the same outfits over and over again. There were only so many variations you can get out of skinny jeans, canvas shoes, and sweaters... "I suspect that you want to impress Preston to some degree?"

He shrugged and started blushing. "Well, I mean yeah... But he knows what I look like."

"So, you just so happened to dress like Saint Agnes' footballs number one fan?" She asked, laughing out loud again. "Harry, I don't get the impression that Preston is looking to make out with Saint Agnes' Best School Spirit award winner..."

"Make out? I don't really think he will want to do that..." Harry laughed a little, turning even more red.

She rolled her eyes. "Where would your Dad's clothes be?"

The two of them walked down the long hallway of North Pointe until they reached the end of the hall. Langley had expected an attic but knew that there was an entire other floor above them that had been a maid's quarters, once upon a time. Instead, this space was just a room filled with boxes that almost looked like an attic but was clearly just one of many spare bedrooms.

Langley looked around the room, rifling through a few boxes. She knew in her mind what she was looking for but wasn't exactly sure how to express it with words. The first box she looked through was full of old ties. Then she opened the second. This was exactly what she was looking for. It was one of those old jackets that sports players wore. She remembered someone saying once that Cliff had been on several teams in high school. She suspected that he had to have owned one. The Kingsley girl held it up and smiled at Harry. She then spotted a straight-color light blue shirt. Very 80's, but with the right pair of skinny jeans and the jacket, Harry could get away with it.

"You want me to wear my Dad's old lettermen jacket? I don't know if he would want me to..." Harry explained.

Once again, she sighed. "Harry, go put some jeans on and put the damn shirt and jacket on. I highly doubt your dad is going to give a damn if you wear this. Damn it!"

SUSAN – 1963

Seamus had insisted on throwing a celebration party, even if his entire family was furious with him. Even though Susan knew that they likely were in the clear, she was still mad herself. She shouldn't need to conspire with Delia to fix her father's now delirious dreams. Yet... Now he was going to get exactly what he wanted. The strawberry blonde was conflicted about if she were happy or just plain annoyed about that.

Mary walked over to Susan and smiled. "Well, you should be proud of yourself. You and Delia did a good thing."

"We broke into an office and forged papers. Aren't you supposed to cast shame upon myself and Delia?" Susan asked her, in all seriousness.

The nun shrugged. "Yes, probably... But I don't particularly like the Knight men. Which, I know what you are thinking, but there is nothing in the Bible that says I can't dislike someone strongly. I just can't hate them."

Susan giggled. Mary had the prettiest eyes. She wished these feelings would just go away. The Fitzpatrick daughter snapped out of it. "Well, why don't we go sit down. My parents are still arguing in the kitchen."

"You didn't tell either of them?" Mary asked.

They sat down, and Susan looked around. "Definitely not. My father would have run over to Knight and demanded they re-read the papers. He honestly thinks that they are helping him."

Brandon walked over with Nadia. He smiled at Susan. "So, Susan, you brought a nun to pray for us before we are homeless?"

"Hello, Sister Mary Newman," Nadia said.

"Hello, children. Please join us." Mary said.

Susan frowned a little. She had been hoping the two of them would have the evening to themselves. "Brandon, don't worry. I think things will work out in the long run."

Nadia put her hand on Brandon's shoulder. "See, that is what I've been telling him all day."

There was clearly something brewing between Brandon and Nadia. Susan and Mary could both tell, but it was clearly too soon for anyone to bring it up. The phone rang from the kitchen, and one of her parents must have picked it up.

A minute later, Ida walked out. "Susan, phone for you."

Susan got up and took the call. "We need to talk," Delia said on the other end.

HARRY – 2018

He felt ridiculous, but Langley made him drive to the stadium anyway... Harry got out of his Knight car and took a deep breath. Between his dad's jacket and all the product that Langley put in his hair, he felt like people would start looking at him. It wasn't that he thought he looked terrible. It was that he wasn't sure how everyone around him was going to react.

The parking lot was already filled, and Langley was actively holding a can of pepper spray as they walked side by side. "Ok, this is coming from me, but you are being overly dramatic," Harry told her.

"Oh, I'm sorry that I want to be safe. It isn't like I didn't carry pepper spray on me in NYC. I just didn't have it out in my hand." Langley admitted.

"Do you think that Preston will see me in the stands?" He wondered out loud.

Langley stopped walking and looked at him. "Damn it. I forgot to make a poster for Brad!"

While he wouldn't put it past Langley to lose it for no reason, Harry had to admit he had no clue what she was talking about for once. "What do you mean?"

The blonde gave him a dirty look. "I overhead that all the other players' girlfriends were making posters to support their boyfriends. I'm going to look like a moron out there in the stands."

Harry stopped and thought... Preston invited him to the game. Did he expect him to make a poster? They weren't dating, but even so… Now he had butterflies and bombs going off in his stomach at the same time. "Langley, maybe we should just go see a movie."

"You know damn well I'd rather be anywhere but here right now. We have no choice to go in, though. Brad is playing, and he expects me to be there for him." She turned and looked at him. "Plus, he is your cousin; you should really be there to support him. Also, Preston invited you, and I'm not letting you get out of this."

She grabbed his arm, and they continued walking to the gate. He paid, and they walked into the stadium. Supposedly, his sister Hannah was going to be there, but he couldn't see anyone he really knew even from school. It wasn't like he was friends with any of them. He just thought he would recognize a lot more people.

There were a lot of alum like he predicted. Some of which he did indeed recognize. Some of which clearly had been part of classes before his father's time, even. It was weird to think that some of these people had maybe had conversations with his grandfather when he had been a child. Harry often wondered what Rodrick Knight would have been like before he was an adult. Could a person be born pure evil, or was it something you learned how to be? He guessed he wouldn't know…

"So, do we go sit in the stands, or are we just going to stay by the sidelines?" Langley asked him.

"I suppose we can stand for a little bit. I mean, I'd rather not be stuck in a large crowd right now." He wasn't sure he would be able to handle this night for long. The important thing was that Preston saw him for at least a little bit. Then, he could go have a panic attack in his car if he needed to.

The blonde rested on a fence. "This is just all so different to me."

"You really never went to a high school football game?" Harry wondered.

She thought for a moment. "Once. It was for some cousin in Long Island. This just wasn't that big of a deal. Remember, when you take into consideration the number of people in my graduating class and the entire student body- a third of the boys at my school would have had to be on the team." She started looking at her phone.

Brad's school had more students than Langley's old school; it seemed. Harry wondered how things would have been if he had been with Brad, away at boarding school. The curly-haired boy wondered if they would have remained as close as Brad wanted them to be now. Or if they would have drifted apart. He had to imagine that Brad would have found other friends, and Harry would have been left to fend for himself.

As he thought to himself, two familiar faces walked over. "So, are you guys having fun? Because I'm still not sure why I'm here," Hannah said.

Langley turned around. "Xander, did Lucy send you to keep an eye on me?" She gave him a dirty look.

The Kingsley son took a deep breath. "No, Langley... I thought that Hannah would want to spend some time away from the office."

"Oh, so you are being a cheap date?" Langley asked him.

Hannah started to laugh. "I'm having a pretty good time." She assured him. The older sister looked at Harry. "Do you two want to come to sit with us?"

Before Harry could speak, Mrs. Templeton walked by, dressed in head to toe *Templeton Ice Cream* wear. She had one of those flags that you waved to cheer on the team.

Mrs. Templeton turned and looked at Harry. "What are you looking at, boy? Can't a lady enjoy a football game?" She walked onwards towards the stands.

The two Knight siblings looked at each other in confusion. "Apparently, the stadium doesn't count as Saint Agnes property?" Hannah suggested.

"I guess I thought she was banned for life after she was caught stealing holy water during Mass," Harry said.

"No, that's not what got her banned. It was when she tried segregating the pews." Hannah reminded him.

A voice over the loudspeaker went off… *"Please welcome your 2018 Saint Agnes Sailors!"* There was a tremendous roar from the home side. Harry clapped quietly. Langley looked as if she was about to pass out from boredom, even though they had only been there a few minutes. Hannah and Xander went to go find seats.

The team stormed out from under the bleachers. Brad was at the front. He only had to wait a second for Preston to run out. It was as if Preston had been looking for him because he clearly winked at Harry. His heart started to melt. For a brief moment in time, Harry felt like he belonged.

"I swear to God and Tina Fey, Brad better have seen me… I wore a bra tonight just for him." Langley screamed over the loud cheering. It was as if Langley speaking signaled for the crowd to go quiet as the band started to play the national anthem. Brad finally was looking at Langley. She smiled and waved. She then turned to Harry. "I'm guessing you didn't bring a hip flask?"

He looked at her. "I don't drink." He said, completely shocked.

VIVICA – 2018

The children were all gone for the night. The redhaired vixen had instructed that Holly either spend time with her husband or stay at her mansion for the night. Tonight was going to be a special night between her and Cliff. She had ordered takeout from the diner and set it up in the Knight dining room. Candles were lit all over the room, and she sprayed it with the perfume that she had worn back when she was a teenager. It had taken a minute to track down, but she found something that smelled almost identical. She wore a blue sweater and skintight white leggings with blue stiletto heels. Cliff would be home any minute. She knew that the gesture would entertain him. He used to love it when she planned nights together. They never went right though because the children were young or because Tiffany, Nial, or Luke were in town. None of those things were true, now, though, so things would be perfect for once.

The front door opened, and Vivica ran to the foyer to meet her fiancé. "Hello, my Knight." She kissed him on the forehead.

Cliff looked around and started to smell something. "Weston, why does this place smell like your childhood bedroom?" He asked. She could tell he had a long day.

"Well, why don't you come into the dining room and we can discuss all the fun we used to have in my childhood bedroom," Vivica giggled. She walked him into the dining room. The redhead turned to see if he would smile. Instead, he looked like he was ready to pass out. "Cliff, I planned a romantic evening, and you look miserable."

He yawned. "Sorry, I've been dealing with lawyers all afternoon. There is money that has possibly gone missing. Hannah's been telling me all about it lately, and I finally started looking into it myself."

For a moment, Vivica wondered how often she would have to talk about KMC with Cliff. She remembered the first time they had been *married*. She managed to dodge the subject as much as possible. It wasn't that she found the discussion of one's job annoying. It was just that she knew deep down that Cliff had had alternative plans for the future. It was only once Tiffany had shown up that he agreed to stay in the family business and once again live in the family home.

At this point, with his father and grandmother gone, she very much doubted he would want to move. She didn't mind living at North Pointe. There was just a lot of history for both of them within these walls—a lot of not-so-great history. Yet, at the same time, some excellent, beautiful things happened here as well. Vivica guessed that the same could be said about the Fitzpatrick mansion as well as DJ's old house...

Her Knight sat down, and Vivica sat down next to him. He looked down at his food.

Cliff took a deep breath and looked at Vivica. "I just realized we are alone tonight, aren't we?" Vivica nodded and smiled. "Well, tell me what you did today other than plan this dinner?"

"I thought you would never ask!" Vivica said, with her voice very overly dramatic. "I just spent time looking into hiring a chemist for the company." As soon as she said it, she realized that this conversation would kill the mood right there and then.

Cliff nodded. "Ok, Weston, I will support you in whatever you do. I'm just begging you, please don't call my cousin."

That was the last thing that Vivica intended to do. The last time she had spoken with Luke Knight, they had slept together. This was back when Cliff was still married to Tiffany. So, technically, she did nothing wrong. Technically was still technically, though, and the last thing she needed was for Cliff to find out...

Luke Knight was the son of Clifton Knight and Dallas Bolton-Knight. Clifton and Dallas moved to Amsterdam when they were in their early 20's- supposedly, as an act of rebellion towards both their parents, who didn't like the fact that they were an interracial couple. Vivica wasn't particularly sure if this was true. Delia Knight had insisted she didn't care about that. She cared that Dallas was supposedly trailer trash.

Cliff had gone to visit his uncle and aunt back when he was a teenager. Supposedly, when they were teenagers, the two boys got along very well. Then one day, Luke showed up out of nowhere to declare what was his in the company. Cliff had won the battle, but that didn't stop Luke from sticking around. Vivica had been in-between marriages at the time and fell for Luke. There had been nothing malicious about it. However, Cliff took it all very personally.

"Oh, Cliff, relax. I'm not going to do anything stupid. Let's not talk about any of our exes." Vivica hoped he would listen.

"Did Harry end up going to the football game?" He asked his Weston.

She nodded. "Yes, I was instructed by Brad to stay home this week. I think he wanted to spend as much time with Lactose as possible. They won't get as much quality time together soon."

Her Knight nodded. "Oh, and why is that?"

Vivica smiled. "Well, Brad and I will be moving in here. Lucy will have her own house again very soon."

"I didn't realize that Lucy had found a new home?" Cliff pondered. He looked at Vivica. "What are you up to, Weston?"

Why did he always think that she was always up to something? "Nothing for once... I actually did something good. I found them a home to rent from me."

Cliff nodded. "Where is it located?"

"Oh, it's actually perfect. It's the old Martin house." Vivica explained.

He shot her a look. Vivica knew that he would shoot her a look. But please- it wasn't as if this was a bad thing.

"Vivica, you bought back your mother and DJ's old house? Do you have the keys?"

She looked at him, confused. "Yes... Why do you ask that?"

"I mean... Do you want to take a tour of it, maybe right now?" Cliff suggested.

It took her a moment to realize what he meant. Considering it was already dark outside... "Cliff Knight, are you trying to get me to let you seduce me in my childhood home?" She smiled. "Screw dinner let's go!" She got up and raced towards the foyer.

LUCY – 2018

The eldest Kingsley daughter sat down in Vivica's living room next to Holly, who was on her laptop. Lucy looked at the maid. "I'm not trying to be mean, but Vivica's not here tonight... Why don't you spend some time with your family?"

Holly turned to Lucy. "My husband is working, and the kids are both having sleepovers... We are all doing brunch tomorrow. Why don't you spend quality time with Langley and Xander?"

Lucy took a moment to think. Had she really ever spent quality time with Langley? She supposed that eventually, she would have to. "Langley and Xander are both at the Saint Agnes football game."

"I remember being dragged to those back when I was in high school. They used to have those at the practice field back then, though. Were you a football fan back in high school?" Holly asked.

Lucy didn't even remember there being a football team, if she was honest. "It wasn't really that big of a deal."

"Clearly, you weren't from the Midwest. I'm shocked that Austin never dragged you to any games... He was Mister Football back in the day." Holly explained.

If only he hadn't... The blonde remembered being forced to go straight from work to the insipid football games with Austin. He would find his old high school friends and start drinking. "Whenever I think about Austin, I start to wonder what I really saw in him..."

Holly put her hand on Lucy's shoulder. "He had some decent qualities deep-down."

"Was he really that bad in high school, though?" Lucy asked.

The maid looked away. "He wasn't an obnoxious jock type. He was more... Upper-middle-class. Rich boy obnoxious. You wouldn't understand the type." "Holly, I grew up rich." Lucy pointed out.

"Well, yes, but there is a difference between obnoxious filthy rich and obnoxious, can-afford-the-latest-tennis-shoe rich. You wouldn't understand because you probably didn't have much of a middle ground where you were from." If Lucy really thought about it, she probably didn't.

"Holly, you didn't exactly grow up poor yourself." Lucy reminded her. She knew that Holly grew up in this area herself.

Holly shrugged. "Well, yes, but I was one of those moderate middle-class homes."

"So, what is your opinion on Perry Fitzpatrick?" Lucy asked.

Holly looked at Lucy for a second. "Oh, you mean Perry Fields. Um, elitist type, to be honest. I only really remember him from the summertime. Margot didn't really raise him during the school year. Her other son was five or six years older than me."

Lucy hadn't known that Margot didn't raise Perry. "Well, they seem to have a pretty good relationship now." She shut her laptop and sighed. "I need to find a decently-priced house. I don't know what I will do. I realize Vivica isn't looking to throw us out, but even so."

"I have a secret for you, but you can't tell Vivica... She bought the Martin house back from Austin's father. She planned on letting you rent it out." Holly explained.

Why on Earth would Vivica buy that house? She then remembered that Vivica had grown up in that home herself.

"That honestly isn't a bad idea. I mean, the kitchen was completely redone. I always did like that house. It is also is close enough that Langley could walk here but still be a safe distance from Brad." This was actually one of the first good ideas that Vivica had ever had while Lucy knew her.

DELIA – 1963

What was taking Susan so long to meet her? Delia sat at the Harper Inn diner by herself. It would be closing in an hour. Susan didn't live that far away. Then all of a sudden, a strawberry blonde walked in.

"Get over here." Delia, whisper yelled.

Susan sat down. "What happened?"

"Well, I think we are in the clear. However, a lawyer double-checked the papers and now they are furious." Delia rubbed her forehead. "Susan, we screwed up the numbers completely."

The Fitzpatrick daughter's eyes widened. "Oh, great... Let me guess; my father is going to have to pay them now."

If only that were the case. "Susan, your father's business could actually more than succeed with these numbers. Benton and Heathcliff have been going at it with one another all night, trying to figure out which one screwed up."

"So, they don't suspect us, then?" Susan asked.

"Well, no. However, they also both insist that someone tampered with something. Nobody apparently saw or recognized us. We somehow got away with this..." Delia admitted.

Susan sat there for a moment. "I have spent most of my life listening to my father go on and on about making it big. Yet, now here I am listening to you say that he did it... Yet, he didn't. I did."

Delia knew exactly what she was getting at. It was a man's world and probably always would be. When they lived in California, before she was pregnant with Clifton, Delia was always helping Benton out at the office. On more than one occasion, she was responsible for how a business deal went down. She got no credit. However, back then, Benton was more willing to admit in private when she helped him. Now that they were living with Heathcliff, it was a completely different battlefield.

"We can never tell anyone what we did," Delia explained.

Susan nodded in agreement. "I understand. I don't know how I honestly feel right now."

The Latina knew how she felt… It was both satisfying and horrifying at the same time. "Well, celebrate with your family, and things should be fine. The contract was signed. One thing we didn't change was the clause in the contract. If KMC breaks the contract, they owe Seamus an obscene amount of money. So, either way, you are in the clear."

LANGLEY – 2018

Brad had won the football game and was sure to be in a good mood. Langley waited in the parking lot along with Harry to congratulate him. She would leave Harry to congratulate Preston. Overall, it wasn't that horrible of an experience watching the football game with Harry. She managed to speak with a few people from her classes, who seemed semi normal. Though, she really just wanted to spend time with her man.

The locker room door finally opened, and Brad walked out with a few of his teammates. He walked over to Langley and gave her a look. "Did you really have to say that right at the national anthem?"

He had just won the first football game of the season for his team. Yet, all that was on his mind apparently was a mistake she made.

"Brad, I'm going to spend the night at Harry's. You have fun with your teammates." Langley walked away.

She understood that Brad had traditional values. The issue was that Langley wasn't willing to change everything about herself. Yes, Brad was attractive, and at the end of the day, she liked him a lot. The blonde girl admired Brad's morals and standards. The issue was they were Juniors in high school. Not associates at a prestigious law firm. They were allowed to break a few rules every so often. She wasn't asking or expecting him to break any laws. It wasn't even like Brad was ultra-religious. His moral views were literally *What Would Nial and Vivica Do? Ok, do the opposite.* While yes, his father was an asshole, his mother had clearly grown since a bulk of her real scandals took place. This was one of the things that she didn't like about small-town life. People never let it go. People always remembered in NYC, but they spoke of it behind closed doors. You were able to move on with your life. If anything, Brad's harbored feelings were what kept Vivica from being able to move on.

Langley honestly wasn't even sure where she was going. She knew she was going to Vivica's to grab something to wear. It was just that it was clearly not two minutes away. The Kingsley daughter sighed and sat down on a bench. If she texted Lucy, she would never hear the end of it. If she texted Xander, she would be interrupting a date. And speaking of dates- the last thing she needed was to be the third wheel with Harry and Preston right now.

A car pulled up. It was Brad... "Langley, please get in."

She pouted. "I don't want to talk to you."

"Well, I don't care if you want to talk. I'm not letting you walk home in the dark." Brad said with a tone.

The blonde reluctantly walked over to the passenger side. "I'm only letting you drive me home because I'm too lazy to walk." She crossed her arms.

"Look, I'm sorry," Brad said, looking at her. He had the most gorgeous eyes. She was still angry, though. "I know I get angry at you."

"Brad, I'm going to stop you right there. I know you get angry at me too. I like you; I want to be your girlfriend, but I'm sick of having to remind you that I'm not going to change my personality for just to suit you. Nobody around us, cares that much." Langley screamed at him. She didn't mean to, but this conversation happened like every other week since they started dating.

He nodded. "Do you want to break up with me?"

Did she want to break up with him? The fact is when she first fell for him at the hospital gala, it was a lust thing. She wanted to see him naked. That was about it. Then she befriended Harry and spent time with Brad. It wasn't as if they had much in common. Yet, they did enjoy hanging out together.

"Look, whether you want to admit it or not; you're embarrassed of your parent's past and present actions... My father is in jail and made me call him A-King. I randomly learn new things about my mother every so often. I'm pretty sure she was an ex-porn star before she had Lucy. She may even do porn now. Who the hell knows? Clearly, she doesn't care about me. Yet, your mother loves and adores you. She obviously doesn't like me." She realized she wasn't answering his question. Langley took a deep breath. "Brad, do you see yourself sleeping with me?"

Brad turned red. "I mean, if we get married one day."

"Ok, well, we are sixteen-years-old right now. I assume you want to graduate college before getting married. So, that would be twenty-two or twenty-three? I can live without sleeping with you. I can't live without being myself, though." Langley explained to him.

"I want you to be yourself," Brad told her.

"Then you need to accept me for me. I can't do this otherwise. I know how to act in public, no offense, but the Kingsley's are North Eastern old money. I'm a literal WASP, as opposed to Fitzpatricks." She thought about it, and she knew for a fact that he never gave her a chance around some of the more prominent people in his life. Whenever he had a luncheon or something over the summer; she wasn't invited. Langley knew this was because he was worried about how she would act.

The Fitzpatrick boy took a deep breath. "I'm willing to start over. You just have to understand; my whole birth wasn't even normal. I lived with Anthony Costa, for crying out loud. My dad sent me away to boarding school because he thought that is what you do." He started to cry. "It's not that I don't want to make love with you. It's that I want it to make love to the right person. I can't be my father, hurting women over and over again. I can't be my mother, being in love with someone who kept ignoring her."

This was the most serious conversation the two teens had ever had with one another. Langley smiled. "Brad, I can't promise you we will be together in a year. I don't know if we are soulmates. I believe in fate, though, and I think fate wants us to both help one another."

He nodded. "I can help you." Brad wiped his tears.

She put her hand on his shoulder. "Only if you let me help you." Langley looked in his eyes. "I'm serious, Brad. You can't continue judging me. If I'm doing something outlandish, fine, but if I choose not to wear a bra or something, you have to deal with it. Also, you are taking me to Drag Queen Bingo."

"Can't you have Harry take you?" Brad asked, confused. Then he clearly thought about it for a second. "Ok, fine, we will go. Only on the condition that you will be my date to the back-to-school dance."

Langley kissed him. She could agree to those terms.

HARRY – 2018

Preston parked his car in an abandoned parking lot. He wanted to spend time alone with Harry, and Harry had reluctantly agreed. Harry definitely wanted alone time. He just wasn't sure how he would handle himself outside of a crowed. Though, he wasn't any better with one.

"It's awesome that you guys won tonight," Harry explained.

The Costa son put his phone down after checking it. "Yeah, totally. But I don't really want to talk about football. I want to talk about you."

"What on Earth do you want to talk about me for? I'm not interesting." Harry told him.

"Harry, you are very interesting. For one, you have the most amazing eyes. Sorry, but it is really true." Preston said, really flirty.

Harry's stomach was about to explode. "I mean, tell me what it is like to grow up a Costa..." He really wished he hadn't said that.

Preston laughed and started to nod. "Fair enough question. I assume there is both curiosity and a bit of worry in terms of being around someone with my last name?"

Well, he hadn't actually thought about it that much, but everyone else around him had. "I guess. I mean you-you don't have to say any... I mean, maybe we should just change the subject."

"No, really, it is a good question. Harry, my family is crazy, but I love them." He laughed and looked at Harry. Harry felt embarrassed. When Preston looked at him, he intently looked at him, with a suggestive twinkle in his eye.

Preston said, finally. "Look, I will say this about my family. My dad's business can get dangerous. I hope that won't turn you away from coming and visiting me at my house. I'd like you to meet my parents." Preston explained.

The curly-haired boy looked at Preston. He wanted to meet his parents. Harry had to imagine that it was a big step for someone like Preston, when his parents were Anthony and Jackie Costa. "Do you introduce a lot of guys to your parents?"

He shook his head no. "I've never introduced anyone in general to my family. At least not in Grosse Pointe. You're kind of special... At least I think you will be."

"Why am I special?"

"I don't know. I kind of want to spend more time with you. You know if you want to spend more time with me, that is." Preston explained.

More than anything, Harry did, At least he thought he did. He turned to Preston again. "Look, I'm going to -ask straight up... Do you like me, Preston? As in, more than a friend?"

It took a moment for Preston to answer, which worried Harry for a second. "I don't know you very well. However, I want to know you more. I think you are beyond beautiful, Harry... I know that sounds so stupid." Preston blushed.

Harry wanted to kiss Preston but knew that he didn't have it in him. Instead, Preston kissed him. It was the most amazing kiss ever. He had never kissed a boy before. Todd Roberts wouldn't kiss him. Why did he think about Todd? Preston Costa was actually kissing him. Preston Costa. Harry wondered what his middle name was. He wondered what it would actually be like in the Costa mansion. Would there be guards? He knew that they had a brick wall surrounding the entrance.

As he was held up, trapped overthinking in his mind, he felt a hand go up against Harry's leg and closer to his crotch. He stopped Preston. "I'm not ready to do anything like that."

Preston moved his hands. "Oh, yeah, no problem. Sorry, it was just the heat of the moment."

Harry took in a deep, stuttering breath. "Look, I know that I'm known for doing certain things because of what happened with Todd Roberts last semester. You have to understand that I was manipulated. I wouldn't have done it with him otherwise." Harry really wouldn't have. Todd was the first and only person ever to show a romantic interest in him. He wanted to keep him in his life at all costs, and Todd forced him to have oral sex in order to keep him. Little did Harry know that during one encounter, Todd had filmed it from Harry's point of view and used it as blackmail.

"I'm not going to force you to do anything you don't want to do. I'll admit that I have seen the video." Preston said. For a moment, Harry was about to die. "I turned it off after five seconds. It was disgusting. You deserved better Harry, and I want to be the one to give you better."

He tried holding back but he couldn't. Harry started to cry. "I'm sorry. It's just aside from Langley, nobody who isn't related to me has ever tried to make an actual effort to be my friend."

Preston reached in and gave him a hug. "It's the dawn of a new era for you, Harry Knight. Let's just make one thing clear." He looked Harry directly in the eyes. "Langley is your best friend. I want to be more than that with you."

BRANDON – 1965

A week ago, Brandon turned sixteen years old. His father just announced that they would be moving. Almost immediately, Brandon started to freak out. If they moved, then that meant the end of his friendship with Nadia. He wanted so badly for it to be more than just a friendship with Nadia. He was relieved to find out that they weren't moving far, just out of Detroit and into a home in Grosse Pointe. It wasn't a large house by any means, but it was going to be a step up from the apartment they had down the street from the bar.

When the little old lady owner sadly passed a year ago, they had inherited it. The family had helped the lady run the bar, and she was forever grateful. However, had she passed on a year before, they would have probably had to sell it and live off that money for a while. Instead, they were able to keep it open, and Susan was able to run it. Then, his mother became a full-time secretary for *Fitzpatrick Steel Group*. It was a surprise to everyone that the Knight deal actually worked out. However, he couldn't figure out why, but he could tell that Susan never really seemed shocked by the outcome. He felt it best not to ask what that was all about.

They were taking a break from unpacking, and Brandon decided to take a walk. He was actually going to be getting a car within the next few weeks. Seamus insisted on it being a Knight car, even if the rest of the family, including his mother, was still jaded by the Knight's. Other than Delia Knight, that was. She had become a staple at the bar. However, she seldom ordered drinks. It seemed when she did, though, she *really* ordered them. He had also met Clifton Knight a few times, along his girlfriend, Dallas Bolton. They were both seniors now, and he often overheard Delia go on and on about how she didn't really want them to be together. He didn't understand why. Though he really didn't think it was about skin color.

Brandon walked down the block, and of course, he just had to run into a familiar dirty blond boy... "What the hell are you doing walking down this street?" Rodrick Knight asked.

"I didn't know you owned this street..." Brandon rolled his eyes.

"Oh, you are so funny..." Rodrick rolled his eyes.

Brandon had realized that Rodrick wouldn't have heard the good news. "Just so you know, Rodrick... I just moved in down the street. I live in Grosse Pointe, just like you."

The dirty blond boy started to turn a little red. Brandon knew that he had always known the deal had not gone the way his family had intended. Rodrick constantly accused him of stealing from his family. Brandon had no answers for him, though. It made Rodrick look bad, not the other way around, though.

"You live on the poor side of town, Fitzpatrick..."

DELIA – 1965

Delia was supposed to be meeting Susan and Mary at the bar in a little bit. However, she still wanted to spend some time with her husband. Things had been somewhat quiet as of late. Delia walked down the foyer staircase with the intention of finding her husband in the drawing-room. Instead, she heard screaming from the dining room.

"We owe them *how much money* this month?" Heathcliff screamed.

Delia was in complete shock. In the last year, he had started to become frail, and yet he managed to sound even more frightening than usual. She wasn't sure if it was proper of her to go into the dining room, but Delia knew she needed to listen in.

"Well, the contract is up in a few months. Once it is, they will be ruined," Benton explained.

"You moron! We have no choice but to renew with them, and they will expect a better deal than the last," Heathcliff screamed.

Delia decided now was time to step in. She walked into the dining room and nodded. They were still having lunch. Clifton was shockingly still in the room, reading a book.

"Good afternoon."

None of the Knight men acknowledged her. Then someone stormed in through the front door. She heard footsteps as they walked in.

"Why are the Fitzpatricks moving in across town?" Rodrick demanded to know.

Clifton finally looked up. "Why do you care?"

"I care, older brother, because it means property values for the entire town will go down. That white trash shouldn't be allowed to roam the streets wild."

"Oh, will the three of you get over yourselves?" Delia stepped in and said. "The Fitzpatricks have money because you screwed up on a deal almost two years ago now. It's not as if we don't still have money Delia groaned. She was sick of the constant bickering over this. "It's not as if they are opening a car dealership."

Rodrick looked the most offended by what she had said. "They might not be opening up a car company. That doesn't mean they aren't expanding. When I was at the yacht club a few weeks back, I overheard talk of the Fitzpatricks buying a space in a building downtown."

Benton started to rub his forehead. "Great, so now they are opening up office space..."

Heathcliff hit his son over the head. "Why are you a failure?"

Lana walked in with a pitcher of lemonade. "Here you are, Mister Knight."

"We are having a family discussion right now, woman," Benton screamed at her.

"Don't talk to Lana in that tone, boy" Heathcliff screamed at him. "She is the only competent one in this household."

The maid didn't stick around long enough to respond. Clearly, her family was obsessed with hating the Fitzpatricks. She wanted nothing of it.

Delia said, "Well, I'm going out for the afternoon." She would come home after Benton was out drinking to avoid listening to them bicker.

Heathcliff grabbed her hand. "You aren't going to that bar, again, are you?"

She looked back at him. "Well, that really isn't any of your concern."

"It is when you are fraternizing with the enemy." Heathcliff looked at Benton. "You just let your wife act out like this? I thought I raised you better than this. A woman should stand behind her man."

VIVICA – 2018

"I don't understand why you won't give me details of your date night with Cliff," Holly said as she sat down in the kitchen of Vivica's mansion.

Vivica sat a few bags on the table. "I don't kiss and tell, Holly," the redhaired vixen smiled.

"That's a downright lie." Holly sighed.

Last night was honestly the first night since their engagement that Vivica felt like they were in love again. Though, she knew neither of them stopped loving the other.

As the two ate breakfast, there was a knock at the front door. "If only I had a staff member who could open the door for me."

"Well, you let them all go last week," Holly said. " It was nice of you to give them all severance packages since you will be moving into North Pointe again." Holly said as she ate a fruit bowl.

"You just can't take a hint…" Vivica knew that eventually, she would need to have a serious sit-down with Holly. She wanted to continue their friendship as is, but the Knight household already had a full, trained staff Holly was obviously going to be welcomed into the house. It was just that at this point, Vivica knew that Holly didn't need the job. She only stuck it out for Vivica, who would be back to work full-time soon.

The redhead walked out of the kitchen with the maid, following her into the living room. Holly looked down at the coffee table. "Why do you have a copy of *Xanadu* in here?" Vivica rolled her eyes.

"I wanted to have it just in case Harry and I wanted to watch it together," she explained as if it was a practical explanation.

Holly stopped her from going into the foyer. "You bought a lousy movie to possibly watch with your nephew? Why?"

Holly knew exactly why, and yet she still wanted her to say it out loud. "Let's just move on, ok?"

"Vivica, you do realize that just because Harry is gay doesn't mean he is going to be into every stereotype, if any at all, right?"

Yes, Vivica knew this. She just wanted to be as supportive as possible. Tiffany was clearly incapable of accepting her own son. After all, she wasn't even in the picture. Cliff was overly supportive himself, but he was also *Cliff*.

"We will talk about this later. We have to get the door," She reminded her. The two walked into the foyer, and Vivica opened the door. The redhead and her maid looked at one another.

"Hello, Preston…"

"Hi, I was wondering if Langley was home?" Preston explained.

"Long Island isn't home right now. I don't know when she will be back." She was hoping never. Vivica looked at Preston, who wasn't moving. "Is there anything else I can help you with?"

Preston took a deep breath. "Ok, I'm going to level with you. I really want to ask Harry to the back-to-school dance. I just don't know how to go about it." He smiled.

"Aww," Holly said with hearts practically forming in her eyes. Her pay was already being docked for the week. Vivica wasn't even really sure how much she made. There was little to no chance that Vivica was going to help a mob boss's son hurt her precious nephew's heart.

"Harry probably wouldn't be interested in a dance," Holly said. Which was probably the truth.

The mob son sheepishly shrugged. "Yeah, I kind of figured. I just want him to get out of his shell a little. I think going to the dance might not be a bad idea."

If this were any other boy, Vivica would be helping him plan the perfect proposal. This wasn't any other boy, though, and Vivica wasn't about to have her precious nephew going to a dance with that bitch Jackie Costa's son. She then came up with an almost brilliant idea.

"Have you ever heard of a brilliant 80's movie called *Xanadu*?" Holly immediately shot Vivica a dirty look. Vivica just smiled. "It happens to be one of Harry's all-time favorites. The roller disco numbers, the

"You mentioned that twice," Holly said, irritated.

"I'm aware." The redhead stuck her a dirty look. "It's an iconic movie, Holly. Harry watches it like twelve times a day."

Preston looked confused as he continued standing in the doorway. "I don't think I've ever heard of it."

This was almost too perfect. Vivica quickly ran into the living room and grabbed her recently purchased Blu-Ray copy of the movie. Vivica ran back in. "Here, Harry finally wore out his copy. I was going to send give it to him as a back to school present. I'll get him a new copy."

Her maid continued giving her dirty looks. "How is this going to get Harry to go with him to the dance, smart one?" Holly crossed her arms.

How was it? Vivica thought for a moment. "If you act out one of the numbers, Harry will get all emotional and go to the dance with you in a heartbeat. Now, you go home and watch that movie!" She slammed the door on his face. Vivica rolled her eyes at Holly, who was still glowering in the corridor. "I don't want to hear it."

"Vivica, they clearly like one another. Plus, he isn't his parents. I mean, just think, Brad is definitely nothing like you. Hannah and Harry really aren't like Tiffany and Cliff." Holly pointed out.

"Yes, but we have had limited interaction with him. Do you remember when the Costa's used to come over to the Fitzpatrick mansion?" Vivica couldn't stand Nial's insistence for dinner dates with the Costa's... Jackie Costa was a nightmare of a human being. Anthony Costa was at least charming and charitable. She was never going to like the man, but she could tolerate him. It was a mutual toleration. Though now that she was divorced from Nial, all bets were probably off.

HANNAH – 2018

While she was feeling better about herself in general, Hannah still was reluctant about moving forward with Xander. She did think he was a good friend. That didn't mean that he would be a good boyfriend. It would have been one thing, had he not officially dated Hope. He did, though, and that was hard for her to get past.

It also still bothered Hannah that Hope had not made any contact with her since she took the English internship. She never really expected that they would be talking for hours on the phone. It just would have been nice to get a text message once in a blue moon. They were still identical twin sisters.

Then again, Hannah realized that she hadn't heard from her mother in an even-longer time. Tiffany had been living somewhere in Europe since late May. She hadn't contacted anyone. If Hannah was completely honest, this wasn't really that sad to her.

Hannah walked out of her office and locked the door behind her. Usually, she would have kept it open for the janitor to clean, but as of late, with the missing-money scandal, she felt the need to be a little more secure. As she walked down the hall, she noticed her father's door open and decided to step in.

"Hi, Dad. Didn't expect to see you here on a Saturday."

"Well, I always work on Saturday mornings. Not usually from the office, though. I've been trying to track the missing funds. Hannah, could you close the door?" He asked her.

She did and then sat down in a chair by his desk. "Why did you want me to close the door?"

Cliff looked around. "The money is definitely missing. The issue is that the money is being taken out in multiple payments of three thousand dollars. The more digging I did, I discovered that the money started going missing in 1986."

Hannah really didn't know the significance of 1986. "Did something special happen that year?"

The Knight CEO looked guilty. "Several things... Your aunt and I first started officially dating that year, actually. That really has nothing to do with this, though. I actually think that your grandfather must have had something to do with this."

"It would fill in a lot of blanks if he had."

Hannah knew that Rodrick Knight was far from a saint. She remembered what it was like when he had lived with them when she was a toddler. There were no fond memories.

"We can't just halt payment, is the issue. For all we know, your grandfather was keeping one of his many scandals under wraps by using company funds." He explained.

Hannah nodded. "That's understandable. We should probably investigate further. Especially since Grandfather is dead now..." She frowned. "Should I feel bad that I don't have any fond memories of him?"

Cliff rubbed his forehead and sighed. "I don't think I have a single fond memory of the man, myself. He was an egotistical bigot who made everyone else around him miserable. Your Aunt Phyliss made the right choice by getting the hell out of there as soon as she was old enough."

Hannah never really thought about her Aunt Phyliss. Phyliss lived somewhere in the world and was not interested in returning, as far as she knew. "Well, I guess we will look into things."

LANGLEY – 2018

"So, he told you that he wants to spend more time together? Langley was triple checking to make sure that Harry was certain.

"Yes, Langley. We kissed for a long time. He wants to date me." Harry admitted to his closest friend.

That sure sounded nicer than her night. Currently, the two, Langley and Harry, were walking laps in the park together. She felt like she hadn't worked out in months, but Lucy wouldn't give her the money to join a gym. She had been told that Vivica and the Knight's had home gyms, but how was she going to people=watch?

"Well, Brad and I talked a few things out," Langley admitted.

Harry smiled. "I was hoping that would happen."

They had talked things out, and she believed that they would be starting anew. However, she felt still felt reluctant with Brad going forward. More than ever, Brad was probably reluctant with her.

"I want to take things as slowly as possible this time around. If he can't accept certain things about me, then this time might be it."

"I was also hoping that I wouldn't hear that." Harry crossed his arms and stopped walking. "I just like being able to spend time with both of you."

Langley put her hand on his shoulder. "Oh, don't worry even if we do break up, I doubt it will be the end of our friendship." She had to be completely honest with herself. She had never actually spent time with someone after breaking up. However, all of her past relationships had been more sexual than romantic.

"Well, I hope you could hang out as exes, because I don't know how I would pick sides in that," Harry said, almost shaking.

Clearly, he would pick Brad. She would assume, at least. The blonde started to doublethink this relationship for a second. Harry was more important to both of them than a high school fling. The fact was that she couldn't really picture a world where

Vivica would allow her nephew to choose her side over Brad's in a breakup. Though, she didn't really see there being pettiness, then again, she could very much see pettiness coming just from Vivica alone.

"Why on Earth is everything in the Midwest so over-complicated?" She screamed.

The curly-haired boy looked at his friend, a little concerned. "I don't know what you mean."

She shook her head with annoyance. "I'm going to need to speak with Brad." She started to walk off. "I'll talk with you later..."

***

The blonde girl sat outside of the boy's locker room at Saint Agnes for several hours. Langley knew everything she was going to say and understood every counterargument that Brad could use. The blond boy finally walked out. He smiled when he saw her.

She stood up and put her fingers to his lips. "We need to talk."

"Ok, what about?" Brad asked her.

"I like you both as a person and sexually. I think it is clear you think the same about me. We've talked about it enough, obviously. That all being said, I think we both love someone more." Langley explained.

Brad looked at her like she was nuts. "I don't know what you are talking about."

He was so smart and yet so dumb. "Obviously, I mean Harry. He isn't emotionally stable enough to handle whatever breakup we could potentially have. It was one thing when I was just lusting after you. It's different now. I don't want to break up, but we are in different places emotionally."

He stayed quiet for a whole minute. Langley wasn't even sure he was breathing. "Are we breaking up?" He asked, annoyed.

"Please, don't be mad. I'm not breaking up because I'm mad at you. I do like you a lot. More than I think you realize. However, Harry's friendship bizarrely means more to me right now. It's not even officially Fall yet. Let's be realistic here; if we stay together, we will be in a different fight every month for the next year. Which might work perfectly for us, but during that off time, it will be a strain on Harry."

"I understand what you are saying, but at the time, Langley... I just don't want to lose you." Brad sighed. "I thought we worked all this out last night."

They had, and that was why this made all the more sense. "This isn't goodbye. I'm not calling it a break, but I do think we will find our way back to one another eventually. Right, now we will work best as best friends to a boy who needs us." Langley smiled. She kissed him on the cheek. "Now, how about you drive us home. I have been walking all morning."

"What if I'm not ready to say goodbye once we do go home?" Brad asked her.

The Kingsley daughter smiled. "Who said anything about saying goodbye? We never really took enough time to get to know one another as people. It was always about what was best for Harry and sexually. Now come on, let's go home." She needed to cry in private.

MARGOT – 2018

"Are you done being an idiot?" She asked her younger brother on the phone. "Well, lct mc know when you are, and you better come home a single man. A single man, Nial!" She screamed as she hung up her phone.

She sat on the back patio and looked out at Lake Saint Clair. Her family was full of morons, and she was beginning to realize that the only sane ones were her and her nephew, Brad. Margot supposed that Perry wasn't a complete failure, but she wasn't going to tell him that. The last thing she needed was for him to think she was going soft.

The back door opened and out walked Lucy. The blonde girl smiled as she sat down. Margot had no idea why she was here. "Hello, Margot."

It only took a moment to realize what was going on. "I'll give you a job but know that I'm not going to treat you any better just because my son is fucking you. Also, keep in mind I actually might like you a little better, so if you break up, don't be shocked if I choose your side." She got on her tablet for a minute. "I might have one fit for you, but it is a step-down from what you are used to."

"I've worked for a woman whose secondary education consisted of the gay ballroom scene of the early '90s in New York City," Lucy said. Then, she shook her head. "That's not why I'm here. Perry wanted to have lunch, and your maid must have gotten confused."

Margot knew her son. This was not a mistake. He purposely had her sent out here. "Back in the '90s, my mother wanted to open a hotel. She did, and then she got sidetracked when her arch-nemesis came to town. It's been a revolving door of managers since then. The Fitzpatrick Group still owns it. It functions; it just isn't anything special. It could be with the right person running it, though."

Lucy rubbed her forehead. "No, really I'm happy with working for Vivica right now." Margot could tell very easily she was lying.

"Word on the street is that Vivica and you have everything you need except a staff and a chemist or two. Unfortunately, I've known your aunt since she was a child. She is never going to agree on a chemist, and unless she forces her maid to go back to college, I doubt she ever will. There is only one person she will ever hire, and she isn't allowed to." Margot knew how Vivica operated. Cliff was the love of her life, but Vivica was addicted to Luke. When it came to Nial, that was a sad story on its own. He was the one who had always been into her... He would just always catch her at her lowest, which happened often.

"I'm sure I'll find a chemist that she will approve of," Lucy said, not sure of herself. "Plus, it has been almost six years since I worked in the hotel game."

The CEO scoffed. "I swear, this town is obsessed with the last five years. Can we just move on? I would certainly like it, too. Having to deal with Vivica and Nial on the regular was not a highlight of my life."

In general, people loved to reminisce about the past. She had people stop meetings just to talk about the time her parents saved the world from being flooded. Or her parents' wedding. Just basically anything to do with her family. Apparently, her own achievements meant nothing when Nadia and Brandon or Nial and Vivica also existed… It was probably all for the best, considering some of her past relationships, but even so.

Margot wrote down a number on a piece of paper and handed it to Lucy. "It's probably less than you are used to."

Lucy looked at the paper, clearly reluctantly. Margot would never know what sort of spell Vivica held over people. "Good lord." Lucy looked shocked at Margot. "This is… Wow."

"I'll give you a few days to consider," Margaux told her.

The blonde stood up from the table. "I need to go to the restroom…." She walked away while Perry walked out.

The son sat down across from his mother. "Why does she look so dazed? Mother, what did you do?"

The redhead sighed. "Exactly what you wanted. I offered her a job."

Perry looked at her in complete confusion. "I never asked you to offer her a job."

"You've been hinting at it for a few weeks now. I don't have time for games. If she wants the job, then it is hers for the taking. If she doesn't, though, then I'm done dealing with her." Margot knew that it wouldn't be the end of her relationship with Lucy.

The backdoor opened again. This time it was a very short woman who looked like she had escaped her coffin. "I let myself in. I was in the area." Mrs. Templeton explained.

Margot rubbed her forehead. "What were you doing in the area exactly?"

"I like to spy on the Costa family. One of these days, I'm going to find proof to get them locked away." Mrs. Templeton took a sip from Margot's own glass.

Mrs. Templeton- this was a woman who had a portrait of Hitler above her fireplace mantle. She claimed it was a picture of her father. "You realize that the Costa family has armed guards on their property, right?"

Mrs. Templeton smiled and nodded. "Bulletproof vest." She lifted up her shirt. "Unfortunately, I didn't see anything, though. Their fairy was roller skating to Oliva Newton-John on the backyard, though."

The mother and son both looked at one another. "Fairy?" Perry asked her.

"Oh, right political correctness." Mrs. Templeton giggled, and then she exhaled. "Their homo son. I bet he has a Cher record somewhere."

"I have a Cher record somewhere," Margot said.

Mrs. Templeton nodded. "I don't care much for the Armenians."

Lucy walked back out and over to the table. She sat down.

"Oh, hello, Mrs. Templeton."

"What is your opinion on the Armenians?" The old bat asked.

HARRY – 2018

The curly-haired teen sat down on the couch in the drawing-room at North Pointe. "What do you mean, you guys are breaking up?" He looked at Langley. "I thought you said you were all right now, Langley?"

Langley looked at Harry, clearly sad. "Well, we are all right. We are going to remain friends. We will still probably see one another just as much."

"Did I do this?" Harry asked. He couldn't believe that his best friend was breaking up with his cousin. Harry knew that this had to have something to do with him. "Please tell me this had nothing to do with me?"

Brad sat down next to him. "Look, man, everything will be fine."

Everything would be fine? He knew that wasn't going to be the case. "You guys seemed so happy."

"It isn't that we aren't happy, Harry. It's just that we don't make much sense as a couple." Langley admitted.

That wasn't how he saw it, though. In Harry's mind, they were one of the best couples. Yes, he knew they hadn't been together that long, but they made sense. At least in his mind, they did.

"Who will you go to the dance with?" Harry asked.

Langley looked at Brad and then sat down on the coffee table. "Um, well... Did Preston ask you?"

The curly-haired boys' eyes widened. "I don't think we are allowed to go to a school dance..." He whispered.

His cousin took a deep breath. "Look, if Preston asks you to the dance, then I will make sure that you get to go to the dance."

Harry took offense. "What if I wanted to be the one who asked Preston to the dance?"

"Harry, I love you more than anything, but for fuck, sake don't make me answer that," Brad said, now rubbing his forehead.

"So, there is no chance you two are getting back together?"

"I suppose we could talk about it at some point. I just don't think it will be until we've really explored ourselves and each other, though." Langley admitted.

This would be so hard for him. Harry knew that he would have to accept that his cousin and best friend were no longer going to be a couple. The home phone rang as he processed this. No one seemed to be answering it.

Harry got up reluctantly and went to explain it. "Hello?" He could clearly hear heavy breathing, but no one was answering. "Hello?" The door opened, and Cliff walked in. "Dad, someone's on the phone, but they aren't saying anything."

Cliff took the phone. "Hello? Who is this? Is this Nial? Whoever you are, don't call again." Cliff looked over at Brad. "No offense..."

"That was weird," Brad said as he looked at Langley. "I have to get going to Study Group..." Brad waved goodbye to her and left.

Langley walked over to Harry. "You two are acting like you have never received a creepy phone call. We used to get them all the time. Sometimes they were men obsessed with me. Sometimes, women who were obsessed with my father. Other times it was the FBI trying to catch my father laundering money... The options are limitless." She smiled and nodded her head as if this was normal.

His father hung up the phone. "We should be fine." He left the room without saying anything further.

Harry turned to his best friend. "What on Earth happened between this morning and this afternoon?"

Langley raised her shoulders. "I don't know. I guess I just thought about it for another minute. Harry, I like Brad a lot, and I think he likes me. I just don't think we like one another in the *same* way. And I don't know if we ever will."

"You could try." Harry pointed out.

"We have been trying for a while. It's not that easy. I do love him but not in that way. I think he was under the impression that I did. Yet, he wanted me to be something else- I don't even know what. It clearly wasn't his mother. Which then again, that was essentially exactly what he wanted." Langley sat back down this time near the front window. "I guess I'm not going to the dance."

The young Knight walked over to the window. "You've been looking forward to this for a while, I thought?"

Langley thought for a second. "I've been to so many dances, galas, and events that some middle American high school dance is something I can afford to miss."

"You could just go by yourself," Harry stated.

"I could also start wearing crocks and eating snack cakes at *Saks.*"

BRANDON – 1965

"You just need to leave him be," Nadia said as she rubbed his shoulders. "Rodrick is not capable of being a good person."

It wasn't that Brandon didn't realize this. It was that Brandon was sick of dealing with it on an almost daily basis. At one point, he tried to get his parents to let him transfer to a public school. They refused on the grounds that now that they had a little money, it would be foolish. Plus, if he were being honest, he would miss Nadia.

Neither of them had really discussed what they were to one another. It was clear they were more than friends, but they both seemed to be fine with not defining it as of yet. Everyone around them was a different story. His parents insisted that they were dating. Nadia's mother and grandmother insisted the same. Even Lana's semi-boyfriend himself, David Brash, seemed to agree, which was kind of hypocritical because neither of them would admit that they were dating themselves. This was what worked for them right now, and they were fine. It wasn't as if they were sleeping together. Though as time went on, Brandon had to admit he thought about it a lot.

Nadia brushed up against him as she fixed her apron. "Now, if you don't mind, I have to get ready for my shift," Nadia said as she walked out into the bar. She was a busboy working for Fitzpatricks and Susan.

Brandon followed her out. "So, what are you doing after work?"

"Probably studying. Which you should be too. I saw your grades. If we both want to get into U of M together, you have to improve." Nadia explained.

A few years ago, Brandon would have agreed. He had to admit, though, that his father had discussed just starting him out at the company instead. He would make enough, and he would still be living at home. The only issue was that he would be far away from Nadia. He wouldn't like that. "I think we need to discuss our future plans a little bit."

The Latina teen got into his face. "Brandon Fitzpatrick, you are going to college, whether you want to or not. A stroke of luck hit your family. Luck that can change any minute."

It wasn't that she wasn't right. It was that she could be even more of a nag than his own mother sometimes. "When does your shift get off tonight?"

"I'm probably closing tonight. I could use the money for a few things." Nadia told him.

"If you need a little extra money, I could always loan it to you," Brandon suggested.

Nadia gave him a look like he already knew what her answer would be. "I don't take handouts. You know that very well."

He was aware, but it didn't change anything. He would have given her the money. He knew it was for things like clothes and records she wanted. Brandon was well-aware that things were tight in the Bloom household. "Well, fine, you have some fun cleaning dishes. I'm going to go catch a late show at the Fox."

"That place is a dump..." Nadia told him.

"While that might be true, you are only saying it because you want to come along." Brandon pointed out.

She crossed her arms. "I made a commitment to your sister. I intend on keeping it."

Susan walked over as the two were talking. "Brandon, let Nadia get some work done, please." She said as she took out a rag and started to wipe down the counter herself.

The younger brother looked at his sister with wide eyes. "Would it be alright if I took Nadia to the movies tonight?"

"Well, if she can get her work done, I don't mind." Susan grabbed a box from behind the counter and walked into the back.

Nadia looked at Brandon. "We can go to the movie, but don't think you are off the hook with anything."

VIVICA – 2018

Sitting in the drawing room of North Pointe, Vivica looked at her tablet. She was looking through applications for a chemist as well as for a few other employees. Lucy was supposed to be helping, but she was out doing something, and Vivica was left in the dark about whatever it was.

It was becoming more and more obvious that the chemist wasn't going to be needed. Lucy would be lost to her sooner rather than later...

The door opened, and Cliff walked in. He looked at her, a little startled. "I didn't realize you were in here."

"I needed a scene change from my house," Vivica explained. "I feel like I spend the entire day in it lately. I don't have any furniture at the office yet, so I decided to come here. I hope you don't mind."

Cliff sat down next to her and kissed her on the cheek. "Not at all. This will be your house again soon."

She looked at her tablet and slammed it shut. "I think my cosmetic company is a pipe dream."

The Knight man nodded. "Well, I can help you if you need it."

She gave him a look. "You know nothing about cosmetics. I only know how to sell them with my face..." The only reason she had been in the cosmetic game the first time around was because Nial wanted her to work and gave her a cushy business venture. The same had been the case during her event-planning business for the last five years. It gave

Vivica a stake within the company, which annoyed Margot to no end as well. Nial seemed to think that stock in the Fitzpatrick family fortune equaled to a suitable wedding gift...

"If you don't want to work, you don't have to. I mean, I want you to be active. Not just a bored housewife. Unless that is what you want." Cliff explained to her.

Vivica had never just been a housewife. The closest probably would have been her fake marriage to Cliff, where she raised the children. However, she loved every minute of it. It wouldn't be the same though, this time. Brad and Harry were teenagers, the twins and Laura were all grown, and she very much doubted that another child was on the horizon.

"I have to do something." There was a knock on the door. "Come in." Vivica said.

It was Lucy. "Oh, hi, dear."

Cliff looked at the two women. "I will see you in a little bit," Cliff explained to Vivica.

Lucy sat down before Vivica could say anything. "I ran into Margot today... Vivica, we need to talk for a moment."

The redhead took a sigh. "You don't want to open the cosmetic company with me anymore, do you?"

"It's not that I don't want to work with you. It's that we are way in over our heads. We don't have a proper chemist, we don't have a business model, and your idea for a launch is unrealistic unless you plan on getting married in a year and a half." Lucy told her boss.

That, for sure, wasn't going to happen. She wanted to marry Cliff right away. Vivica had spent far too many years not being Mrs. Clifton Knight. That wouldn't be the case for much longer.

"Well, when would we ever even see one another?" Vivica asked.

Lucy continued, "Margot offered me a job running a hotel that the Fitzpatrick's own. Do you have a location for the wedding yet?"

"Well, not yet. I guess I could have the wedding there. Then you could help me plan it. It would be just like old times." Vivica thought out loud.

Lucy's smile fell quickly. "Just like old times..." She put a smile back on. "We will always be friends, and I'm eternally grateful for all you have done for myself and my brother and sister."

The redhaired vixen thought for a moment. "Oh, my goodness, I almost forgot!" She stood up. "Lucy, I have a house for you all to live in."

The blonde girl looked at Vivica in confusion. "Please, tell me you didn't buy me a house."

"Sort of- kind of. Obviously, I knew you would refuse to live there for free. So, I will be your landlord. The best part is that it is the old Martin house where you used to live." Vivica smiled.

"The house that my ex-fiancé died in?" The Kingsley girl asked.

Vivica sighed. "I swear... If we were to go through every house on this block alone, you wouldn't find one where a death didn't take place. Plus, it has been redone, and we obviously will get new furniture. Or you can take furniture from my house. I won't be needing it for much longer, and there are so many rooms I don't even go into in that house."

Vivica didn't even know what would become of her house. She wasn't allowed to sell it because Luke owned part of it with her. She really didn't see him moving back to Grosse Pointe. The only reason that Luke Knight ever moved to Grosse Pointe was because Delia had begged to spend time with her grandson. He had spent most of his life isolated from his family, aside from his parents. When he moved to town, at first, Cliff and Luke had been close. They had spent several summers together in their teens. The most prominent one in Vivica's mind was the first summer where they were officially a couple. Luke had heard many stories about her and all their friends. He clearly used his knowledge of her as a way to get into his life. It had worked well.

Luke was a charmer. So, was Cliff though. They were alike in many ways but also completely different in many others. Luke had the benefit of being raised in a country with a completely different view on things. Whereas Cliff had been raised in conservative Grosse Pointe during the Reagan era where everyone turned red, regardless of financial views. Vivica blamed *Dynasty*. Though she also loved *Dynasty,* so she easily forgave it.

"So, do you want to live in the house?" Vivica asked. "I mean, I have no issue with you continuing to live in my house. I just figured that you would prefer something that you were financially responsible for. I know you have crazy views on things like that." She never understood why Lucy was so dependent on being independent. It really made no sense.

It took a minute or so for Lucy to speak... "Well, yes, but I expect you to treat me like any other tenant."

The redhead smiled. "That's fine with me. Just don't expect me to fix any leaky roofs. That's what Holly is for. That maid is about to do even less than she did before with the North Pointe staff at her leisure."

LANGLEY — 2018

Watching Harry get asked to the dance in the most ridiculous and over the top way possible was making Langley think. She wanted a man like that. She wondered if Brad was still that man. Clearly, he would never have done something like Preston had done for Harry, though. Brad might have been extremely liberal in terms of politics, but he was extremely conservative and reserved otherwise.

Why couldn't things have been simple? She just broke things off with Brad. She did. Not him. Her. *Stupid girl,* she thought to herself. The Kingsley daughter sighed. This was the most complicated relationship she had ever been in. After years of not really being interested in men aside from just having fun with them, she slowly started to turn into this bubbly romantic with Brad. It made her sick. She blamed Brad as well for this. Langley knew, though, that it was her own fault.

All Langley wanted to do was go and talk with Brad, but he was still in the gym. She was in a study period where she was locked in the library with Harry.

She turned to him. "I've made an awful mistake…"

"Why what happened?" Harry asked.

"I thought that breaking up with Brad was the right thing to do. But I'm not entirely sure that it was, though." Langley sighed.

The curly-haired Knight boy looked at her with a blank face. "I can't keep up with this anymore. So, now you want

Brad? How many times do you possibly plan on changing your mind on this subject?"

At least four times a day, if she could help it. This was a matter of love. She always knew one day she would get married, but she honestly never thought about having to actually date someone. Langley had no idea if Brad was going to be the man that she would marry. However, she knew that he was the man who was going to prepare her for whatever love was.

She started to smack her forehead with a book. "Why can't I stop thinking about your idiot cousin? Your idiotic but brilliant cousin..."

"Maybe take a deep breath because people are starting to look at you funny..." Harry pointed out. "Look, at the end of the day, I obviously want you two together. However, I'm just trying to accept the fact that you won't be together. If I have to keep accepting that you will keep getting back together only to break up every five minutes, my head might explode."

He had a point. She knew he was right. It was starting to make her own head explode. "Do you have any Xanax on you? I feel like I'm going to have an anxiety attack."

Her friend gave her a dirty look. "I only take that in emergencies."

"It's probably for the best. I'm already on like four different pills."

"You mean medications?"

"No, I mean pills. Medication is something that is prescribed to you by a doctor. Pills are something prescribed by me and the internet. How else would I stay so focused?" Though in hindsight, she realized that they clearly weren't working for her now. She couldn't stay focused to save her life. Once again, she started to smack herself with a book.

Harry quickly yanked the book out of her hand. "If you don't stop this right now, I'm going to need my medication." The two looked at each other as they both thought about the magic that came from a prescription pad.

Langley quickly shook her head, trying to change the subject. "So, what have you and Preston spoke about since he asked you to the dance?"

"Just normal stuff, I suppose. He wants me to formally meet his parents."

"*Formally meet his parents*. What does that even mean?"

He shrugged. "I've met Anthony and Jackie Costa before, in passing. My parents and aunt have always tried to rush us along, though, whenever the Costa family was near in the past."

It was hard for Langley to understand why the whole town hated the Costas so much. Maybe it was because she grew up around the New York mob scene? Her father's business with them had really desensitized her to it. She had never been around when anyone was being shot; however, there were days in which certain people were there, and then all of a sudden, they were never seen again.

"I wonder if Preston or his family know any of the New York mob?"

"I doubt they would tell you if they did. What kind of mobster actually comes out and says what they do for a living?" Harry reminded her.

This was very true. "I could come with you if you want." She was sensing hesitation in his response.

"Well, maybe. I mean, Preston hasn't even mentioned when he wants me to meet them. Just that he wants me to meet them."

"So, has your father picked a wedding date for him and the bitchy redhead that doesn't like me?" Langley asked, deciding to change the subject away from their love lives.

"I'm not entirely sure. I know they want to rush things, but my aunt was going to start a cosmetic company. Now she isn't. It almost is as if she was trying to give herself something to do to remain relevant." Harry said.

HARRY — 2018

Langley kept rambling on about different things that were on her mind. It was weird to have a friend who talked so much about herself, and yet actually wanted to hear his opinion. Not only hear his opinion, but also expect him to talk about himself. Harry's life was forever changed by a girl whose only claim to fame was not getting arrested on Spring Break one time when she was thirteen, and he loved it.

Preston had been texting him all morning. It was weird to be getting text messages from a boy, without feeling threatened at the same time. He just wanted the school to be over for the day so he could go and do nothing, alone in his room. He, for some reason, missed that. However, Harry knew that part of his life was over.

Preston wanted him to watch his football practice. Which meant that Langley would tag along and *spy* on Brad in plain sight. Which Harry had no issue with, he just wished that she wouldn't ask him if Brad had seen her or not. After all, she was extremely loud and abrasive when needed.

"Earth to Harry Knight!" Langley whisper-screamed at her friend. "What did you get for the math homework?"

The curly-haired boy shot up in shock. "Sorry, I had something else on my mind."

Langley laughed. "Well, of course you did. You always have something else on your mind!" She pointed out.

She was correct. Harry hated to admit this. He couldn't get Preston Costa off his mind. Preston Costa, with his amazing eyes and perfect body. Preston Costa, who was always so nice to him for no reason and yet every reason. This boy liked him. He liked him back. Harry needed to get out of his mind...

"Right, the homework. Well, I actually had trouble with it."

"Math is your favorite subject. How on Earth did you have trouble with it?" Langley inquired.

"I was up all night texting with Preston again."

"You need to learn how to prioritize.," Langley pointed out to him.

He didn't know how to prioritize Preston, though. Harry had always been so good about prioritizing up until now. "Sometimes, I wonder how my aunt prioritized the men in her life."

Langley rolled her eyes. "Not very well. I mean, look at how she treated your father."

His father? "My dad actually probably treated her worse. I don't actually know the reason why they didn't just get married in the first place. I suppose it is technically a good thing they didn't. I wouldn't have existed, and Brad wouldn't have, either."

"Well, you don't know for sure. I mean suppose a universe where you were a redhead and Brad had curly Knight hair. Brad would look good with curly Knight hair." Langley started to daydream.

Somehow Harry doubted that would be the case. On top of that, Harry still had the redhead gene...

MARGOT – 2018

After months of waiting, it was finally happening. Margot was finally getting around to painting the mansion the color that she actually wanted it to be. This was decades in the making. The drab blue walls felt so dated at this point. A coral green color would work so much better with her overall mood. She had informed her parents of the change, and they were not happy. Brandon Fitzpatrick had helped paint many of the rooms in the home himself. Margot didn't really give much of a damn. The Fitzpatrick mansion was finally hers after years of when the Whore from Beverly Hills walked in and out of the family home. If Vivica wanted to change the curtains, then Vivica would totally get her way. When Margot tried to change the toilet paper brand, she was ridiculed to the high end.

Perry walked downstairs. "Mother, why are there people painting?"

"Didn't you get my memo? I'm redoing the house," Margot explained. "The new furniture will be here tomorrow. I found a place that would torch Nial and Vivica's mattress. I thought we could roast a pig or something. Misses Templeton loves a good pig roast…"

Her son rolled his eyes. "Grandpa and Grandma are going to kill you when they see this." He crossed his arms.

Nadia and Brandon wouldn't even let her paint her room when she was a teenager. Margot had been stuck with a pink room up until she was in her twenties. It was beyond pathetic, in her mind. She had never even liked pink all that much.

"Mother and Father can complain all they want. This house will be mine one day."

"That's extremely morbid." Perry pointed out.

"It's not like I'm wishing them dead. I'm just being realistic." Margot pointed out.

There was a knock at the front door. Perry walked over himself to get it. "Oh, hi, come on in."

Lucy walked in. Margot was unsure if she liked the Kingsley girl with her son. It was nothing against Lucy. Margot saw a lot of herself in the girl. It was the fact that she saw a lot of her father in Perry. That wasn't a good thing in her mind. Though it was at least a small blessing that Perry wasn't anything like his own father. "Hello, Lucy." "Hi, Margot. Thank you for meeting with me so early in the morning."

She looked nervous. Margot already knew why she wanted to meet. She had just given her the deal of a lifetime. A deal that she had made her work for. If she had handed it to her five years ago, then it could have been a disaster. Margot was not about to get involved with a Vivica 2.0.

"I hope I'm not too early for you."

Margot laughed. "I'm up at four every day regardless. I really don't believe in sleep, and neither should you or anyone."

"So, why did I have a bedtime growing up?" Perry asked.

The mother looked at her son. "I needed a break from you." She walked over to Lucy. "Now I was thinking that we could go over to the hotel later today. We will get you started right away, of course. There are a few contracts you must sign, of course. The most important one being that you won't be able to work with Vivica anymore."

The eldest Kingsley child looked at her new boss and looked taken aback. Margot knew this would be an issue for

Lucy. Margot knew better, though. If that slimy redhaired tramp got involved, then all of this would just be a lost cause.

"It isn't like Vivica had any intention of working at a hotel." Margot reminded her.

"Well, I suppose you are correct. I'm just thinking about in the long run. Would it be a contract stating I couldn't work with Vivica at the hotel? Or a contract stating that I couldn't work with her on any project in the future in general?" Lucy inquired.

"In general. It's for your own good." Margot insisted.

Perry grabbed Lucy's hand. "Mother, we are going to go into the library and read over the contracts a little. We will meet you at the hotel in an hour or so."

Margot shrugged. "Well, all right. Just remember that this is the best deal on the table for you right now. It's either that or you go work with your con artist father."

Lucy turned to Perry and looked at him in horror. She then turned back to Margot. "How did you know about that?" She asked.

"I know everything. Do you think that I wouldn't look into an employee in the upper management of one of my businesses? It was a simple background check." It might have sounded harsh, but any other company would have done the same rightfully so.

LUCY– 2018

This was just never going to get any easier. Lucy should have known better than to think that this would be easy. She sunk into the armchair of the Fitzpatrick Mansion. She had fallen into the chair so many times over the years, and each time was out of being distraught over something that Vivica had done. This time it was the slightly older redhead's doing.

"Well, I guess it does make sense that she would look into my background. I just, I don't know... I feel like she knew enough about me already."

Perry rubbed his forehead. "I mean honestly, she still has her PI check up on me from time to time. She really needs to outsource the position. It's difficult to investigate privately when I know exactly what he looks like."

"Why does she have a person check up on you every so often?" Lucy didn't even think that made sense.

"I'm her son, and she is crazy. That's honestly the only answer I can give you. I mean, I get the feeling that your father probably checked up on you every so often," he pointed out.

Lucy supposed that he wasn't wrong. In some ways, she kind of hoped that Perry was right. The concept of her father caring enough to have someone check up on her sounded like a wonderful notion. The only issue that she had was it sounded loving and caring as a child and teenager. As an adult, it sounded creepy. Lucy also had the issue of realizing that if someone was checking up on her, it was probably a mob boss. Which honestly still sounded appealing to her.

"I suppose I'm just worried about the idea that Langley or Xander might find out about my meeting with our father."

"Do you find it at all odd that Xander was never contacted by your father?" Perry inquired.

It really wasn't that shocking to her, if she was being honest. Langley knew that in her father's mind, Xander was the future police officer. She, on the other hand, was the righthand eldest child. This was what worried her when it came to Langley. Her father could easily influence Langley if he were to return to her life.

"I doubt very much that he even looked into Xander."

The redhaired boy flipped through the contact. "I mean, based on what the person in the position was paid before you, I think this is a beyond generous deal, considering my mother underpays the maids."

"Is that really a smart thing to say when the maids could be listening in?" Lucy wondered.

"The maids are just happy that Vivica's maid is finally gone. Was Holly really that bad?" Perry asked.

Lucy laughed hysterically... She really didn't know why she found the question so funny. "Well, yes and no. She kept Vivica from going completely overboard. However, I don't think I ever saw her clean anything, other than maybe dust a table or something. I'm sure there is a wall or two that is extra-clean in comparison to the rest of the house outside of Vivica and Nial's old bedroom."

"Considering the fact that Mother is repainting, all that cleaning might have gone to waste." Perry smiled.

Lucy loved his smile so much. It was so calming and just made her feel warm inside. Could she really see herself with someone like Perry? A man who was from a different part of the same world? Austin was middle class all the way, and that was the main turn-on for her: he was a man who was outside of her own world. Yet, Austin had been a cheater and liar. He betrayed her constantly.

Vivica had once made a comment about how it was impossible not to fall for a Fitzpatrick man. They had the best eyes and the best bodies. Lucy couldn't fault Langley for falling for Brad. She could fault her for falling for Vivica's son, though.

It just hit her... Vivica was no longer going to be her boss or business partner or whatever it was they were to one another. Would they just be friends? That was all right with Lucy. They could be good friends. Lucy guessed that Vivica would be her landlord. Which was fine, she supposed. Lucy already knew that Vivica wasn't going to fix a leaky faucet.

Percy kept talking. "I'd personally demand another two grand and talk it down to another solid grand. It might sound like a nerve-wracking idea. However, it's Margot..."

"All right. I feel confident with this." Lucy sighed.

SUSAN – 1965

Running a bar had never crossed her mind when Susan was younger. She always just assumed that she would be a secretary or teacher. Housewife clearly was out of the question, even if her parents now more than ever were up her ass about it. In their mind, now that they had a little bit of money, that meant that Susan could start looking for a man. It was obnoxious how her life only became important to her parents now that they had finally succeeded in a fever dream. Something that *she* was responsible for getting them. Which she probably would never be able to tell them.

Susan often wondered what her life would be like as she got older. Would she ever have children? Or find someone that she wanted to spend the rest of her life with?

She had found someone. She had found two people. Two best friends that she would have the rest of her life, she was sure of that. It was funny how throughout school, the concept of a best friend was something that was so important to children. Yet, most of those friends were gone by the time they graduated high school. It wasn't even as if the people she graduated had left the area. They all just sort of drifted further apart as the years went on. A lot of them left the Saint Agnes Parish, and many were starting to explore different faiths altogether. Susan herself never thought of the concept.

She turned to Sister Mary Newman, who was enjoying an iced tea at the bar. "Do you ever doubt your faith?"

"Oh, every day," Mary said right away.

The strawberry blonde was taken back by the quick and shocking response. "Really? I never thought that you would have any issues with God or the church."

Mary nodded. "Well, my faith in God never really goes away, I suppose. It's more or less my faith in how the world works. I mean, you look at the people in this town for instance..."

"They aren't that bad. Grosse Pointe is definitely a little snootier, but the same sort of people could be found anywhere. Even in a rougher area."

Susan believed this to be true. She had grown up on the outskirts of Grosse Pointe in Detroit. The people she met in the city really were not any better or worse.

"Well, yes, you can find the same people all over. It's more or less the kind of people that I get to deal with on a daily basis. Rodrick Knight somehow continues to be placed in classes that I teach. He continues to misbehave the older he gets. One would assume that he would have requested to be moved out of my classes by now." Mary said.

Mary might have been the only person that Susan knew who disliked the Knights more than she did. Actually, Delia disliked them more than both of them combined. Delia's hatred for her own family name was both amusing and sad at the same time.

"Is Delia joining us for dinner today?"

"I'm not entirely sure. She might have to have dinner with her wonderful son..." Mary rolled her eyes. Clearly, not the average nun.

"Well, at least Clifton seems normal. Plus, Brandon says that Heathcliff is apparently very nice and understanding towards the Bloom family. Though he hates Delia. And he also tried to destroy my family. So, there is that as well."

Susan guessed that certain people in this town really were that bad. The Knights were not the picture-perfect family that they displayed in their publicity adds.

"Do you remember those adds from when you were a child when Heathcliff, his late wife, Benton, and the daughter would be sitting by the fireplace?"

Mary looked at her, confused. "Vaguely, but yes."

"It's just so weird to think that we actually interact with them to some degree. I mean, you know what I mean."

After all, the Knight family that seemed so unhuman in those old ads seemed even less human in reality. Benton and Delia loved each other only on days that didn't end with Y. The two sons hated their parents. Heathcliff had become famous for his *welcoming to all* attitude over the years and yet still hated most minorities, it seemed, which also included most women.

As the two women were deep in thought, another voice joined the conversation. "I need a refill on my gin!" Mrs. Templeton screamed.

"I just poured you half a bottle worth..." Susan said in shock.

The old bat gave her a dirty look. "It tasted watered-down. When are you assholes going to start selling Templeton ice cream? I gave you a good deal." She said with a straight face.

Templeton ice cream was probably the most disgusting brand on the U.S. market. If not the global market.

"We are having issues our distributor and are waiting on getting some more," Susan lied.

"Well, I can easily fix that for you. We don't sell chocolate, though. I don't trust or have faith in dark things." Templeton explained. She coughed. "I need to go use the shitter." She excused herself and walked towards the men's room but quickly went into the lady's room, swiveling around, confused.

Sister Mary Newman cleared her throat. "And that is why I have no faith in humanity."

CLIFF – 2018

Hannah was not letting up on the money. It wasn't that Cliff was against the idea of looking into this lost revenue. It was the fact that it most definitely had something to do with Rodrick and some sort of payoff to someone. A payoff that could end up hurting the company, family, and who even knows?

The one thing that Cliff did wonder, though, was why something that probably involved his father was only just now coming to the surface. Why was his daughter the only one who was discovering it? Back when Cliff took over as CEO, he had a team of private investigators dig into every corner of the company to get his father's dirty doings out of the way.

Cliff closed his laptop and sighed. Someone had knocked on his home office door. "Come in."

Harry walked in, holding two shirts. "I need your advice. Which one should I wear?" He asked.

Cliff's son had never come to him for clothing advice. It honestly was a weird feeling. "Wouldn't your aunt or Langley be better options?"

Harry sighed. "Langley keeps shifting between going to the dance with Brad and going into hiding. Aunt Vivica hates Preston, so she would probably tell me to dress in bellbottoms or something."

"What makes you think that your aunt has an issue with Preston?" Cliff asked. Aside from her tricking him into doing a roller disco number... "She just has an issue with Anthony and Jackie. They aren't exactly..."

His son sighed. "I know the rumors."

Cliff wasn't entirely sure what to say. "Well, yes, rumors. Harry, those rumors might have some truth to them."

"I'm already aware, Dad," Harry explained. He sat down across from him. "Are you ok with me seeing Preston?"

No. Cliff would rather Harry be with a forty-five-year-old leather Daddy... Ok, maybe not that. He wanted Harry to have a non-controversial man his own age.

"I just want you to be safe." He realized how cringe-worthy that sounded, coming from him. "You aren't five years old, anymore. You must hear the rumors going around town about the Costa family. I'd say at least half of them have some truth to them."

Harry nodded. "Well, I have to be honest with you. I'm not as freaked out as I should be."

It took Cliff a moment to process this. For whatever reason, Preston Costa did not make Harry's anxiety flare up. At least, not in the ways that it would have a few months ago.

Cliff sighed. "I'm happy for you, Harry. Your aunt is happy for you. Or at least she will be- once she takes a moment to realize how happy you are."

"Why do I have trouble believing that?" Harry murmured.

Cliff stood up. "Let's put it this way; your aunt loves you. If things work out between you and Preston, she is bound to fall for him at some point. Then, she will understand about your feelings for him."

Honestly, Cliff was semi-lying. He wanted to point out that who cared about all the issues that Vivica might have with Preston? After all, Harry's own mother, Tiffany, would have an all-out tantrum that would never end.

Lately, Cliff had been asking himself the same questions over and over again. Why on Earth did he fall for Tiffany? She was cold towards people. Tiffany had always judged everyone. Ha it really been her own vanity that made Cliff love her?

These weren't the types of things he should be thinking of. These weren't the type of things that he should be thinking about, with the son of his ex-wife right in front of him.

Meanwhile, Harry glanced down at his phone. "Langley wants to talk with me," Harry explained.

Langley always wanted to talk with him… He was starting to sound like Vivica… "Ok, you have fun."

As Harry left, Hannah walked into his office. "Dad, we have an issue, and it might be my fault."

Cliff rubbed his forehead. "What exactly did you do?" He was now having flashbacks back to Hannah in high school.

"I requested tax information from the government to help track the paper trail of this missing money. Different transactions were reported as taxable income," Hannah explained to him.

It didn't take a genius to know where Hannah was going with this. "The IRS is going to get involved?" Cliff rubbed his forehead. "We should be fine." He quickly said. The IRS was always down their throat for one thing or another.

"If you say so, Dad. I mean, this paper trail goes back to 1986." Hannah pointed out.

1986… Cliff started to think about all the things that happened in 1986. That was the year that he first started to officially date Vivica. That was the year that he lost his virginity. It was also the year that DJ Brash *died*. The year that his father murdered DJ Brash. That's what his father made a point in telling Cliff right before he died- that he killed DJ Brash to protect his family. After all, killing him kept DJ Brash from inheriting any money from the Knight family.

He looked up at Hannah. "I have to go." He grabbed his coat and marched out very quickly. Vivica was in the hallway as he started walking by, without even turning to say hello.

VIVICA – 2018

Walking into Cliff's office, Vivica found Hannah sitting there, looking a bit shaken-up. "What's going on with your father?"

The brunette Knight girl brushed her hair back. "Oh, um… We are having some issues locating where certain money has been deposited."

"From Knight Motor?" Vivica wondered.

"Yes, Hannah said. "Since 1986, we have been losing large sums of money each year. It started when Grandpa was in the CEO chair, obviously."

Vivica grimaced. If the missing money had to do with Rodrick Knight, then Vivica knew exactly why Cliff wouldn't look at her before leaving the room.

1986… What a weird year in her life.

As she continued to think about it, Vivica started to hear the music of Olivia Newton-John again. She looked at her niece. "Please tell me- am I the only one who can hear that?"

Hannah walked outside of her father's office. "Holly, why are you standing out here, playing music?"

"I'm just taunting your aunt for a few more days." That's when Holly walked in and saw Vivica look both annoyed and worried at the same time. "What's wrong, now?"

Her niece looked back at her maid. "Apparently, there is some corrupt business deal that dates back to 1986. It is worrying my father, and Aunt Vivica, as well."

"Oh, good Lord, that's the year you lost your virginity and step-father- all on the same night!" Holly screamed out loud.

Vivica looked mortified at her maid. "I'm so glad that I shared that bit of information with you..."

"That was information I didn't need to know" Hannah said out loud, putting her hands over her mouth.

The beautiful redhead looked out the window. "1986 was such a different time. Your father and grandfather were always arguing. I would threaten to call the police on Rodrick constantly, but Cliff would always tell me not to. Meanwhile, my mother and D.J. could barely handle me. This might be shocking, but I was a very difficult teenager."

Her maid and niece both ignored the statement. She looked at them for a moment longer. "It's ok to say that I probably wasn't."

Holly rolled her eyes. "We can tell you whatever you would like, but we've seen your yearbooks and went to Saint Agnes ourselves... You weren't exactly winning any awards for Star Student."

"That's why I liked having Lucy here. She always butters up her answers." Vivica crossed her arms. Things were definitely changing. Lucy wasn't going to be around as much. She would be able to see Hannah much more often, though, and Harry, for that matter.

There was no word if Hope would be coming back from Europe anytime soon. There was also no word on if Tiffany was ever going to come back, which Vivica was perfectly fine with. Things were clearly different now, and Vivica wasn't entirely sure how she was supposed to adjust to all of it.

Vivica turned to Hannah again. "What was it like for you to go from your mother to me, back to Tiffany?"

Her niece sat back down. "It was weird. I mean, we legitimately thought that Mom was dead. I was also really young at the time. Then, when you started to watch the three of us, it just felt normal. We were like a big family that worked well together, and then Mom came home..."

Then Tiffany did come home, and she ripped them all apart. Brad went off to boarding school because of his idiot father, and Harry was left to his own vices. The girls, including Laura, went off to college, and Laura moved away. Vivica really did have to admit that Hannah was the *daughter* she was closest to.

"I should probably go find Cliff." Vivica grabbed her purse and walked out.

BRANDON – 1966

Nadia Bloom was the most beautiful girl that Brandon had ever seen in his life. Everything always worked so well for her. She was clearly the rational one of the two of them- but also the adventurous one. It was obvious, though, that she wanted him to go off to college with her…

Brandon murmured, "If I go to college, are you going to visit me?"

The Latina teen looked at Brandon like he was being an idiot. "Brandon, if you go to college, I would be there with you, obviously."

Brandon sighed. "Yes, but you already said that you wanted to go out on the East Coast or something. I really don't have much desire to travel away from home." As he admitted this to her, he realized it was the truth. He wanted to work at the company and get married. Then, a few years down the line, he would have a couple of children. The concept of moving away from Michigan never crossed his mind. "I like Grosse Pointe."

Nadia smiled at him. "Well, then we can go to school in Michigan. That being said, you have to promise me that we will travel the world one day. My dream is to see the world."

Brandon sighed. "Nadia, I can give you the world. Dad and I were looking over our business prospects last night, and while it might take a while, by the time we get out of college, we will be in the same boat as the Knight family."

The girl rolled her eyes. "Brandon Fitzpatrick, I don't want you turning into a Knight. Do you honestly want to be anything like Rodrick or his father?"

Brandon was taken aback. "Well, obviously not. I just mean that money-wise, we will be in a very similar boat to them."

Brandon was never going to be like the Knights. After all, Rodrick clearly was never going to grow up. And according to Susan, his father had been hanging around the bar as of late. Susan had heard from that annoying old crone, Mrs. Templeton, that he had been kicked out of the Country Club for excessive drinking.

Brandon didn't know how to speak with Nadia. She wasn't like normal girls. She wasn't looking for her M-R-S. She really wanted to go to college, and she wanted grand adventures. Brandon really couldn't figure out just how *grand* she actually meant. It was obvious that she didn't just mean she wanted to see Paris. Nadia had mentioned places like Africa or the Middle East, and places that just didn't seem your typical sightseeing trip.

Nadia turned to him again. "Look, we still have some time to think about the future. Let's just enjoy the present for what it is."

LANGLEY – 2018

A year ago, Langley had been through five boyfriends in six months. It really wasn't something she thought that much about. Langley cared about having a good time, and a good time was meant to be spent with many different people. Yet now, here she was- head over heels in love with Brad Fitzpatrick. But they were broken up now. The saga of Langley and Brad's relationship was getting both repetitive and obnoxious. And Langley couldn't stand dealing with these sorts of feelings. On top of all that, Lucy decided to tell them that they were all moving back to that tiny house a few blocks from Saint Agnes. This just wasn't going to work. The youngest Kingsley girl felt like she should have just been able to stay at Vivica's mansion. She suspected that this was all Vivica's idea.

There was another thing... Vivica Fitzpatrick clearly didn't like her. Since when did parents not like her? All her ex-boyfriends' parents liked her. She was so over this. She needed to sleep with someone. It really couldn't be as hard as she was making it out to be. There were options.

Langley walked down the hall at Saint Agnes. It was the end of the day. In front of her was Tad Lucas; he had a great ass but was also dumb as shit. Then there was Holden Gray, who had a great face but was scrawnier than Harry in terms of build. Langley continued to judge each boy based on how they would be as a sexual conquest. Still daydreaming about sex, she wandered towards the boy's locker room. It was a dream of hers to one day spend an entire day in a men's locker room. Those types of thoughts were sure to get holy water scrubbed all over her body at this school. But at her old school, it was pretty natural. Langley watched as the broad-shouldered Brad Fitzpatrick walked over. He had the perfect ass, and she couldn't even see it from this angle. She needed him. She wanted him. He was perfect.

"Hey, Langley!" Brad said with a smile. She was undressing him with her eyes. The boy was such a prude that he refused to even play doctor with her. When they went swimming at his own damn pool, he got freaked out at her seeing him shirtless. "Do you want to wait around, and I'll give you a ride home?"

She wanted to ride him. She realized that he had been standing; there for a moment longer than was considered normal for a response. "Sure, Bradley. I'll wait for you." She smiled. She would wait and wait until she could touch his flesh. That smooth body was all she wanted.

"Great, we just have to drop off Selena first," Brad explained.

"Who the fuck is Selena?" Langley asked, both confused and pissed off.

Brad looked taken aback. "Just a friend from Purity Club."

Oh, for fuck's sake, she thought. Now he was dating some girl who wanted to be fingered by him just as badly as she did. "I'll get a ride from Harry..." She stomped over towards the exit, towards the football field. She couldn't believe this. He was cheating on her with some girl named Selena...

The blonde girl found Harry in the stands and sat down. She gave him a look to tell him that she knew about Selena and was not amused. "Why didn't you tell me?"

"Tell you what?" He asked.

"Selena... Who is this girl?" Langley asked.

The curly-haired Knight boy took a deep breath. "Oh, Selena... She is just some girl that Brad has been talking to. I don't really think they are anything but friends."

"Yet, you didn't tell me about her." Langley pointed out.

"I didn't really think you'd want to know. I thought you and Brad weren't going to go out anymore?" He reminded her.

Langley sighed with a pissed-off look on her face. "Harry, I say a lot of fucked up shit in the spur of the moment. I've changed my mind, and I want him back. I also want his body. I want sex."

Harry nodded his head, looking away. "Well, um... You realize that you can't have both, right?"

"Yes, Harry Knight. I get that I cannot have Bradley Fitzpatrick in the way I want Bradley Fitzpatrick, but I want Bradley Fitzpatrick, damn it!" She screamed. Why on Earth was she calling these boys by their full names? "I, Langley Lorelei Kingsley, want Bradley Fitzpatrick, and I'm desperate to have him!"

Harry turned back to look at her again. She felt like several other people probably were looking at her at this point as well. "I will support you in getting him back," He smiled. "Your middle name is Lorelei?"

The blonde rolled her eyes. "My mother was a *Gilmore Girls* fan. At least that's what Lucy told me, once." She looked at her phone. "Do we have to stay here? You got your man, and he isn't going to stray off. So, why don't we go back to your house or something."

Harry asked her, "What did you do after school when you were in New York? I've always wondered. I can't imagine you just going back to your house."

He was right… "The PG-13 version of what I did after school was going shopping with friends."

"What is the R-rated version?"

"Mixed study group with different colored lipsticks. That's as much as you are getting out of me." She said, continuing to look at her phone.

It was obvious that Harry wanted to ask more, but it was also obvious that he was scared to. He grabbed his backpack. "Let's just go hang out at my house."

Langley grabbed her bag. "Thank freaking God!" She screamed. She looked out into the bleachers for the potential Selenas. Each one looked like a pure girl waiting to unleash their inner slutty side with Brad.

VIVICA – 2018

It wasn't that Vivica didn't trust Cliff. It was just that she just *really* didn't trust Nial. So, they had put a tracker on Cliff's phone, just like she had for Nial. Cliff knew about it. So, she didn't feel guilty following him to the cemetery. The only issue was that he wasn't where the other Knights were buried. It was clear that someone had spit on Rodrick's grave, but that could have honestly been just about anyone.

She passed Mrs. Templeton and asked, "What are you doing here?"

Mrs. Templeton explained, "I just like to be around my ex-husbands. I take pride in knowing that minorities are dead, and I'm not." That woman was a truly horrible person...

If Cliff was here, then he was hiding himself. Vivica decided to use the opportunity to visit her mother and D.J.'s plots. That was where she found her familiar curly-haired man kneeling over. This confused her. As much as Gail had pretended to be all right with Cliff after he had left her for her sister, things clearly shifted between them and never really recovered.

Vivica walked up to his side and put her hand on his shoulder. "Cliff darling, what on Earth are you doing at my mother and D.J.'s graves?"

Cliff stood up. "Vivica, I have to tell you something..." He rubbed his forehead. "I don't know how you are going to react."

Vivica crossed her arms and looked into his eyes. "I'm listening."

"Do you remember the night that D.J. died?" Cliff asked her.

How could she ever forget? That was the night that she had lost her virginity to Cliff. They had assumed that they were alone at North Pointe when Rodrick walked in with Margot. It was then that Cliff answered the phone call that would forever change their lives... Vivica's mother called to meet them at a construction site that D.J. had been overseeing. He had an accident and died. It took Vivica and her mother months to start recovering, and her mother took far longer than she had.

"Cliff, what exactly does D.J.'s death have to do with anything?"

Cliff stood up and looked away from her. "When Rodrick was in the hospital right before he died, he told me something. It turns out that D.J.'s father was not David Brash Jr."

"How on Earth did you know about that?" Vivica said, a bit unsure of where Cliff was going with this.

The Knight man turned back around. "Wait a minute; you knew that he wasn't David's father?" Cliff looked very shocked by this answer.

Vivica nodded. "David and Lana married after years of would-they wouldn't-they romance. And apparently, Lana had a short-lived relationship with someone else. David didn't care that she was pregnant and proposed to her anyway, and they raised D.J. together. Lana died before D.J., so he never knew who his real father was."

This news was not sitting right with Cliff. "So, no one had any idea who D.J.'s father was?"

"Not that I know of. I suppose we could try asking Nadia Fitzpatrick, but Nadia was so weird when it came to her brother especially after I married Nial. They had always considered me a niece… It's a very weird family. I mean Christ, you should look at those journals that Harry has been reading. Apparently, Brandon Fitzpatrick had an older sister that was a lesbian. Huge news to me. After all, we both grew up spending holidays with that family. And then, we lived in that house off and on for years…" Vivica knew that the public perception was to love the Fitzpatricks and hate the Knights, but really they both were equally fucked up when you really thought about it.

"Vivica, I know who D.J.'s father was…" Cliff explained to her.

How on Earth would Cliff know? Vivica thought this was all getting very strange. "Cliff, what is going on?"

He sighed. "Weston… Lana Brash was the maid when Rodrick first moved into North Pointe. Apparently, she had some sort of a one-night stand with my grandfather Benton in order to make my great-grandfather Heathcliff jealous."

D.J. was a Knight? David Brash Jr. was really David *Knight*? A brother to Rodrick? Which would have made him Cliff and Luke's uncle? Which would have technically made Vivica a Knight by marriage, years before she had even dated Cliff…

"Why on Earth did Rodrick tell you this?"

"Why did he ever tell me anything? I don't know… Are you upset with me?"

She had no idea what to think. Yes, she was angry, but she wasn't sure why. This information really wasn't upsetting, and yet it was. Vivica looked down at D.J.'s grave. All she could think about was his overly corny, almost Sitcom Dad-like attitude towards every damn situation. Had this information been revealed back when he was alive, he probably would have just smiled and moved on. That was the D.J. way. He would have acknowledged the fact that Delia would probably have been upset, and he also really wasn't a fan of Rodrick.

Yet, then, Vivica thought a bit more about it. D.J. had left her money when he passed, which wasn't very much, considering everything he had was his and not the Fitzpatrick's. Yet now that she was really thinking about it, he would have been owed money from Heathcliff and Benton's estates.

Why was she thinking about this from a financial standpoint? She didn't really need or even this money. In a few months, this money would be hers regardless. What on Earth was she thinking about money for? Vivica felt like a gold digger about to get her payday, and it was sickening.

Earth Vivica looked at Cliff. "I have to go..."

LUCY – 2018

The lobby of the Inn was not exactly modern or vibrant. It all felt very late 90's, and it still needed major updates to it. The actual hotel rooms needed new carpet and curtains desperately, and some of the rooms still had boxed. T.V. sets. If Lucy hadn't already been promised a certain weekly salary, she probably would have turned this down in her old life. But in her new life, she had no choice but to take on this crazy adventure.

"So, are you excited to officially start?" Perry asked her.

"I'm excited to have a job where I'll be the boss. I mean, aside from Margot." Lucy had to keep reminding herself that technically, Margot was her boss.

Perry laughed. "I honestly doubt that the two of you are going to have much interaction with one another. As you can clearly see, this is a forgotten entity of The Fitzpatrick Group."

She could see that this was fairly obvious. "Why on Earth did they buy this in the first place?"

"Actually, they inherited it shortly after the original steel company took off. Originally, the pub was the only part that they owned, but my grandparents bought the rest of the property in the late 70's I think it was turned into the hotel. I don't think it really ever has been the main priority for anyone, though," Perry explained to her.

This was going to be awkward because her first instinct was to eliminate the pub. It felt awkwardly out of place, compared to the rest of the hotel. Lucy liked the idea of having a restaurant on location, but the pub was so dark and impersonal. She was about to voice her concern when a familiar redhead came tumbling in. "Oh, for goodness sakes..." She looked at Perry. "Sorry, let me just deal with this."

Then, Lucy walked over to Vivica and crossed her arms. "Vivica, what on Earth do you want? I'm trying to work, and I have no idea if Margot has cameras in here or not."

"I need to talk with someone, and Holly is on a date with her husband. He threatened to have me arrested if I interrupted another one of their date days." Vivica sat down dramatically on the couch in the lobby.

Lucy had no idea why this was shocking for her. She might not work for Vivica anymore, but she still worked *near* Vivica. It was never going to end with this woman, and Lucy really didn't know why this shocked her. She sat down, next to Vivica on the couch. "Ok, what is wrong?" Lucy asked her.

Vivica looked up, onto the ceiling. "I think there is a crack in the ceiling... Lord, this is why we never hosted the hospital gala here. It's falling apart."

"Vivica, I'm trying to work! If all you are here to do is critique the place, we can do that later." Lucy quickly looked up, and she was right though... This place was a disaster...

Vivica said, "I just met with Cliff at my mother and D.J.'s graves. Apparently, Rodrick told Cliff on his death bed that D.J. was really Benton Knight's illegitimate son with Lana Bloom Brash. Oh, and apparently, Rodrick had D.J.- his own brother- murdered on the same night that I lost my virginity to Cliff. If you want to get really fucked up, I think he was fucking Margot that night." Vivica saw Perry and waved at him, who was looking at the two women.

Why on Earth was it that Vivica never had anything normal to tell her? It was never that she bought a new dress. It was always that she bought a new dress that happened to belong to a witch or some crazy shit like that.

Lucy took a deep breath. "Ok, well, obviously, Cliff had nothing to do with it, and Rodrick only died at the beginning of the summer. I mean, did you expect him to inform you of this?"

It took a minute for Vivica to respond. "Well, yes and no. I mean, I've kept more fucked-up secrets for far longer. The issue is the fact that there is missing money that is somehow involved in all of this. Plus, the fact that the first thought to come to my mind was that technically, D.J. would have been owed money from the Knights. Which I don't know where that came from."

VIVICA – 2018

This was all too much, and Lucy was not helping her at all. She desperately wanted to call Holly, but Holly's husband scared the hell out of her, and she was not allowed to talk to them on date nights. Even though tonight wasn't date night, Lord knows that technicality wasn't going to fly.

"Am I a bad person?" Vivica wondered.

Lucy looked at her former employer and friend for at least three minutes. "No... You are not a bad person. You just tend to do things that are not very logical."

Not very logical? That was far from the truth. At least Vivica didn't think so.

"What am I going to do? Lucy, I need you to be honest. Do you think that I need to go away for a while to think about this?"

The blonde former assistant smacked Vivica across the face. "You can't keep running away from your damn problems! Going off to California or Europe is *not* the answer to your problems. You either are going to marry Cliff, or you aren't. You have a teenage son who needs you now, more than ever because he breaks up and gets back together with my slutty teenage sister, who is ready to fuck him in public. Your nephew can't handle you being away for more than five seconds without thinking that he did something wrong. The only other person he seems to turn to is, once again, my crazy ass sister. Oh, and the son of the mobster. Then there is Hannah. I don't think I have to say anything more on that subject. Your fucking maid who, mind you, I don't think I've ever seen clean anything in the five years I've worked for you-she goes into detective mode trying to find you every time you leave. Do you really think that hiding somewhere is the way to go?" Lucy stood up and stormed away from her.

In the five years that Vivica had known Lucy, this was the first time she had ever gone off on her. "Well, don't forget that you are chaperoning the dance tonight!" Vivica screamed after her. She had a lot to think about. She knew what she was going to do about Cliff, though...

HARRY – 2018

Harry held two different options for the dance in his hands as he looked in the mirror. Harry turned to Langley. "Do I wear the sweater or the sports coat?"

The blonde girl was too busy looking at his tablet. "I don't care, Harry. I'm trying to figure out who this Selena girl is."

Harry sat down next to her. "If I agree to show you who she is, will you stop obsessing and help me out?"

"You could have just done that in the first place..." She handed him the tablet.

It took him only a few seconds to find the girl's name. "Here, Selena Cross..."

Langley looked at him as if he were joking. "Oh, it's only going to take me a few damn minutes to end this bitch's career as a man stealer."

It worried Harry that Langley was clearly about to hurt this innocent girl. Yet, he was too concerned about making a good impression for Preston to really care, right now.

"Do you think Preston will be dressed up?"

"Who the hell knows? He wore short shorts to ask you out. That is so damn midwestern," Langley scoffed. She put her phone down. "Well, Selena is not going to any dances anytime soon."

Once again, Harry was worried about this Selena girl, but he was even more worried about his date. "Shouldn't you get dressed for the dance?"

Langley scoffed again. "Fine... I'll go get dressed and then give Brad dirty looks all evening. Selena won't be there, though." Langley walked to the door, where someone was standing there, about to knock. It was Preston. Langley looked him up and down. "Spread the word, Selena Cross is sleeping with her cousin!" Langley walked out the door.

Preston looked at Harry. "What the hell was that about?"

"I feel like the less we know, the better in this situation. So, what are you doing here?" Harry asked him.

"I just thought that maybe you would want to get ready for the dance together?" Preston smiled.

Preston had the most beautiful smile in the world, Harry thought to himself. Everything about Preston was so beautiful and pure. "Yeah. I just don't know what to wear." Harry explained.

The mobster's son got up and went into Harry's closet without asking. It took him a minute... "Well, I'm going to be wearing a blue button-down with a white tie. So, why don't you wear the same?"

Harry blushed at the concept of wearing matching outfits. "You really want to go to this dance with me? I mean, it could be social suicide or something like that."

"Social suicide? Harry, who the hell talks like that? It isn't *Beverly Hills, 90210*. Though, I feel like someone needs to remind Langley of that sometimes. I don't care if people stare at us all evening or call us fag and queer and all the other names they can think of. I just want to spend the evening with you." Preston explained to him as he sat down next to him on his bed.

"I like you a lot, Preston Costa." He leaned in and kissed Preston on the lips. He couldn't help himself. Preston had luscious full lips, and Harry had to kiss them as many times as possible.

Preston stared into his eyes for what seemed like a full five minutes as they held each other's hands. "I like you a lot too, Harry Knight." He kissed him back.

SUSAN – 1965

The strawberry blonde Fitzpatrick sat down in Delia Knight's kitchen, along with Mary. The three women had grown so close in just a few years. She wouldn't have it any other way.

"So, what are we doing this weekend?" Susan asked.

"I have a church thing I can't get out of," Mary explained, tapping her fingers. Susan loved the way that Mary tapped her fingers.

Delia yawned. "I'm actually going to be meeting with a counselor at the local college. I'm thinking of going back to school."

Susan smiled. "Oh, I'll go with you if you would like! What do you want to study?"

"I've been considering nursing. I've wanted to since before I first met Benton. The children are almost fully grown now. It seems only right that I start getting out of the house a little bit more."

Delia said this with a smile on her face. Susan was so happy that Delia had been able to stay off of wine more or less the past few years.

Mary took a sip of her lemonade. "I think that is really wonderful. Benton will be ok with it?"

"That I have no idea, and honestly, I could care less," Delia explained to them.

Rodrick walked down the staircase. He had on the same evil look that he always had on his face. "Mother, when are we having dinner?"

Delia sighed. "I don't know… When Lana decides to make it. Have a snack while you wait."

The boy gave a look as if Delia weren't aware of something. "Well, Lana has been slipping in her work lately. Father doesn't seem to mind, though." Rodrick walked out the back door. He was snickering all the way out.

The Knights were definitely an acquired taste. Susan doubted that there would ever be a time where people respected them in the same way they used to. Times were changing, and the Fitzpatricks were finally on their way up in the world. She really had Delia and Mary to thank for helping her with that. Things were finally getting better. That is all she ever could have asked for. The future was finally looking bright…

HANNAH- 2018

Hannah had no idea why on Earth she agreed to go to the Saint Agnes homecoming dance. Hannah maybe went to a handful of dances during her entire time in high school, and she always regretted each and every single one of them. It was always just Hope and her idiot friends acting like assholes, and yet Hannah always seemed to be the one to get in trouble. Xander was insistent that they check it out, though, because he wanted to keep an eye on Langley, and apparently, because Lucy was going to be supervising it.

"We really don't have to stay that long," Hannah explained.

Xander rolled his eyes at her. "Oh, come on, just enjoy yourself for five minutes."

As they spoke, Mrs. Templeton walked over to them. "Your dress looks slutty," she screamed and then walked off.

Hannah blinked. "I thought she was banned from this place?"

Sister Mary Newman walked over. "She was, but she donated more money... The church can't afford to turn away large donations. Even if they are from people who were probably at the Last Dinner." She patted Hannah on the back and went back to dancing with a bunch of underclassmen. Hannah had to admire that Sister Mary Newman was still this crazy after all these years. Then, Hannah spotted her own father standing by the punch bowl. She excused herself from Xander to go and talk with him.

"So, did you figure out where the money has been going?" Hannah inquired.

Cliff sighed. "No... I have a few theories, but no."

CLIFF-2018

Cliff didn't know what was going on with the money. He suspected that Rodrick had been paying off a hitman, but for crying out loud, a hitman didn't need to be paid off for something that happened in 1986.

He looked at his daughter and said, "On Monday, I'm going to cancel the payment to whoever it is. We will be done with it once and for all. If the person comes forward, then, great."

That's when she finally showed up. Cliff looked up as Vivica walked into the room, swaying on her feet. Instead of making her way right to him, she found Lucy and Holly leaned forward, sneaking him a few quick glances. The three women were clearly talking about him.

The Knight CEO looked around his old gym. He hated this place. He hated it when he was a student, and he hated even more as an adult. Why on Earth did he send his children to this school? Saint Agnes was nothing but painful memories for him. The only good thing about this place was standing across the room from him, clearly ignoring him. He fucked up his relationship with Vivica so many times over the years and honestly regretted everything except having his children. He should have married Vivica, not Tiffany. Vivica was the love of his life. Vivica was his destiny, and he might have fucked it up yet again.

Cliff sighed. He looked onto the makeshift dance floor and saw his nephew Brad arguing with the Kingsley girl. He spotted Harry dancing romantically with Preston. Cliff couldn't help but smile at how much Harry was growing up. Even though Preston was nothing like Vivica, he was reminded so much of him and Vivica at that age when he looked at his son and boyfriend. It was crazy to think that Harry had a boyfriend. It wasn't that Harry was with a boy. It was the fact that Harry was with *anyone*. Cliff never thought that he would get to see the day. Cliff often worried about Harry living with him for the rest of his life and never leaving his room, and that had all changed in such a short amount of time. Then, there was Hannah, right next to him. His troublemaker was a smart young woman with actual aspirations. The only thing that was missing in his life right now was his Weston.

LANGLEY-2018

Langley yelled, "I'm telling you, Brad; I didn't do anything to that Selena girl. I don't even know what she looks like."

Langley had been trying to enjoy herself all evening, but Brad was being a buzzkill. A very fuckable buzzkill.

"Look, I know you were somehow responsible for this. Can you just admit to it and we can move on?" Brad asked.

Langley rolled her eyes. She wasn't going to admit to anything she may have obviously done. "Ok, I will admit to this. I still love you," Langley said. She didn't know why she just said that. Brad didn't say anything, but then he kissed her.

"I love you too, Langley. I only broke up with you because you seemed to want to. I mean, the only issue, though, is clearly wanting different things," Brad explained to her.

They really didn't want the same thing. Langley wanted to show she was going to regret this instantly. *Screw it*, she thought to herself... She was just going to have to take more cold showers or get a vibrator.

"The Midwest has changed me. Good bad or indifferent, I want you, and if that means no sex, then that means no sex. You and I belong together, though."

Langley really did believe it. She grabbed on to his shoulders, and the two started to dance together. She rested her head on his shoulder. His broad shoulders made her cringe. This wasn't going to be easy...

VIVICA-2018

"Oh, for goodness sakes... Lawry's special season is dancing with Brad now. Is this night going to get any worse?" Vivica was not feeling up to this at all.

"I still can't believe that you didn't call me to tell me about this!" Holly screamed at her.

Vivica wished that she had. Lucy had been absolutely no help, and she could tell that Lucy wasn't having it, even now.

The redhead looked in the gym. This dump clearly hadn't been updated since before she graduated high school. Why on Earth did she send Laura and Brad to Saint Agnes? She never even liked going to school in the first place. Her mother only sent her here because she thought it would make her disciplined. That clearly worked out a whole lot... *The Whore from Beverly Hills*... That would forever be her damn calling card.

Vivica could still remember spending time watching Cliff play basketball in this gym. He looked great in a basketball uniform, especially after he started developing his legs. Vivica needed to get with the program. Why on Earth were things so difficult for her and Cliff? They loved each other so much, and yet, the universe clearly didn't want them together.

Vivica turned around as someone tapped on her shoulder. It was Cliff. She knew it was Cliff; he had been wearing the same cologne since he was twelve. Which, of course, she had picked out for him.

"Yes, Cliff?"

"I'm sorry..." He gulped.

She knew he was sorry. Vivica was sorry herself, and she really wasn't sure why. "I still want to marry you."

He smiled and nodded. "Good, because I want to get married right away."

The redhead smiled back at him. She could tell that all the usual suspects were looking in on them. "Holly, why don't you go talk with your husband?"

The maid crossed her arms. "I want my drama!" She screamed. Lucy took her by the arm and dragged her away.

Vivica turned back to Cliff. "I want everyone important at the wedding. Even if that means having to invite Lunesta and the Costa family."

"Anything for me, Weston." He kissed her like he had kissed her so many times before, only this time was especially different because they both knew that this was the beginning of the rest of their lives. For the good and the bad this time, it was going to stick....

Will Vivica and Cliff make it down the aisle? Is Langley really going to be able to handle a sexless relationship? What about A-King? Is he done messing with Lucy and his other children? Will Holly and her husband ever make enough time for one another? How about Hannah and Xander? Will they go past the friendship faze of this relationship? Is Mrs. Templeton's age ever going to be revealed? What about Preston and Harry? Where are the Costa parents? Where is Nial, for that matter, and will he continue to cause trouble for Vivica and his sister Margot?

All will be revealed in the next exciting installment of "Between Heaven and Hell!"

ABOUT THE AUTHOR

L A Michaels was born in Troy, Michigan and raised in Lake Orion, Michigan. L A has also lived in Wichita Kansas and Rock Hill, South Carolina over a two-year period. Currently, L A lives in Warren, Michigan.

A major fan of Soap Operas, L A grew up watching the *ABC* daytime lineup with his late mother, while discovering shows like *Guiding Light, As The World Turns, The Bold and the Beautiful, The Young and the Restless, Days of Our Lives,* and *Dynasty* on his own. Comic books, world history, and theatre have also played a large part in his life.